To Chelsea, Nicholas / Gra

AVERY'S CROSSROAD

—BOOK TWO—

Peace

DEANNA K. KLINGEL

Deanna K. Klingel

Greenville, South Carolina

Library of Congress Cataloging-in-Publication Data
Klingel, Deanna K.
Avery's crossroad / Deanna K. Klingel.
p. cm.
Summary: Quaker Avery Bennett earns his degree from the Medical College of Virginia in 1863, but questions whether he wants to practice medicine after the Civil War.
ISBN 978-1-60682-193-0 (perfect bound pbk. : alk. paper)
[1. Quakers—Fiction. 2. United States—History—Civil War, 1861–1865—Fiction. 3. Medical care—History—19th century—Fiction. 4. Virginia—History—1775–1865—Fiction.] I. Title.
PZ7.K6799Ave 2011
[Fic]—dc22 2011006279

Cover photos: Craig Oesterling (young man); iStockphoto.com © photoGartner (dog beagle); Library of Congress (burned district); Library of Congress (ruined buildings); Library of Congress (siege guns); Library of Congress (street view); Thinkstockphotos.com (soldiers)

Design and page layout by Nick Ng

Greenville, South Carolina 29614
JourneyForth Books is a division of BJU Press

Printed in the United States of America

ISBN 978-1-60682-193-0
15 14 13 12 11 10 9 8 7 6 5 4 3 2 1

Table of Contents

1863 "NOT HOW IT SHOULD BE, BUT HOW IT IS"

PART ONE

1864 RAINBOWS AND CANNON FIRE

PART TWO

1865 GOING HOME

PART THREE

Acknowledgments

Many thanks to family, friends, and associates who have persevered in their support of Avery and Gunner and shared their special expertise:

Royal Scribblers, who rained enthusiastic critique and encouragement for years.

Wendy Ricci, for education on the Gypsy Vanner horse; Col. Albert Busck (Ret.) for all things military; Jeff and Laurie Klingel of Appleseed Nursery for sharing honeybee and historical Virginia agriculture knowledge; Carole Clark and Ann McLeod for sharing historical artifacts and suggestions.

In memory of Tom Pierson, for the use of his amazing Civil War library.

Dr. Roberta Butler-White for original editing of a very rough draft and for all you taught me about editing and rewriting, thank you.

Thank you to Chris Godsey for reading, and rereading, so patiently.

Dave, always my rainbow, thank you.

Nancy Lohr, JourneyForth Books, BJU Press for piecing together my pieces of rainbow.

Thank you all.

PART ONE

"NOT HOW IT SHOULD BE, BUT HOW IT IS"

1863

CHAPTER ONE

ODD COMMUNICATIONS

The headlines of the Richmond, Virginia, morning paper screamed in large print:

EMANCIPATION PROCLAMATION
ISSUED BY PRESIDENT A. LINCOLN.

The words of the proclamation were on page one, and Avery read them carefully. He was surprised to see that the President, oddly, had freed the slaves in only the slave states. *What about the others?* he wondered. He read through the document hopefully, but when he got to the end, there was no proclamation to end the war. He didn't think there would be.

Rarely did he see a newspaper on the very day it was published. He normally picked up the tattered, passed-around copies left behind by others. He had bought this edition of the *Richmond Daily Dispatch* on the way to work, deciding to give this one a thorough reading to see what was going on in the war today—the first day of the first month, his sixteenth birthday.

"Let's check the post office column, Gunner. It's been a while since we've had a letter from home," he said to his hound.

Avery counted on those letters to keep him grounded. When he'd left home in 1861 in search of his uncle, he'd never planned to be gone this long. But circumstances and opportunities

had come his way. Now here he was studying to become a doctor. It was almost too good to be true. But he missed the farm and his family. Their letters were so important.

He checked the post office column and was glad to see there was mail being held for him. As the city filled with more and more people, the post office holding list was growing longer every day.

"From the looks of this holding list, we'll be standing in a long line, Gunner. I hate to stand in line."

Finally arriving at Chimborazo Hospital, he shook off the cold and handed the newspaper to an ambulatory patient. Since it was too cold to go outside, the ambulatory patients now gathered in a large ward tent to play cards, exercise, and share their war stories, while trying to heal. This large Confederate Army hospital was where Avery and the other students at the Medical College of Virginia were training to become surgeons, while enduring the ravages of the battlefields.

Avery was in a glum mood today, totally unlike himself. *The war changes everything. Perhaps the war is changing me too,* he thought sadly. He couldn't seem to shake himself out of despair this morning. Gunner, looked up at him and whined. Avery smiled, bent down, and hugged his dog. He suddenly felt much better.

"You, dog, are the one thing in life that never changes. Even the war hasn't changed you. Thanks be to God for that!" He put his cold hands in his pockets, whistled a tune, his step much lighter, and he went to work—just another day. Later that day a volunteer slipped a communication to Avery secretly and then disappeared quietly without a word.

"What's that all about," Avery mumbled. He looked at the envelope, and seeing a postal code rather than a stamp, he knew it had come from a Union soldier. He pulled out the message and quickly concealed the envelope in his pocket.

Dear Sir Doctor Bennette,

I am tolde by many that you hold dear medicines to relieve infekshuns in the body. I inquire not for myself but for another who is unable to speake for himself. Can you meet us please at the ferry landing outskirt of towne? It is as close as we dare to come to Rebel camps. We will meet just at dark please. And also I will pay you in Greenback your fee. Please it will be of such importance.

Yours in the service of the president,

Lt. William B. Woodruff.

"I'm not sure I like the sound of this. It's a very odd note, Gunner. I think I'll ask someone else to accompany us." He quietly passed the note to his roommate during the day. At the end of the workday, without any words about it, the two doctors left together as usual with their medical bags. But instead of going to their dormitory, they headed for the ferry landing. Gunner, of course, trotted along ahead of them, nuzzling the snow drifts and rolling his shoulders in the snow. Avery was disturbed.

"We shouldn't have to be so secretive about this, Jones. I mean, they told us when we started our studies here that there are no sides in medicine. We doctors have to treat both sides equally. And yet—"

"And yet, we are in Richmond, Bennett. We need to use good sense. Not a word of this to anyone."

"That's what I thought too. Thanks for coming along."

"I wouldn't have missed this!" Jones winked and slapped Avery on the shoulder. "Can't wait to see what this big mystery is all about."

The ferryman was disappointed that they didn't want to pay for a crossing, and as the other ferry was making its way across the waterway to the landing, he grumped off to go about his business of doing nothing, happy to leave his post. When the

ferry landed, a strong-looking Union soldier peered suspiciously around, and seeing no one but the doctors, jumped ashore and extended his hand.

"Thank you kindly for coming. I'm Lieutenant William Woodruff, United States Army." He pumped their hands excitedly. Avery gave him a quick look up and down but didn't see anything that looked like it needed treatment.

"It's not me," the soldier explained. "It's another soldier."

He led them back to the ferry. On the floor of the ferry, wrapped in two woolen blankets, was a very small form. Avery bent down to examine him.

"This is a child!"

"It is, sir, but a fine soldier indeed. He is my son. A good little soldier, and he's very sick."

The two doctors examined the feverish child and determined that he had an infected throat, swollen tonsils, and a high temperature. Avery told the soldier how to create a gargle and mouthwash for the boy. He gave him a little bottle of astringent made of gold seal that he carried in his bag. Dr. Jones prescribed lots of clean water and rest, and they both thought honey would bring some comfort. Avery then suggested chilling the water with snow or icicles.

"That's what my mother did for me when I was a boy," he told the soldier. "Perhaps you could wrap some snow and icicles in something and apply it to his throat for the swelling. It will give him some relief," said Avery. "Maybe flavor it a little with peppermint or vanilla and let him swallow that. He will recover, but he needs to be kept inside. Do you want us to take him to the hospital with us?"

"No! Uh, no, thank you," the soldier blurted. He glanced around nervously.

"How is it that the army employs such a youngster?" asked Avery.

"Richard is eleven years. He's too young to carry a rifle, but he helps to tend the wounded. At the Battle of Savage Station, he helped to bury our dead. He's a good boy," said the proud father.

"I couldn't leave him home with his mother and his six sisters. They would turn the lad into milk toast. A boy should learn from his father, so I have him with me."

Gunner was nuzzling the boy's cheek, and now the feverish eyes were wide open in amazement. He sat up, looked around, coughed, and then laughed in spite of his sore throat.

"Look, Father, it's a dog doctor!"

"As always, Gunner is the surgeon in charge," laughed Jones.

"Thank you so much, doctors. We'll be on our way now. I'm beholden to you. If anything should happen to the lad, I'd have his mother to answer to, you know."

"Put him into bed as soon as you get back to camp," Avery reminded him. "Keep the fever down, and be sure he eats."

The soldier shoved the ferry into the water and waved to the doctors.

"Never a dull moment," said Jones. Avery thumped Jones on the shoulder, and the two watched the ferry disappearing into the evening.

"Just a child, Jones. That father took a great risk to get him here to a doctor. Yet that's the best we could do for him. Do you ever regret studying to be a doctor? I mean, sometimes do you just feel like quitting or going home?"

Jones shrugged. "No. I don't think so. I can't think of anything else I'd like to do. Why? You getting homesick or something?"

"I don't know. I've always been interested in healing and medicine, even as a boy. My mother is a healer, and my grandfather was a surgeon. But I never really planned to be a doctor. Doctoring sort of found me, and then circumstances made the plan. I mean, it's okay. I guess I do want to be a doctor. It's just not quite how I hoped it would be. I mean, a child soldiering? He should be home in front of a fire. This isn't how I thought doctoring would be. War changes everything."

"Yes, I guess, but, Bennett, you're a top-notch doc, why would you want to stop?"

"I don't know. I want to be like my mother. She uses herbs to make medicines and helps people. I want to help people be healthy. I thought doctoring would be more about living. Now with the war, doctoring is mostly about dying. I really do get discouraged and depressed with all this . . . this dying, all the broken people, and sickness and infections that we can't help. I always thought doctors could fix everything."

"You give us too much credit. Doctoring will be easier when the war is over. We'll deliver babies and treat bunions! And we'll sleep at night. You're a good doc already, Bennett. And I imagine you'll keep on studying and be a modern doctor in some big city."

"I don't know. I'm really a farmer, you know. I'm not so comfortable in a city."

"So you'll be a doctor for farmers. Don't worry about it. Now take me, that's a different matter. I'm thinking I might go out west when this war is over. Might do some gold mining. If it doesn't work out, I can always doctor the gold miners, right?" Jones laughed and shoved Avery playfully with his elbow. "You're a doctor, Bennett, through and through. Even if you were a farmer, you'd still be a doctor. It's who you are."

"Well, it's good for us today that we've helped that little soldier boy. I need a few successes now and then to keep from being discouraged over all the dying. That squeaky little cot in the dormitory will feel good tonight, huh? Let's go home and go to bed. Gunner, lead the way."

CHAPTER TWO
KABOOM!

K*aboom!* A tremendous explosion shook the tents and huts. The hut windows rattled, and terror flew on invisible wings through the tent wards where shell-shocked veterans thought they were under attack. Nurses lost their footing, and basins and cups scattered across the floors. Gunner felt the vibration and darted quickly to Avery's side. Avery was in the wound ward when the shock hit. Patients grunted and groaned when their cots rattled, shaking broken bones, opening wounds, and waking all but the dead.

Everyone talked at once, and volunteers ran to the wards to keep the soldiers calm and to check for fires around the hospital tents.

"The Yankees have reached Richmond for sure, boys," said the Confederates.

"Maybe it's a signal that the war is over," offered some of the more optimistic.

"No one is allowed to fire upon a hospital. What are they doing?" an indignant student doctor sputtered. Everyone who was able to move jostled for position to look outside to identify the source of their terror. Those unable to move tried to hide in their blankets. One of the orderlies ran out of the tent.

"Smoke!" he shouted.

"I see it!" shouted another. "Down the hill. Toward the river."

"Over there. I see flames."

"Huge flames!" screeched a volunteer standing in the yard. A series of smaller explosions followed, shaking the floors, rattling the camphor lamps, and vibrating everything. The huts shook, the tents flapped, water sloshed, and tremors of terror shot through ailing bodies.

Finally one of the soldiers lying on his cot slowly drawled, "I'd say the Ordnance Factory just went up in smoke and flames."

Everyone who heard him stared at the patient, digesting what he'd said.

"What do you mean?" a soft-spoken nurse asked the patient.

"You from around here?" he asked her.

"No, sir, I'm from Philadelphia."

"Well, I'll tell you, miss. The Richmond Arsenal is an ordnance factory down near the James River Bridge. You've seen it, I'm sure. Huge storehouse for arms and military supplies. But it's also an ammunition manufacturing plant. Most of the employees at the arsenal right now are women and girls, doing their patriotic duty for the Confederacy while their men folk are off soldiering. Lots of explosive stuff over there. I hope I'm wrong."

Avery consulted with one of the deans and the surgeon. "We're most certainly going to be getting burn patients in the next few hours. We're going to need a lot of honey to treat those burns. We should start requisitioning immediately. We haven't much on hand. I'm worried about what I've been hearing. I'd like to take a run down there. I understand there are lots of women and children in that factory. Can I take some orderlies and maybe one or two others with me?"

"You're right. We need some first-hand information. Go," the surgeon in charge told him. "We'll cover for you here. Staff, volunteers, visitors, coming and going all day, will bring bits and pieces of information, but we need to know the truth about what to expect."

Avery gathered a few orderlies, two other student doctors, and some supplies. They jogged down the hill and across town

to the factory. The patient, it turned out, was right. The laboratory next to the arsenal had exploded. When the doctors arrived, flames and smoke, screams and horror stopped them several yards in front of the disaster. Several of the hysterical, burned victims were staggering toward them. Burned bodies littered the grounds. Avery swallowed hard. *Will I ever get used to this?*

As soon as Avery and his team arrived back at the hospital with a few of the injured, they sent volunteers with litters back to the factory to do the best they could to locate other victims and bring them in for treatment.

The next few days brought some unusual visitors to the hospital to see these new patients, who were technically not military and were mostly women and girls who'd been working at the ordnance factory when it exploded. The first visitor came in looking quite important, dressed like he was going to a party—gloves and shiny shoes, top hat in his hand. He was definitely out of place here. Avery scowled as he watched the man.

"How do you do, I'm Mr. Josiah Gorgas," the visitor announced to anyone looking at him. "I'm Chief Ordnance Officer of the South and the director of the arsenal." He had a newspaper reporter with him from the *Richmond Dispatch* to be sure his words of condolence to the victims of the fire were all spelled properly and placed on the paper's front page. Avery stood in the corner with his arms folded, watching the man who wanted to make his tour of the hospital an "official visit." Gorgas requested that a doctor accompany him and his entourage as they visited at the bedsides.

The dean saw Avery observing and gave him the job. Avery wasn't happy about it, but did as the dean asked. He had quickly realized that the man's visit had little to do with his burned and injured factory workers. The visit was to make sure the world knew he'd done an exemplary job of keeping the Confederate Army armed, despite lack of money and supplies.

"The army never ran out of ammunition. Not on my watch," Gorgas pointed out repeatedly. He held the lapels of his

coat and looked proud and important. The explosion wouldn't blemish his record.

Pompous, thought Avery. *He's wasting our time.*

"Let my record speak for itself. We kept our army armed," Gorgas continued.

"I'm not sure the patients here think that's terribly important right now," Avery murmured.

"Just want to extend condolences and give my regards to those recovering," Gorgas announced loudly to the reporter.

"I'm not sure you can do that without looking at them," Avery said. "You say the right things, but you never look at them."

"You are an insolent young man," Gorgas huffed. "I'll report you to your dean. You may be excused." Gorgas was aloof and agitated. He checked his timepiece frequently as if he had something more important pending.

Avery stepped away from the man.

"What was that all about?" asked Jones. "Didn't the dean ask you to host him?"

"The dean probably thought Gorgas was sincere. But he's not. He's wasting our time. Look at Gunner. He knows it too." The dog, who was usually ready to accompany anyone on rounds, eyed Gorgas warily and kept his distance.

The second unusual visitor that week was also not military. He was a gentleman from the Young Men's Christian Association, the YMCA. He never gave his name, but he wanted to know the names of the victims, and he used their names when he spoke to them. He came by to console those injured at the explosion and to tell them that along with his organization, all the employees at the arsenal had set up a fund to help relieve the victims' suffering and the suffering of their families. He placed a collection box near the hospital door in case anyone cared to contribute. He spent most of the afternoon praying with the victims of the explosion and giving hope to the injured, unemployed ordnance workers. He helped the staff feed the patients, and he reassured them that everything that could be done for them, would be, and not to worry.

Gunner kept him company for much of the afternoon and walked him to the door when he left. Avery and the other student doctors shook hands with him and thanked him for coming by.

"Now that's a different story, isn't it, Gunner?"

CHAPTER THREE

ELMO SILAS, HONEY MAN

When he had first come to Richmond last year, Avery had purchased quality honey from a beekeeper named Elmo Silas. Following the explosion, Avery sent a volunteer into the country to find Elmo. The next day the beekeeper showed up in a rickety wagon at the Chimborazo Hospital looking for Dr. Bennett, "the boy doc," as he referred to the young doctor.

Elmo Silas was a comical little man, short and stout. He wore large overalls, rolled up several times. The soles of his shoes were tied on with strips of cloth. Avery had never seen him without his straw hat and wondered if perhaps the man slept in it, which might explain why it was so misshapen. Elmo had a big, blue nose and a wondrous orange, curly beard that had bits of honey stuck to it in several places. His corncob pipe was always smoking and created a little halo around the man's head. He had such unusual accented speech that it took Avery a bit of time to figure out sometimes what Elmo said. The little man was friendly and feisty, and he amused Avery.

"Mawnin, Dockor Bent," he said. He bounced on his tiptoes toward Avery in jerky quick steps, but his speech was as slow as honey drip.

"Hear ya gots to hab moe bee hon. Well, I tricked up some, and I brung it. Bestest in da coundy, I tell ya da trufe," he drawled. He shook Avery's hand, leaving it sticky.

"Ah brung sumpin else fer it too. Ah brung a hibe to sit oud yonder dere and c'lect mo bees 'n hon. Yes sir, I picked ya oud a good c'lect place, an ahm thinkin them bees'll be so happy dere, they can make ya lots a hon."

Avery thought about that for a few seconds. "You're setting up a bee hive here?" he asked.

"Thas what ah sayd." Elmo scowled and puffed his little pipe.

"But there isn't anything out there for the bees to work," questioned Avery. "Everything is barren here."

"Ah know," Elmo drawled, "an we're gon fix it. They's helpin me." Elmo motioned to the side yard where Avery saw several ambulatory patients with small buckets, busily tossing something into the air. It looked like it was snowing!

"We's plantin da clober. Bees love clober."

Avery mulled that over. "You are planting clover for the bees?"

"Thas what ah jes sayd." Elmo made a puzzled face. "You don' hear too good, do ya boy doc?"

Avery grinned. "Okay then, you're the honey boss!"

Elmo chuckled. "Well, ah don' know bout dat, ah'm thinkin maybe da queen bee, she think she be da hon boss!"

The men shook hands, leaving Avery with an even stickier hand, and Elmo toddled off to his rickety wagon. He sat on the wagon and ate a meal which he'd brought along tucked neatly into an old woolen stocking. He ate a wrinkly apple with a piece of bacon drizzled with honey and all balanced on a piece of hardtack like a little tower. He took quick little bites, and then chewed and chewed and chewed, slowly.

When Elmo finished eating, he lay down in his rickety wagon and took a little nap. The student doctors and soldiers eyed him with amused interest. Following his nap, he hopped off the wagon and carried his little white wooden box out beyond the trees where the clover would soon be growing gloriously.

The soldiers watched him slide the trays into the box as he chatted with the queen bee the entire time. Though no one really

understood what he was saying, it was obvious that Elmo loved his bees. When everything seemed to satisfy him, he hopped onto the wagon and waved goodbye to everyone he saw. He saw Avery standing in the doorway.

"An y'all be da boss a da hon bee medicines is whad ah hear. Ahs happy nuf to gib it to ya fer da troops. Ahl be back!" He waved, and Avery waved back, not fully sure what Elmo had just said. He looked beyond the wagon and saw the little hive sitting in the barren yard.

"Our own little honey factory," he mused. "Sure hope that clober . . . uh, *clover*, grows! Honey's about the best medicine we've got."

CHAPTER FOUR
DESPERATION

The student doctors walked through the city square from their dormitory on their way to class and work at the hospital, and it occurred to them that something seemed just a bit off this morning, though none could quite explain it. It was quieter somehow, though it seemed there were more people than usual in the square. There was tension in the air. Many of the women who usually greeted the doctors watched them suspiciously without speaking. Some clusters of women lurking together stopped talking when the doctors approached.

"Rather an odd feeling about the place this morning, don't you think?" asked Jones

"Gunner senses trouble, Avery, don't you see him?" Edwards whispered hoarsely.

"I've noticed," Avery answered, looking warily around him. "Almost feels like a funnel cloud brewing, but the weather is fine." He shuddered. Gunner stayed close to the men, strangely pensive, tail tight between his legs. The roommates exchanged glances and sped up their pace, anxious to be away from the center of the city.

"What do you think's going on here, anyway?" mumbled Jones.

At the hospital Avery sensed still more change. Some of the local volunteers seemed aloof and very gossipy, whispering in the corners, but they acted as if they were busy whenever the doctors

came near. They came and went alone, reporting back as if they were on picket duty. Avery watched them suspiciously.

"I don't know what's going on here," he said quietly to the others, "but I think we need to be alert. Something's going to happen, and I don't know what." The others nodded in agreement. Gunner stayed at Avery's side all morning, panting and looking alert. His shoulder muscles were defined, his ears at attention.

Around midday they were surprised to hear church bells ringing in the city.

"What are the bells for?" everyone asked as they listened uneasily to the bells pealing. The church bells continued to toll for a long time, and soon they heard all the bells in the city joining in: factory bells, church bells, school bells, and fire bells. Everyone glanced around nervously.

One volunteer blurted, "I'm going to the square. I want to know what's going on." The dean said that since the man was a volunteer, he was free to do what he wanted, but the students were to stay put. Avery noticed that several regular local volunteers were absent this morning.

Just a short time later, two Public Guards came riding hard to the hospital, their snorting horses kicking up dust. They announced loud and clear to everyone that they were all to stay where they were and to consider themselves under house guard.

The chief surgeon and the dean walked to the front door shaking their fingers and said, "Now, you see here—" but the Public Guard was gone.

Several of the ambulatories gathered in the yard and wondered anxiously *who* was holding them under house guard; they didn't want to say "Yankee" aloud. They began to murmur among themselves. Some were reciting prayers. Everyone was beginning to believe the day had finally come; the Yankees must be in Richmond, and they'd soon all be prisoners of war—or shot. Fear hummed through the air. Avery tried to reassure his patients, but he, too, was anxious.

From the hillside beside one of the wards, Avery could now hear shouts of riotous quarreling. It sounded more like an

angry mob of people than a military invasion. In the distance, glass shattered. Gunner growled low and deep.

Outside near another ward tent, the doctors and the students searched the horizon for smoke and flames, but found none. The ambulatories wandered about listening for artillery fire, waiting, and expecting to be taken prisoner.

"Think we should make a run for it?" one whispered to another.

"On crutches with no guns? You crazy?"

The shouting, the shattering of glass, and the screaming continued and got louder and more out of control. It sounded like hundreds of people. The church bells rang for a long time. When they finally stopped tolling, the emptiness was filled with the shrieking angry roar of a mob. And then the crowd began to quiet down as well.

"What's happening?"

"Stay calm," Avery advised them.

"What's going on?"

"We don't know anything yet," Avery said. "We need to keep our heads until we know what we need to do. Try to relax."

"What is it?" wondered the sick and injured, hiding under their blankets.

"What is this all about?" asked the students and the doctors pacing restlessly. Gunner watched Avery and whined.

The volunteer who had taken off to find out was now making his way up the road and running up the hill to the hospital yard. Everyone crowded around to hear his story.

"What is it? What did you see? What's happening?" They shoved their way close to him.

Out of breath and gasping between words, he reported: "It's the women . . . it's a riot . . . the mob . . . angry women . . . they . . . they have no bread . . . you know . . . flour, money . . . their children are hungry . . . for their families . . ."

Avery motioned to one of the nurses who offered the man a jar of water.

He gratefully gulped it, took a breath, and continued. "Their families are hungry, so the women decided to help themselves. The militia is all over the city arresting *women*. They've been caught with bacon and shoes, soup, bread, even fabric to make clothes. The Capitol Square is a mess of rubbish; windows are broken, and merchants' doors pushed down. Merchandise has been stolen. Who would've believed it?" he said in a daze. "Desperate, angry women. They're looting everywhere." His head was in his hands, and he shook his head in disbelief at his own story. "The Public Guard on horses was surrounding them and—you won't believe this—President Jefferson Davis himself is there! He said they had to go home or the Guard would begin firing into the crowd in five minutes."

"What?" his audience shouted in horror.

"They can't do that."

"What kind of madness is that?"

"Firing on women?" Avery squeezed his forehead.

"I left right then and hightailed it back here; I think they mean it." He panted, trying to catch his breath and calm his nerves. His hands were still shaking. Gunner laid his head in the man's lap. The upset man stroked Gunner's head, calming down. He looked up at Avery.

"Just unbelievable," he said.

Everyone began to talk at once. Some asked the volunteer for more information, which he didn't have. Some said they should all stay put at the hospital for their own safety. Others said they should all stay since some of those fool women might be arriving from the square with gunshot wounds. A few of the local volunteers wanted to go home to make sure their mothers, wives, and sisters hadn't been involved. Others looked strangely sorrowful . . . or maybe guilty.

"I think," said Avery, "some of you knew this was going to happen. But I'll bet you had no idea it would turn out so badly." A few of the local volunteers dropped their heads sheepishly and moved into other ward tents away from Avery. The surgeon in

charge, a bit bewildered and uncertain how to restore order at his hospital, wrung his hands.

"Oh dear," he murmured as he paced in a small circle.

Avery felt sorry for him. Avery stepped up onto one of the outdoor chairs, put his fingers to his mouth, and gave one shrill whistle. Gunner jumped to his side in anticipation.

"I think," said Avery, "that our chief surgeon would like to say that it's time to get back to work now. Our patients are waiting."

They tried to shake off the events, and the crowd of employees, patients, and students began to disperse. Within the hour everything was restored to business as usual at Chimborazo Hospital. The chief surgeon nodded his thanks to Avery for his leadership, but continued biting his fingernails.

"As if the war between states wasn't enough," Avery said. "Now we have war between women and shopkeepers. A bread riot! What do you make of that, Gunner?"

Gunner lay at the doctor's feet, his chin on his paws. His tired amber eyes looked woefully up at Avery.

CHAPTER FIVE

SPRING FEVER

The springtime gardens all around Richmond were sad replicas of their former glory. The ladies of the city despaired that there would be no annual garden parties this year. Careless foot traffic, the removal of trees for firewood, horses hobbled near shrubbery, and the Bread Riot damage doomed the Richmond gardens, now mires in the spring rain. There were few traces of green in the city of gardens in spring of 1863.

Avery thought about the springtime in the Kanawha Valley. He imagined his family sitting on the old quilt under the blooming apple trees, eating a picnic supper, talking, and reading, while listening to the honey bees working the blossoms. *I never meant to be gone so many springtimes.* He longed for the peacefulness of home away from the cities of war. He sat at his desk to write an overdue letter to his family. It was the next best thing to being there on their farm.

May 16, 1863

Greetings to my dear family,

How I miss all of you and the fresh smell of springtime in the valley, and most especially in our own holler on our own farm. It must be the most beautiful place on earth this spring.

It stays very busy at Chimborazo Confederate Hospital here in Richmond. Richmond is teeming with people, and the war activity is all around us. There is no fresh smell of springtime anywhere. There are no gardens, Mother, and no fields to be plowed, Father. Some days I wonder what I'm doing here. I think I could be more help to you at the farm, a better farmer than a doctor. No matter how hard we try, soldiers die. I've now seen more dead men than live ones in my life. And every day there are more with no end in sight.

The most recent excitement here was just a week ago. A highly revered Southern General, whose name is Thomas Jonathan Jackson, lost his life and was brought here to Richmond to "lie in state" at the Capitol Building. He is quite legendary here in the Confederacy. I don't know if you would have heard of him, but if his name appears in the Wheeling Press at all, it may refer to him as "Stonewall Jackson" as that's his popular nickname here among his troops. He has earned a great reputation for skills in battle. Unfortunately his injury, which led to an amputated arm, was inflicted accidentally by one of his own Confederate troops. That would be funny, if it weren't so serious. He died of pneumonia while recovering. I've heard it said by both sides that General Jackson was a deeply religious man of good character, a good General, a loving husband, and a fine gentleman. I might have liked the man.

We have also recently had a huge fire in Richmond. The woolen mill, which is one of the few employers left in the city, has burned near to the ground, catching many other buildings nearby in flames. We worried the entire town might burn down. The city was filled with black smoke, and we covered our mouths with our

handkerchiefs when going outside. For days we were brushing ash off our hair and shoulders. You should have seen me with gray hair, like an old surgeon! Many complained of burning throats and noses, and everyone has coughs. The greatest sadness is now even more people have no employment, and the air we breathe is more poisoned.

Gunner is fine and sends his greetings. He enjoys making his rounds every day. His jobs are quite separate from my own. He's a true doctor and healer for sure, but he brings relief of a different kind for the injured. It would be fine if I could make rounds as cheerfully as that dog.

I am beginning to get used to being called Doctor Bennett. At first it seemed strange. I'm often in charge of a ward, and I'm called on to confer with the surgeons about serious wounds. We use a lot of your recipes, Mother, and the surgeons are impressed. I've been combining a couple of them and created a good poultice.

My classes are all interesting, and I'm learning a lot. I enjoy the hospital work very much, but wartime makes it difficult and sometimes quite overwhelming. We are all terribly busy all the time. Some of our nights are quite short. When I work the night shift, I have trouble staying awake. I find myself longing for my loft at home and the quiet of the farm.

Jones, one of my roommates, has told me he plans to get married after our diploma ceremony in August. That leads me to ask you, Father, a private question, which is on my mind. I do wish my roommate good fortune in his marriage, of course, but I'd like to ask you man-to-man, how does a man know when he should marry? Jones seems so certain that they are meant to marry

that I was wondering if you might share some counsel for my future. I should like to know.

All my love to all of you,

Avery Junior Bennett and Gunner

"Father will be pleased to see my handwriting improving. Right, Gunner? Let's make a little inky paw print on this, and you'll sign it too. Mother will definitely think your writing has improved."

Spring warmed quickly, and now, in the midst of the heat and stench of early summer, Avery sat with Gunner on the dormitory steps catching the evening breeze. He'd picked up his mail at the end of his shift and eaten supper quickly so he could read his letters before dark.

"This is an exciting day, Gunner. We've got three letters to read. We've never had three letters at one time. It's almost like having a new book to read." Gunner sniffed the envelopes and whipped his tail with enthusiasm.

The first letter was from his mother. She'd heard of Stonewall Jackson and was interested to learn that Stonewall was more than a legend and thanked Avery for telling them all about him. She planned to share it with her pupils at school. She wrote that she wondered how she ever got along without her farm hands Banjo and Maize, who had come from South Carolina with Aunt Caroline. They'd added some hens to the flock that were all thriving. Avery imagined the eggs frying in butter with hash. He could almost smell them cooking.

"The school is wondrous for everyone," she wrote. "Everyone in the entire valley will soon know how to read. The shy and backward boys and girls of the hollers are learning to know each other by name and get along well together. I am very much pleased."

Avery mulled over that. He'd never played games or talked much with any of the children in the hollers. They were all just there, part of families who worked and prayed together in

their valley. He rubbed Gunner's throat and tried to imagine the little girls and boys talking, playing, and reading together at his mother's new school.

"Mother's school is making some changes in the valley. Maybe if I'd talked to Nurse Claire as a child, I wouldn't be so tongue-tied now. What do you think, Gunner? I wonder if it's too late for me? Part of me is becoming a man, but the other part is still a shy boy from the holler who can't make sense talking with a girl. I need to work on that part, don't you think so, Gunner?"

Gunner rolled over and put his feet in the air, doing his dying trick. Avery laughed and rubbed Gunner's belly.

"You're right; it feels like I'm dying whenever I talk to that girl!" Thinking of Nurse Claire McDougal back in Alexandria brought a smile to Avery, though seeing her filled him with dreaded shyness. "We grew up in Kanawha; we should be old friends. But we really just got to know one another at the hospital in Alexandria. I think Mother's school is a good idea, Gunner."

His second letter was from Aunt Caroline, who told him what a wonderful lawyer his brother Clayton was becoming. She wrote that Phoebe loved collecting eggs in a little basket that Maize wove for her. Avery couldn't imagine his baby cousin walking around gathering eggs in an African basket. Gathering eggs had been one of his earliest chores as a little boy too small to even reach the roosts, but he had felt so proud to be trusted with the precious eggs. *I really miss the farm.*

The third letter was from his father. It was getting too dark to read outside anymore, so he and Gunner went to their room. He lit the desk lantern and sat down at his desk to read. Gunner curled at his feet.

To my dear son Avery,

I was deeply touched by your request to advise you on the subject of marriage. That is a very important matter indeed. I send my congratulations to your roommate and my best wishes for their happiness.

Your mother and I have had many happy years together in our marriage. On the day we married, did we know that? No. We knew only that we vowed before God to do the best we were able. How does one know if it's a good choice, you have asked me? I think, dear Avery, that it's more a matter of the heart knowing than a matter of the mind knowing.

When you enjoy her company more than you enjoy your own, when everything you dream of for your life includes her, when you can no longer imagine your life without her, when she's in your every thought and your every purpose, this is your heart speaking. It might not make sense to your mind. When you receive good news, and she's the first one you want to share it with, when you are sorrowing and you seek her comfort, when her suffering brings you pain, and when you celebrate her joy, then you have received a wonderful gift from God. This, son, is love.

Then your mind must catch up with your heart and make the decision to make her your wife. Then you'll marry her, comfort her, provide for her, and pray at her side for as long as God deems it to be so. And it won't be a chore; it will be a blessing, as God blesses such a union. So you needn't worry about knowing, son. Your heart will tell you. Your mind must listen.

There is much more to this question of love and marriage. But for now, I believe this is what you need to know. There will be time when we are together again that I can tell you more. When you get home, we'll get our poles out of the shed and head to the pond where we can fish and speak privately about these very important matters. We have time for that.

You are young, Avery; take your time. You will want to marry your best friend, not a stranger. And it takes time to recognize a best friend.

All my best,

Father

Avery exhaled, realizing he'd been holding his breath through most of the letter. He folded the letter and pressed it into the pages of his textbook. He wiped the moisture from his eyes and smiled, thinking of his parents together at home, missing them both.

CHAPTER SIX

BOYS ON THE TOWN

The next evening he unfolded his father's letter to read it again.

"Hey, roomie," said Jones. "What are you doing studying? It's a fine evening; there's girls out there, and there are no classes tomorrow. We're going out on the town; care to come along with us?"

Avery wanted to read his father's letter again, and he wasn't sure he wanted to go. He knew when they went out on the town, they walked to the other side of the town to talk to the girls at the Ladies Seminary School. He'd never gone with them before. Why would they want to go talk to girls? But, since he and Gunner had decided that he needed to work on talking to girls, he thought maybe he *should* go; this might be a perfect opportunity to talk to one and get in some practice. *I need practice,* he thought, *like Mother's school children.*

"Yeah, well, okay, I'll go."

"All right! Now you're talking."

The roommates slicked down their hair and put peppermint on their tongues. Avery watched them tuck in clean shirts and spit on the toes of their shoes, shining them on the opposing leg. He only had one clean shirt, and he didn't want to waste it. He deplored spitting on his shoes, and they were beyond shining anyway. He slicked his straight unruly hair, tucking it behind his ears, and went as he was.

He discovered quickly that the boys "on the town" were quite different from the men in the dorm, who were diligent students, quiet and relaxed, making good roommates. The boys on the town were bawdy and loud, drawing attention to themselves. Avery walked behind them, head down, embarrassed and uncomfortable. When they got to the iron fence around the Ladies Seminary School, they grew more boisterous and whooped and shouted; Avery thought they acted silly. They lifted each other up like acrobats and kept checking to see if the girls were watching.

Some of the southern ladies came to the fence smiling and acting very shy. One pretended to accidentally drop her fancy handkerchief through the fence. Avery thought it was certainly no accident. One of his roommates picked it up and, with a grand show, smelled it, acted silly, and passed it back to her. They held hands briefly while exchanging the handkerchief, and the girl giggled. *Not a real giggle, just a made-up giggle. I don't see anybody talking.* Another of the roommates yanked a branch off a small tree and with a great playful flourish presented it to another tittering, giggling girl on the other side of the fence. When she took it, he yanked it back, pulling her up to the fence, where she pretended to be shy. They stood closely a moment before he lurched forward and kissed her. They both pretended to be shocked and surprised as if it had been an accident. Avery thought this was the silliest game he'd ever seen. *When are they going to talk?* He scowled and scratched his head. Gunner cocked his head and flicked his ears. Avery wondered what Jones was going to do since he was planning to marry Nancy after he got his degree. Jones leaned against the fence, talking to one of the girls.

"Okay, Gunner, come on, finally we're going to talk to someone." He and Gunner started off in that direction. Jones and the girl giggled at the secrets they were whispering, and they held hands through the fence. Jones was caressing her arm.

"We're going to meet Nancy," Avery said to Gunner. The two of them approached the fence. He had a bit of a lump in his throat, but he would be polite to Nancy. *I can do this,* he encouraged himself. He cleared his throat.

"Hello. My name's Avery. I'm Jones's roommate. You must be Nancy, his fiancée. It's nice to meet you. Congratulations to you on your upcoming marriage." He extended his hand through the fence to the girl. She glared at Jones. Jones turned to Avery and scowled.

"Uh, oh, uh, my mistake," Avery stammered. His face colored and burned. Avery kicked walnuts and pinecones all the way back to the dorm, with Gunner at his side. He was disappointed in his friends and their silliness, but he was also puzzled. *Something isn't right about all this.* He wondered if Jones and his fiancée Nancy would fit into Father's criteria for marrying. He didn't think so.

"Gunner, I'm confused. All along I thought since I was the youngest student, the youngest doctor, I was the only one who couldn't talk to girls. But these men tonight acted like school boys. I don't think they know how to talk to girls either. At least, Gunner, we don't make donkeys of ourselves. At least we know manners!"

His roommates were cool toward him the next day. Jones, especially, seemed uncomfortable, but Avery said nothing about their disappointing behavior.

"We'll just say no to their next invitation, Gunner." He looked at Gunner who rolled his eyes up at him.

"You're right. There won't be another invitation. They think I'm a wet blanket. But I'm getting to like myself that way. But you . . . I know you like the ladies, don't you, Gunner? Well, we'll be back in Alexandria after graduation, and Mrs. Simpson will fill your bowl nicely. And Claire . . . yes, you'll see Claire. Now, Claire . . . there's a sensible girl. She wouldn't giggle and titter and pretend to be shy. She just says how things are, honest like. She's a sensible girl. I think when I choose a girl—well, if I ever want to, that is. When I choose a wife—well, I probably will sometime—I'll choose that kind, the sensible kind. Yep. That would suit us, wouldn't it, Gunner? I wish we could talk to Father. I wonder what else he's going to tell us?"

He kicked the stones with a happy step and began to think pleasantly of Alexandria, Claire, and the Simpsons. Somehow his whole world seemed a bit more at peace.

CHAPTER SEVEN

COMMENCEMENT

Through the summer Avery worked and attended classes. In July all the students were out of the hospital for two weeks while they wrote their exams. It was a quiet and tense time on the campus, but the student doctors knew that up on the hill things were not quiet at the hospital. While they were taking exams, the war raged on. Their quiet was interrupted by artillery fire and the sound of the army marching and drilling in the town center. The war surrounded them. The college was like an island for the students in a sea of battles and bloodshed.

"What are you writing your graduation thesis on, Avery?" Jones asked.

"Hospital organization and administration. Dr. Simpson suggested it. He thinks I'd make a good administrator. My essay is on wound care and amputation. My study shows new uses for old remedies; I've kept stacks of notes and recipes of my mother's for years. And my research paper is 'New Therapy to Prevent Muscle Atrophy.' I've been corresponding with a physician in Philadelphia about it. It's a fascinating field of medicine using electricity. He's treating the brother of my friend Claire McDougal. How about you, Jones? What are your topics?"

"I'm still thinking. I think I'm going to write about prosthesis, artificial limbs. We need to come up with some better ones for all these soldiers. There ought to be good money in that field in the next few years."

"Good luck. I don't know if I'll ever do anything with these studies though."

"You still being addle-brained about doctoring, Bennett? You're the best one of us. What's wrong with you? There's money in it!"

"I don't know. Some days I think it's exactly what I was born to do, but maybe it isn't what I *want* to do. Maybe it's only what other people think I *should* do. I'm probably just tired. And I don't think doctoring is about money, Jones, not really."

Avery was exhausted and wondered if he could even finish writing his essays. All he wanted to do was sleep. When the exams were over, there was great relief, celebration, and a lot of nervousness waiting for their results. His roommates went out on the town to celebrate. Avery and Gunner planned to go fishing in the James River, but returned to take a nap instead. He couldn't remember ever feeling this tired.

Avery's family sent him some greenback money to buy clothes for his diploma ceremony in August. He was startled when the clerk at the haberdashery measured him and picked out his size. When the man held the shirt up, it looked like one of Avery's father's shirts.

"No wonder my britches are too short," he said in amazement. "When did I grow taller than Father and Clayton?" The store had a long looking glass, and Avery looked at himself. His head was above the glass. It would've been fine for an average-sized man, but Avery could only see his body in the looking glass. It looked like his father's body. Gunner sat at Avery's feet and looked in the glass too. He looked up at Avery and cocked his head to match Avery's disbelieving stare.

"No wonder my feet hang out of the bed." Avery had never focused on himself or given too much thought to his appearance. Now he was astonished to see the strong body of a man where his own stringy body used to be. He tried on the new shirt and longer pants. He bent down and took a better look in the glass.

"I need to get a haircut." He turned around and looked at his reflection, front and back, and shrugged to Gunner.

"Well, maybe we're going to turn out okay after all. Yes, maybe we will." He was beginning to feel more confident about that. He tucked his hair behind his ear and smiled. "Mother and Father might be surprised, but I'll be the most surprised of all!"

Avery received the summa cum laude award, graduating first in his class. His Doctor of Surgery diploma from the Medical College of Virginia, class of 1863, was written entirely in Latin. He struggled with the translation. His diploma had a shiny gold embossed seal in the middle, the likes of which Avery had never seen. It was the seal of the college. He ran his finger over it. He was now a surgeon. He found that hard to believe. *I don't really feel any different!*

After all the speeches and formalities, Avery was the first in the class to receive his diploma. And the last to receive recognition was the class mascot for "meritorious, tireless, and irreplaceable service." Gunner's gold seal with the college emblem was meant to be stitched onto his little cape as an official mascot, having matriculated at the Medical College of Virginia.

A reception in the dining hall was held for all the new surgeons. Normally this would be a full banquet, but the shortage of food meant only a reception for this class. Some of the graduates had guests in attendance who all wanted to meet Gunner. His reputation had reached the homes of the student doctors near and far by way of the students' letters. A couple of guests commented dryly that Gunner's cape looked like a Union cape. Avery had never thought about that and no one here at the college or hospital had ever mentioned it before, but Gunner took no offense and pranced about proudly in his cape, enjoying the attention and the refreshments.

"You always do like a good party, don't you, Gunner," laughed Avery.

All of Avery's classmates shook hands with him, congratulating him on his honor, and he congratulated all of them for their achievements. They whacked each other on their backs and laughed and joked about their times spent in class and talked about their future plans.

Avery leaned against the wall near the punch table alone, as he often was, watching the proceedings and watching Gunner socializing. Jones walked up and extended his hand.

"I'll never forget what I've learned from you, Avery. I've looked up to you. And not because you're tall," he laughed, looking up at Avery. "It's more than just medicine too. I'm glad to have had this time with you. You're the youngest in our class, but maybe also the wisest. You're a good surgeon. And if you decide to change careers and do something else, go do it! Your future isn't cut in stone, you know. You'll be good at whatever you do. Congratulations and good luck to you."

Avery was astonished at Jones's words. "Thank you kindly. God go with you," Avery responded, and he shook Jones's hand. *Decide to do something else? Just go do it? Not cut in stone?*

There was a toast made to the graduates, now surgeons, and a toast to the college.

"The Medical College of Virginia is the only medical school in the country that didn't close for the war. We have no war on our campus," the dean boasted proudly. Avery thought about his patients and wondered what they'd say about that. The class of 1863 posed for a group photograph, a tradition at the college, in front of the famous Egyptian Building. A photographer had come to make daguerreotypes and promised there'd be one for everyone. The doctors all held their diplomas as they stood in front of the camera. Gunner sat in front of the class and posed proudly.

The surgeons of the class of 1863 shook hands again and said their goodbyes at the dormitory. They carried their footlockers out to waiting buggies and wagons.

"Good bye . . ."

"Good luck . . ."

"Been nice to know you," resounded from all the rooms.

And then the campus suddenly became quiet.

Gunner looked at Avery expectantly, as if to say, "Well, are we going?" Avery hadn't thought about where he'd go after receiving his diploma. He'd lived one day at a time and not given much thought beyond the next day in class, the next day at the

hospital. He had no train ticket, no plans, no buggy, and no one to look at his diploma. He didn't even have a spare, clean shirt that fit him. He was tired, very tired. He stood there leaning against the lantern stand with his foot resting on a hitching post, thinking over what Jones had said. He stared into the distance. While he was puzzling, the dean of the college and the chief of surgeons approached him.

"Dr. Bennett, so glad we caught you. We're glad you're still here," said Chief of Surgeons McCaw.

"Just going."

Gunner heard "going" and looked sharply up at him. Avery was too tired to converse with the men.

"Well, we were hoping to catch you. We wanted to offer you a teaching position here when the next class comes in: full pay, housing, and the use of the laboratory for research. What do you say?"

Avery was stunned. His dream of being a modern doctor tried to flash before him but faded in a haze. "When do I need to let you know?"

"As soon as possible, please," they said. Avery could tell they were surprised and disappointed that he didn't take their generous offer immediately.

"I'll give it some thought and get back to you." He didn't feel able to make a decision right now. He felt so tired and maybe a little feverish. His mind wasn't clear or sharp enough to make a decision about anything, much less his future. They shook hands, and the two men walked away shaking their heads.

Wanting to lie down, Avery went to his room. "Guess we better pack, Gunner." Gunner jumped up on the bed and watched Avery pull out his few belongings. He had only a few clothes, mostly too small; his biggest bundle was books. He could manage without the footlocker. But where was he going? He felt more tired by the minute. He thought about the comfortable feather bed at Mrs. Simpson's. He could be there in a day or two. He thought about his friendly straw loft at home. He could be there in a week

or two. He could stay here and take the job at the college. He was tired, very tired. His head ached.

"I'd like to show Claire our diploma."

Gunner wagged his tail, and Avery tossed his clothes into his cloth knapsack. He carefully placed his diploma between the pages of a book and tied his books together with an old shirt.

"Let's go to Alexandria, Gunner." He paused for a nostalgic look at his desk. He was too tired to smile. He pulled the door closed behind him.

CHAPTER EIGHT
THE DOCTOR IS IN

Mrs. Simpson was surprised to see Avery and Gunner at her door, but she was also delighted. She had enjoyed housing Avery when he'd first arrived in Alexandria with their friend General Keese. And when her husband had arranged a position for Avery at the Medical College, she had made it clear that he was welcome to return anytime. Now he told her about graduation, his honors, and the reception. He showed her his diploma and Gunner's citation, happy to have someone to share them with. She fixed him tea, and then he and Gunner went upstairs to take a nap in his old room with the chintz curtains. He slept for three days.

Dr. Simpson thought perhaps Avery was exhausted from his exams and should be left to catch up on his sleep. But on the second day, Mrs. Simpson urged the doctor to check on him to be sure he wasn't feverish or festering with something.

"Quite warm, swollen glands," was the doctor's report. "Let him sleep."

For supper Mrs. Simpson took him some broth, which he drank, and then he went back to sleep. By the end of the first week he was feeling a bit better and thanked Mrs. Simpson for her care and concern.

"Just a bit of malaise, probably glandular fever," was the surgeon's diagnosis, and Dr. Bennett sleepily concurred. "Lots of students get glandular fever, especially at exam time."

The next week when Avery was feeling stronger, he discussed his dilemma with Dr. Simpson.

"I could go home and start a medical practice in the holler. I could go to Parkersburg and work in the hospital. I could stay here in Alexandria and work with you. I could go back to Richmond and take a teaching post at the college. But I'm not even sure I still want to be a doctor. Maybe I'll go home and farm with Father. I don't know what I want to do."

"Well, now that's a lot to think about," commented Dr. Simpson.

"Sometimes I don't think I'm really cut out to be a doctor. I didn't come here to become a doctor; that just happened. And I'm grateful, don't think I'm not. You've been more than kind, and I appreciate it all. But, I've always loved farming. I like healing, but I don't like dying too much. I've seen so much dying . . . what do you think I should do?"

"You really don't have all those options, you know. You were exempt as a student, but you have a commission in the army. Did you forget about that? If you walk away from it, Private Bennett, you'll be considered a deserter."

Avery's sore throat tightened. Dr. Simpson was right; he hadn't thought about that at all. He'd forgotten he was a private in the army. He sent a note to the dean and Director McCaw.

Dear Sirs:

I am deeply gratified by your offer, and I would like to consider it again at some future date. For now it behooves me to return to my military rank and post with the Union Army. Thank you for a fine education.

Sincerely,
Avery Junior Bennett, M.D.

Finally feeling recovered after four weeks in Mrs. Simpson's care, he reported for duty at Mansion House Hospital wearing

his private's stripes once again and his medical corps shirt. Gunner wore his cape with his new citation stitched on.

"We're in the army again, back where all this started, Gunner. We're out of enemy territory, and now we're real surgeons. So at least for now, we're sticking with medicine. And Father always said, whatever it is you're doing, do it well as if you were doing it for God himself."

With his hands in his pockets and whistling a Union tune, Surgeon Avery Junior Bennett and Gunner went back to work feeling a huge burden lifted.

Nurse Claire was happy to see Avery, and Avery was certain that Gunner was very happy to see her. Claire happily shared the good news that her brother Timothy had left the hospital in Philadelphia and had gone home to Kanawha Valley. The sad news was that he was deaf and partly blind. But he was able to walk and move both arms; he was starting to make sounds and form a few words.

"Thanks be to God," said Claire gratefully. "He could've been dead."

"And thanks to the French doctor and his electricity therapy." *I'll learn more about this electricity, and someday maybe I'll be as fine a doctor as the Frenchman . . . if I'm a doctor at all.* He felt oddly pleased that Claire wanted to share her good news with him. He remembered how he'd wanted her to see his diploma.

CHAPTER NINE

STRANGE BEDFELLOWS

As the summer was coming to an end, Avery began to think about his old friend Rose. He still thought of her as "Mrs. Somebody," and the thought made him smile. She was old and lived alone in the Virginia wilderness. He wondered if she had firewood and enough food for the winter. She occupied his thoughts more and more, until he decided he had to see her.

He requested leave from Dr. Simpson. He told the doctor about his old friend and how he really wanted to bring her to the city where he could watch after her and be sure she ate. Dr. Simpson suggested that Avery take a wagon from the hospital livery in order to bring her back.

"I know a widow woman over on the west side who rents out rooms. Your friend could be comfortable there," suggested Dr. Simpson.

And so he made his preparations; he, Gunner, and his horse Fan set off down the turnpike with the wagon to find her homestead once again. Fan hadn't been keen about pulling the wagon at first, but she was beginning to get into the rhythm.

"Maybe we'll put you to the plow, Fan," he called cheerfully. "Have you missed me while I was gone?"

Fan snorted and shook her head, shaking her mane.

"Guess not," laughed Avery. "I'm sure Leon took good care of you in the livery and spoiled you plenty, I'll bet." Gunner

jogged merrily alongside the horse—when he wasn't sleeping in the wagon.

"Is this better than walking, Gunner?" he teased his dog. "Looks like we might be getting a bit lazy, hound dog."

Avery and Gunner slept the night in the wagon near a clearing. Fan slept tethered in the shelter of the forest a short distance away near a stream.

As dawn broke the second day, Avery thought this might be the day they'd see Rose's farm silhouetted on the flat wilderness plain; he was sure they must be close. He was still lying in the wagon when Gunner went on alert. Avery heard the slow, deep growl; he reached for his gun. He rolled over quietly and peered over the edge of the wagon, knowing full well that when Gunner growled there was a reason. In the early morning mist and pink light of dawn, he saw someone moving stealthily across the road. The figure disappeared into the misty forest.

"Uh-huh; thanks, Gunner. Fan will thank you too."

Avery pulled on his shoes; Gunner's gaze never broke. Suddenly Fan whinnied, and Gunner flew onto the ground. Before Avery could leap off the wagon and run into the trees, he heard Gunner tearing into the surprised would-be thief, who was hollering for mercy. Fan whinnied and stamped, and Avery ran. When he reached the tree line, he could make out the man with Fan's reins still in his hand, backed against the tree. Gunner was close to him, growling and snarling. The terrified thief was pinned against the tree, totally surprised.

"Gunner, off," Avery said quietly. "This your horse, sir?" he asked the thief politely, while pointing his musket in his direction.

"Well, maybe. I mean it's dark, you know. I might have made a mistake, but I think it is." He started to walk away.

"Hold where you are," said Avery. "Let's see your camp."

"Camp? I got no camp. I'm alone. Honest."

"Honest? You know that word? Step out here." The thief looked at Gunner and stayed where he was.

"Step out here. Do as I say, and the dog won't bother you. But I should warn you, he doesn't like liars, and neither do I. Do you understand me?"

"Yeah, sure," he said, while trying to slide past the dog to go toward Avery. Gunner gave him a warning that sent terror through his veins. "I-I don't like dogs much."

"You have reason to fear them. Dogs know when you're up to no good and when you lie. Dogs don't like that."

"Nice dog, nice dog," the man said, trying to win Gunner's affection. It wasn't working.

"Gunner, get Fan." Gunner moved, and the man fearfully dropped the rein. Gunner picked up her rein and brought it to Avery. The man breathed now that Gunner had moved away from him.

"Let's see your camp. Put your hands on your head, please. Lead me to your camp. My gun is pointed at the center of your back, and Gunner will be right beside you—just so you know."

"Okay, then, okay. I'm going."

Gunner walked beside him, watching his every twitch. Avery pointed his gun toward the ground and walked behind him. The man assumed the gun was still pointed at him and walked cooperatively in front. Behind Avery, Fan plodded with her reins draped over his shoulder. Out of the trees and into the morning light, Avery watched the short man's nervous behavior and studied his gray clothing and appearance.

"Looks like we've met up with a deserter-turned-thief, Gunner. What should we do with him?" They had walked a few yards down the road when Avery could see a covered wagon in the trees. He saw someone moving around behind the wagon.

"Stop here. How many people in your camp?" Avery asked. "And remember, the dog will know if you're lying, and he'll go after you. You'd better tell me the truth. How many?" Gunner gave him a low growl for emphasis.

"Only one; we're the only wagon here. Two other wagons went on—me and Billy Ray, just us—the truth, I swear."

"Call your friend."

"Billy Ray, c'mere," the man called. The other man came around the wagon and stood still as he took in the scene. Avery pointed his gun at the thief for emphasis.

"Tell him to put his hands on his head and walk this way away from the wagon." Gunner growled.

"Okay, okay."

Billy Ray put his hands on his head and stepped clear of the wagon. The little procession moved forward. Avery backed both men against a tree.

"Gunner, guard duty." Gunner was in front of the men, close, ears laid back, showing his teeth. The dog looked absolutely fierce; Avery had to look away to keep from laughing. He held his gun in their direction while he looked into their wagon.

Inside the wagon a jumble of merchandise was heaped carelessly. He saw iron pots and pans and someone's prized feather pillow. There was a clock, tools, and dishes. He saw an old quilt, and when he pulled it aside, he saw the cradle. His breath lodged in his throat.

"Where did you get this?" he demanded bitterly. They looked at each other and shrugged, as if they didn't know or didn't care.

"Help them remember, Gunner."

Gunner stood up, lowered his head and before he could growl, Billy Ray said hurriedly, "Up there. Just a ways. In an old farm. We'll take it back, okay? Nobody was home. We'll take it back."

"Nobody was home? You sure about that?"

"That's right. No one was home."

Avery pulled the cradle out of the wagon. He pulled the old mildewed quilt down and wrapped up the cradle.

"This isn't yours," he said to the two.

"We'll take it back. Nobody was home, like we said. We just wanted to save it."

"Sure," he said. "You stole it. I know where this cradle came from, and you'll take it back all right—with me. Watch them, Gunner."

The dog happily complied, and the two men backed tightly against the tree. Avery went into their wagon looking for something to tie the men with. He found rope that he figured was once someone's clothesline. He wrapped them tightly until they looked like moth cocoons and neither could move very well. Putting Gunner on guard duty, he rode Fan back up the road to his own wagon. He hitched her to the wagon, and they brought it alongside the two thieves.

Avery studied the sorry-looking men. Both were dirty and hungry looking. One wore a Union scarf around his neck; his blue shirt was dirty and torn. The other wore a gray soldier's cap jauntily on his mop of greasy hair.

"Huh. One of each. Desertion can create strange bedfellows. Get up there," he said, trying to sound mean. He got the two men up on the wagon, and though they were barely able to move, he secured them further by lashing them to the wagon. They wouldn't be moving at all when he was finished with them. Their black moustaches were twitching, but nothing else moved. Gunner got on board and lay down, staring at them. They were terrorized by his hot panting breath on their faces.

Avery unloaded the loot from their wagon and placed it in his own wagon. He put the cradle, wrapped in the old quilt, on the seat beside him. He tied their pretty gypsy horse to the back of his wagon.

"Looks like you've robbed some poor gypsies of their nice pony too," Avery accused.

"There wasn't nobody around the caravan, so we thought we should take it and feed it."

"Sure," said Avery, sourly. "Not likely that the gypsies abandoned their caravan and their horse. You two aren't very good liars."

About midday Avery stopped under the shade of some trees and poured out some water for the men to drink. He watered Gunner, allowed him a break in the trees, and then Avery took a break himself.

He watered Fan and the pretty pony. He'd never seen such a pony up close before. He'd occasionally seen one pulling a gypsy caravan through the countryside back home. He decided it was about fourteen and a half hands, technically not a pony. It was wide and strong with distinctive black and white patches. The mane and the tail, snow white, were thick and long, the tail reaching nearly to the ground. She had large feet with lots of white fluffy hair around her fetlocks. To Avery it looked like a small draft horse, but her playful demeanor was more like a circus pony. She had bright flowers, bells, and tassels on her bridle and harness. He could imagine the strong horse pulling a colorful gypsy caravan. He thought of his father's matched draft horses pulling together on the farm. One had been stolen at the start of the war. *Father would like this horse.*

Avery asked the men if they needed to relieve themselves, but afraid to move, they nodded no. So Avery clucked to Fan and they continued their journey with the deserters bound and bouncing in the wagon, the gypsy's horse smartly tied to Avery's wagon and trotting merrily along behind, picking her feet up, bells jingling, and Gunner on guard duty.

Avery didn't think it would be much farther, and he sure hoped he was still on the right road. He'd never approached Rose's house from the east going west. He'd always come from the west headed east. But it wasn't long into the afternoon when he saw the lonely farm silhouette standing out on the empty plateau.

"We're here, Gunner." He stopped the wagon and stared ahead at her deserted-looking homestead. He took a deep breath, bit his lip, and snapped Fan's reins. They trotted courageously up the lane to the dilapidated farm.

"What will we find, Gunner?"

CHAPTER TEN
UNDER THE PEAR TREE

"Mrs. Somebody? Rose?" he called. Gunner ran quickly to the house and pushed open the door with Avery close behind.

"Mrs. Somebody? You here?"

Behind him he heard the shuffling feet coming through the door. "Well, lawdy, lawdy, look who come callin' this day. It be my own, and I'm so glad to have you uns back here on account I got to be takin' care o' some bizness with you uns."

"How've you been, Rose?"

"I got me some sickness, Avery. I go in and out to the privy, and I wash up my hands, and go in and out, and wash my hands. I hardly have time to lay down and be sick. But I been washin' my hands, just like yer tol' me. But I got me some sickness."

"I'm sorry to hear that, Rose. Maybe I can help you. I brought you some food."

"Thanks." She sounded weak and tired.

"I've brought a wagon, too, Rose. I want to take you with me to the city so I can look after you in the winter, keep you warm, and feed you."

He watched her stagger to her cot and sit down on the edge. She looked even smaller than when he last saw her.

"I done my livin' right here, Avery; I aim to do my dyin' here too."

Avery quickly changed the subject.

"Rose, did you see some strange fellows here a day or so ago?"

"Strangers, you say? Don't believe so. But, like I said, I been in and out o' the privy about a week now, and sometimes I can't make it back all the way to the house, so sometimes I have me a nap in the barn. So maybe they come callin' when I's out. They friends of yers?"

"No, they're not friends of mine. But, I ran into them up the road. I was on my way here. They had their wagon stuffed full of other people's belongings that they stole."

"Well, I'll be. Why'd they want to visit me? I ain't got nothin' to steal. Except, you know, over in the corner yonder," she whispered, nodding to the chimney corner.

She glanced over to the corner and noticed only a small pile of quilts. Where was the big one? She hadn't noticed it was missing.

"Lie down, Rose," Avery said as he helped her lie down on her cot. "I'll be right back." He went out to the wagon and brought down the cradle wrapped in the old smelly quilt.

"Hey, mister, me and Billy Ray, we gotta relieve ourselves, okay?" called the thief.

"Later," answered Avery angrily. He carried the quilt in to his friend. "They had this in their wagon."

"Oh, glory be's!" She looked faint. Her color was already poor, and she seemed to be running out of life before his very eyes.

"Sit down, my old Farmer Boy Surgeon Avery," she said. "God kept me here long enough to see yer jes this one more time. And now here you come. I'm so grateful. Remember how yer come in here in the rain that day?" she chuckled. "Yer was the first friend I ever had in a long, long time. I didn't even know that word too much, and I might have fergot it altogether if I never did meet yer. I only know the *friend* word in the Psalms, you know, but I wasn't sure what *friend* might really feel like. When I met yer and the dog, then I knew how friend would feel, all warm, yer know.

"An I never would a knowed how friend looked if yer hadn't come back an fixed my eyes so's I could see y'all. An all that

time, I be waitin' to die and wondrin' what takin' that chariot so long, I's ready to go. But I wanted to see yer agin, because I had some bizness I wanted to say t'yer." She paused and struggled to take a deep breath.

"I want t'give yer that cradle, Avery. You's jest a boy, but you's gitten on, and sometime yer might be havin' yerself a young un what might fit in it, and yer kin tell him all 'bout ol' Rose. An they's somethin' else I want yer to do fer me. It's under this here bed. It's tucked up there, and it's a ol' paper that prob'ly don't read too good; but it's a fer sure real paper deed, an it say's all this land be mine. An I want yer to have it. It's all I got in the world, and it don't mean nothin'. But yer and Gunner, yer means it all t' me, and it's how I kin say thanks, and how I kin do somethin' fer yer. So I want yer to take it out now."

Avery's eyes were burning and his throat was closing up. He couldn't breathe. He didn't think he could speak, but there really wasn't anything to say anyway. *I'm a doctor. I should be able to heal her, but I can't.* He crawled under the cot on the floor of dirt, soot, and rodent droppings. He looked up at the ropes criss-crossed under her. She scarcely made a dent in them. He saw the paper, yellow with age, pressed tightly between her straw ticking and the rope. Carefully he made a space around it with his fingers so it wouldn't tear; he pulled it out. It was stained and a totally different grade of paper than he'd ever seen before. He had difficulty reading it and recognized that it was written with berry juice ink and a quill pen; the writing was very fancy. It looked like some kind of a legal form. The date in the corner said 1709. He'd have to show it to Clayton and his father.

"Now I got to make a mark on it," she said. "Then this land belongs to yer and the dog. Then I be's ready to leave it behind. My chariot be comin', Avery," she said hopefully.

Avery handed her the paper and gave her a piece of charred stick from her fireplace. He knew she couldn't read, so he was interested in how she was studying it, as if she were reading every word. On the bottom of the page following the last word, Rose wrote *RMH* with the charred stick.

"That'd be my mark," she said. "I learnt that when I's just a girl. I 'broidered it on my linen. It's official like."

"It is, Rose. It's official. Rose . . . thank you." Avery swallowed hard. He was deeply moved. He knew that she was saying goodbye.

"I need to go tend to the thieves, and then I'll be back," he said.

"You take yer time. It's all done now."

Avery pulled the two men off the wagon and half dragged them with their legs tied together over to the trees.

"Do your business. You can stand there forever for all I care." He gave them a little shove, nearly causing them to topple over. He walked off and left them at the tree, knowing they weren't going anywhere. His fists were balled, and he felt his temper growing. His breathing was shallow, and he struggled against the lump that was swelling in his throat. He punched at the tree and kicked it. *What good is doctoring? People just die. I'm useless.*

"Gunner! Where are you, Gunner?" He whistled, but Gunner didn't appear.

"Gunner, stop playing around and get out here when I call." He was angry at the men for having taken the cradle and all the other possessions from the poor people between here and the city. *It's the war. I hate it. It's turned people into thieves and turned cities into battlefields.* He was angry with Rose because she was leaving this earth, and he was angry that his dog had gone off without permission. He was angry at himself for being helpless to deal with any of it. *I'm useless. Some doctor!* The emotional turmoil roiled within him.

"Some doctor I turned out to be. What is wrong with me?" His balled fists struck his temples, and he buried his toe in the thin soil, kicking up the dust. He pounded the side of the wagon. He leaned against his wagon, turned and looked at Rose's farm. He bowed his head, and he began to cry. He took some deep breaths and tried to sort out his feelings.

"Gunner, where are you? I can't fix any of this. God, help me. I'm so mad at the entire world. Forgive me. But right now I

hate the whole world." He took a deep breath and looked at his fists. He opened them slowly and deliberately and began to regain control of his emotions. His father had taught him to do this many years ago. He talked to his shadow on the ground.

"These aren't bad men; they're victims of the war. God will be their judge. I can only take them to the authorities who can try to get the stolen things back to their owners. That's all I know to do. I can't be angry with Rose. Dying is part of living. You can't have one without the other. I can't begrudge Rose her time to die. She's been here on this earth ninety-five years and known her share of suffering. Now I have to be happy with her; her chariot is finally coming. She doesn't need a doctor. She only needs a friend." His tears fell freely.

"And Gunner? How could I ever be angry at Gunner? Gunner's my—" Suddenly he knew where Gunner was.

He went back inside, and Gunner was lying beside Rose on her bed. Her limp hand rested lightly on his head, her fragile fingers barely moving. Gunner wasn't moving at all. Avery picked up Rose's tiny wrist and tried to feel a pulse. He felt a faint movement, not really a pulse, as if the last bit of life was eking through the fragile vein on its final circuit. Rose opened her eyes and looked at him.

"Under the pear tree, Avery. That's where I needs to be." He wasn't sure what she meant. *Is that where she wants to be buried? Why the pear tree?*

She lifted her arms to him and said, "Let's go now. I think my chariot is there. My mama is there too." He lifted her up. She weighed nothing. He wrapped her in her quilt and carried her through the door, past the pump. He carried her past the barn, past the privy, and up into the meadow. He carried her up the little knoll to where the lonely pear tree stood.

"Probably been here a hundred years," he murmured. He laid her on the grass under the pear tree among the scattered autumn leaves.

"Oh thank ya, Avery; now I's ready." She started to hum a little tune. She smiled. "I got no pain, Avery." She closed her eyes and took her final shallow breath.

Avery wiped his eyes on his sleeve. Gunner was sitting like a sentinel, staring at the tree. Avery walked down to the tool shed and brought back the shovel. He looked across the quiet fallow fields. A quiet breeze brushed across his face. He noticed the stillness. No birds sang, no insects buzzed. Gunner hadn't moved. Avery dug the hole under the pear tree. Gunner didn't dig; he just stared at the trunk of the pear tree. Avery wrapped the quilt around Rose's tiny body and lowered her into the hole. Gunner didn't get up or sniff; he sat still, staring at the pear tree. Avery covered the hole with the dirt and sat down. Gunner's eyes never left the tree, as if he could see to its core. Avery watched him, wondering.

He looked around at all the natural and untouched beauty of Rose's abandoned land. He was grateful that the war hadn't come through it while she lived. He was sure it soon would. Gunner continued to stare at the pear tree. Avery followed his gaze.

"What do you see, Gunner, that I don't see?"

Avery studied the trunk of the old misshapen tree. "Hasn't been pruned in many years—funny little crotches. I imagine it's taken some lightning hits."

Gunner just stared silently ahead at the tree, his ears on alert, his tail still. Avery fixed his eyes on the lichen covered bark where Gunner stared. He rubbed it, and the lichen fell away. He ran his hands around the pear tree's trunk, and then he saw it: *Mother, 1788.* It was carved in the trunk, and the trunk had healed. *David, 1791.* Below it was a misshapen heart that had also been healed by time. It said *D.R.K. loves R.M.H., 1790.* He rubbed the back side of the trunk and felt the bumps with his fingers. *Baby, 1791.*

Avery went back to the wagon, took his pocketknife out of his knapsack, and then returned to the pear tree where Gunner still sat staring. He remembered the day he'd read the family

page in her Bible aloud to her, uncovering a history she had never known. Now he carved:

Rose Marie Holtom. b Aug 15, 1768, d Sep 6, 1863.

He started back down the meadow and whistled for Gunner to follow. Avery looked back at the pear tree where his dog still sat staring. Two birds appeared and were drifting onto one of the gnarled old branches, stretching their wings. Their bright eyes stared back at him. A rapid fluttering on the end of another branch drew his attention. A small gray bird suddenly appeared there. The birds fluttered briefly around the tree and flew off together. Gunner didn't growl or bark or show any bird-dog excitement; he sat quietly and stared. Avery was breathless.

A soft breeze rustled the leaves on the old tree, and Avery thought he heard a quiet voice blowing with the wind: "Not how it should be, but how it is." That's how Rose had described her life the first time he met her. "Yes," he said sadly, "It's how it is. Goodbye, Rose."

Gunner ran down the hill to the wagon. He lifted his leg on a tree and then hopped up onto the wagon. Avery walked the thieves gently to the wagon and carefully helped them up without a word. He gave them water to drink. He studied their dirty faces. *They're brothers. They look just alike. Like Clayton and me.* He watered the gypsy horse, Fan, and Gunner; then he drank the remaining water. They all headed back to Alexandria.

Avery turned the deserter thieves in to the militia. He posted a broadside notice that anyone who recently had goods stolen should check in with the constable. The constable suggested that Avery take the gypsy horse with him as his reward since they wouldn't be able to take care of her and the gypsy owner would be long gone. Taking his deed, his cradle, and his pony, Avery and Gunner began the trip back to the Simpsons' and back to the hospital to work.

"I'm glad I got to see her again. I'll always remember her," he told them sadly. He named his pretty gypsy horse Rose, and Leon made her comfortable in the Simpsons' stable.

CHAPTER ELEVEN

OTHER PERSPECTIVES ON THE WAR

The autumn leaves began to fall in Alexandria, and the days grew shorter. In the long evenings the news was read and discussed. Rumor had it that the Yankees would soon reach Richmond.

"That's been the talk for more than a year back in Richmond," Avery told the rumormongers. There would be no breaks coming for any of the staff and volunteers. Since Avery had returned there had been a steady procession of incoming soldiers. He was surprised at how far some of them had been carried to reach this hospital. From his memory of his father's atlas, he drew a large map of Virginia on the back side of a large sheet of butcher's oil cloth and hung it on the wall. He began keeping a record of the battles where his patients had seen action: Fredericksburg, skirmishes up and down the Rappahannock River, Chancellorsville, Hampton Roads, someplace the soldiers called The Wilderness, and now he added Gettysburg. He kept lists of his patients and their treatments in his journals, continuing to learn which medicines worked and which didn't. *There is so much more to learn,* he wrote in the margin.

All the soldiers told stories of heroism and cowardice, valor and betrayal; they told of great generals and failed leadership. The Confederate troops were sacking, ravaging, and defeating the Union everywhere. Avery wondered if they might run out of men before they won the war. The numbers of dead and wounded

mounted, and those who survived told their stories. Gettysburg, Avery learned, was in Pennsylvania. These soldiers came a long way, and some in deplorable conditions.

"We had them at Gettysburg. We had them. They were right there. We let them get away. They retreated into Virginia, and we lost again. Why didn't we pursue? Why does the Union keep retreating? We could have taken them. If only . . . if only."

Avery heard the same version of this story from several different soldiers. It interested him that as battered as they all were, they all wished they hadn't retreated. *I wonder if they know how brave they are?* Avery wondered. *I wonder if they wanted to become soldiers or if it just turned out that way?*

The Union Army under General Meade had suffered over twenty thousand casualties at Gettysburg. The field hospital tents overflowed, and soldiers lay on the ground. As soon as they were able to be moved, they were taken by ambulance wagon and train cars to the next available hospital. And here they were—the ones who'd survived. Avery listened to their stories, believing the soldiers were relieved of a huge burden when they were able to tell someone their personal versions of battle. Gunner listened and offered them company. They showed Avery on his map where they'd been, where their company was destroyed, where they'd fallen, or where someone they knew hadn't gotten up. Some of them, ignorant of geography altogether, had no idea where they'd been or where they were or where their homes were waiting.

"The citizens of Gettysburg are concerned about the rain and the wind wearing away the soil from thousands of shallow graves all over the battlefield," an orderly told them. "I read it on a broadside."

"So?" growled a soldier.

"Well, a magazine I looked at says they created a soldiers' cemetery right there on the battleground. Pennsylvania's governor, Andrew Curtin, provided some of his own money."

"Generous of the man, that." The surly soldier seemed a bit more interested.

"Yep. He's paying to remove the soldiers and rebury them properly."

"Good on him then. We've still got some decent ones about then, haven't we?"

Patients who'd been at the battle of Gettysburg were interested in this discussion. Avery listened to them, but rarely commented. He'd been trained in Richmond to keep his opinions to himself, and he found it easier to remain quiet. Sometimes he felt angry. Angry at all the wounds he couldn't repair, the lives he couldn't save. At other times he could rejoice that one of his men healed and went home or back to the battlefield. He was frustrated that there were never enough supplies and never enough healthy foods. Some days he came to work feeling confident and strong, but by nightfall was questioning himself again. *Can I do this the rest of my life? Do I even want to? Am I a quitter?*

"Listen to this," one of the volunteers read from the paper. " '*There was a formal dedication of this new cemetery on November 19, 1863. More than ten thousand people came to see President Lincoln.*' Well, now, that's a good crowd, wouldn't you say? '*Mr. Edward Everett, a statesman from Pennsylvania, spoke longer than two hours about the battle.*' "

His audience groaned. "They should have thrown tomatoes at him."

"They probably don't have any tomatoes over there either."

"Stones then." Everyone laughed.

The volunteer continued reading: " '*People were getting cold and restless, but President Lincoln was planning to speak next.*' Says here that he read from a little piece of used, torn paper from his pocket."

"You mean even the President doesn't have any paper stationery?"

"Guess things are bad for everybody, huh?"

" '*His address was scribbled on the used paper, and it lasted about three minutes. Its simple eloquence stunned his audience.*' How about that? Here, Doc, read us what he said."

Avery sat on the edge of the soldier's cot and straightened out the tattered newspaper. He began reading.

" '*The Gettysburg Address.*' I guess that's the name of the speech."

By Abraham Lincoln, President of the United States, November 19, 1863.

Four score and seven years ago our fathers brought forth on this continent, a new nation, conceived in Liberty, and dedicated to the proposition that all men are created equal.

Now we are engaged in a great civil war, testing whether that nation, or any nation so conceived and so dedicated, can long endure. We are met on a great battlefield of that war. We have come to dedicate a portion of that field, as a final resting place for those who here gave their lives that that nation might live. It is altogether fitting and proper that we should do this.

But, in a larger sense, we cannot dedicate—we cannot consecrate—we cannot hallow—this ground. The brave men, living and dead, who struggled here, have consecrated it, far above our poor power to add or detract. The world will little note, nor long remember what we say here, but it can never forget what they did here. It is for us the living, rather, to be dedicated here to the unfinished work which they who fought here have thus far so nobly advanced. It is rather for us to be here dedicated to the great task remaining before us—that from these honored dead we take increased devotion to that cause for which they gave the last

full measure of devotion—that we here highly resolve that these dead shall not have died in vain—that this nation, under God, shall have a new birth of freedom—and that government of the people, by the people, for the people, shall not perish from the earth.

Abraham Lincoln.

Only breathing was heard in the ward. Avery and the nurses read the words from the newspaper so many times to so many soldiers that day they almost knew it from memory. Soldiers who'd been at the Battle of Gettysburg, hearing the speech for the first time, wept unashamedly. Several tried to commit it to memory.

"I won't ever forget this," one soldier told Avery. "I'm going to teach it to my sons. I hope they'll teach it to theirs. I'll teach it to my nephews too. Their pa's laying out there somewhere. My brother. He ain't goin' home with me."

My brother, thought Avery, *is at home, where I should be. Are they reading this at home? I'm going. Maybe tomorrow. Leave all this behind with Mr. Lincoln. It's not my war.*

CHAPTER TWELVE
MIXED BLESSINGS

"Did you see the broadside in town this morning, Matt?" Avery said. "In spite of the hardships, President Lincoln reminds the nation there are still things to be grateful for. Secretary of State Seward has written a proclamation signed by the President. The third Thursday in November is going to be a day dedicated to giving thanks. And this year, along with giving thanks, he asks everyone to pray for healing for the wounded nation."

"Things must look different in the capital. I'm not sure folks here are feeling too grateful," Matt snickered. "Nor can most folks recall a lot to be thankful for right now."

"Listen though. He's calling it Thanksgiving Day. He wants it to be a feast day. That's a good idea, isn't it?"

"Most folks don't have much to feast upon these days, Avery, with food and staples so scarce. What's he expect?"

"It's a day for families to unite in prayer."

"Even though most heads of families are absent?"

"It's supposed to be like a homecoming or a visitation day. But since most people's horses and wagons have been sequestered, I wonder who can go visit? Not many will be going home, that's for sure."

"Well, I wish the President luck with his plan. Sounds good on paper, but I doubt it will catch on," said Matt.

Avery shrugged. *Maybe I'll go home for Thanksgiving Day.*

But later that day when Avery returned to the Simpsons', he discovered the undaunted women of the city had already begun to plan. Several churches announced special Thanksgiving Day services. Lacking the fruits, vegetables, and ribbons they normally used to decorate the town square for festivities, the creative housewives crafted fake ones from wax, papier-mâché, or wood. The city of Alexandria and cities across the nation were taking this new holiday seriously. Homes, storefronts, and churches exhibited wreaths and garlands, fake fruit, colored leaves, dried stalks of grain, even corn shocks, unlike any festive decorations Avery had ever seen before. Mrs. Simpson had arranged dried weeds and vines on the table. She ironed scraps of fabric with her flat iron, making them look like ribbons, and then she tied the strips around the stems of her bouquets that would soon hang on the church doors.

"Huh. Looks like folks do still believe they have some things to be thankful for," he said.

Mrs. Simpson invited neighbors and told the doctors to invite Claire and Matthew Mason to join them for their feast dinner.

"You're inviting Claire?"

"Well, of course, Avery. She's a lovely girl far from home. I enjoy her company, and I do believe that you do as well. Am I wrong?" Her eyebrow lifted suspiciously over a twinkling eye.

"Oh, well, no, I mean, well . . . I'll ask her. Uh, Mrs. Simpson? I've been thinking about something, but I don't quite know how to explain this."

"Well this sounds like something serious. We'll probably need some cider for this. Come, come. Out to the kitchen, dear boy."

Mrs. Simpson seated Avery at the table and poured two mugs of watered-down cider. "Now then, what's on your mind?"

"I've been wondering if I'm really cut out for doctoring. Maybe I should go home and farm. Maybe I'll go at Thanksgiving time. You know, the family time the President wants. Everyone expects me to be a doctor—a really good doctor, first in my class and all. Maybe I can't be that doctor. Maybe I'll disappoint everyone."

"Who is everyone?"

"Dr. Simpson. My parents. My patients. My teachers. I just don't want to let everyone down. How do I know what I really want to do with my life?"

"Avery, no one can prescribe your life for you. But you are so young. You don't have to decide everything now. You have time to try a lot of things, and just because you try something doesn't mean you have to do it forever. Right now you're trying to be a doctor. And from what I hear, you're a really good surgeon. You have a lot of responsibility on your shoulders for a young man. But you've got broad shoulders." She smiled.

"It's all those men. All the ones I couldn't save."

"You? That's not up to you. You do the best you know how. But saving them? That's not on you, Avery. And if you think it is, then you are thinking too highly of yourself." She paused and sipped her cider. "What would you be if you weren't a doctor?"

"Probably a farmer. I like farming. I'm good at that."

"Uh-huh, I'm sure you are. And when the drought comes and the corn shrivels up, will that be your fault? When the wheat is ripe, will you take credit for that? We can only do the best we know how, Avery. We aren't God! Do what you enjoy, and do it the best you can. If you choose wrong or get tired of it, you can change your mind. Do something else. But don't be in a great hurry now to cut your entire future in stone. It's not necessary. You're only human. Now shoo. I've got work to do."

Just go do it? Isn't that what Jones said? Not in stone. That's what Jones said. I could change my mind later and that's okay. I'm not a quitter. Saving them isn't mine to do.

Mrs. Simpson spent days accumulating rations. Where she found them, Avery couldn't imagine. He planned to go goose hunting to help, but he wasn't too optimistic. Feeding two armies and two capital cities, most of the game in eastern Virginia was depleted.

When Claire arrived for dinner on Thanksgiving Day, she carried a wrinkled brown paper bag and wore a radiant smile. She held out the bag to a surprised Mrs. Simpson, who carried it to the table to open it. Gunner pushed his head up in the midst of all

the guests so he could see what was happening on the table. Mrs. Simpson opened the bag and rolled the contents out on the table: small, hard, beautiful potatoes. Gunner smacked his jowls.

"They're sent from my parents' potato farm. They're givin' thanks to you for your kindness to their daughter," Claire said sprightly. Everyone looked at the potatoes as if they were nuggets of gold. Gunner licked his lips.

"Praise be to God!" exclaimed Dr. Simpson. "These are the most beautiful potatoes I've seen in a while." He gave Claire a little peck on the cheek. "Mrs. Simpson, let's see what kind of miracle you can produce with these, my dear."

"Oh, Claire, what a wonderful gift this is. I must write to your generous family. Thank you so much. Who would've guessed how appreciative we'd learn to be for a simple brown potato?" Mrs. Simpson shook her head and carried the potatoes in her apron out to the kitchen.

"I'll help you," said Claire. Mrs. Simpson put a kettle of water on the fire to boil while Claire diced the potatoes and dropped them into the water. Fragrant steam hovered under the kitchen's low ceiling.

The friends gathered and bowed their heads around the Simpsons' friendly table.

"I'm sorry there's no tablecloth on our table. I've torn it into strips for the Committee on Sanitation to use for bandages. We'll just make do," Mrs. Simpson said.

Dr. Simpson asked the blessing. "Come Lord, our Guest to be, and bless these gifts bestowed by Thee. Bless our loved ones everywhere, and keep them in Thy loving care. Amen."

Claire helped Mrs. Simpson bring the food to the table in a grand procession. Since there wasn't an abundance of anything, they gave great importance to the small amounts. Avery and Gunner had produced a small wood duck and a carp from the river, but no goose. The neighbors brought a slice of smoked ham; it was the last piece in their smokehouse. Mrs. Simpson baked bread using very coarse flour and grain. It was hard to chew, but it had Avery's honey on it. Claire's potatoes were diced in small pieces

to be sure everyone would get some. The neighbors had obtained some yams from a local market, and Mrs. Simpson had discovered some exotic raisins at the port. She had also made a wonderful rhubarb cobbler. All summer she'd been tending the rhubarb hidden behind the carriage barn.

"Nobody bothers with the rhubarb," she said, smiling as her guests raved about the cobbler. "They think it's just a big weed. I brought these old plants from Boston many years ago. It might be the only rhubarb growing south of the Mason-Dixon."

"Mrs. Simpson, I'm from New England, and I just love rhubarb." Matt beamed his radiant smile. When the meal was over, Avery was asked to give the closing blessing.

"Gathered around our table, our hearts unite in praise to Thee, our heavenly Father, Who blesses all our days. Help us always to have grateful ways. Amen."

It warmed Avery to know that across the state at the Bennett's own Thanksgiving table, his father would be saying exactly the same thing. He wondered what they might be eating and if little Phoebe was now sitting at the table with them. He was happy knowing that General Keese would be with his family in Kanawha Valley. Gunner was under the table with his head on Avery's knee. Avery reached under the table and passed a little cube of potato to his friend.

"Happy Thanksgiving, Gunner. I give thanks for you, my friend." He looked around at the table and made a mental image of the moment. It would remain in his mind just as clearly as a Matthew Brady ambrotype.

Later that afternoon following their guests' departures, the doctor's and Gunner's naps, and Claire's and Avery's kitchen cleanup, they all decided to take a walk on the glorious autumn day. As they strolled through the town, they spoke to many Alexandrians who were all out walking on the peaceful Thanksgiving Day. Looking about, one would never guess the city was under occupancy, full of spies, and that the enemy lurked only a hundred miles away in Richmond. There were many soldiers strolling with

ladies on their arms today, and none looked ready to defend the perimeters of the city.

Avery noticed their escorting styles. He thought he might offer his arm to Claire the next time Dr. Simpson asked him to escort her back to the nurses' dorm. He wondered what Claire might think of that. He noticed that some of the soldiers talked to the ladies, but some of them didn't. He quietly observed all the ladies and gentlemen that afternoon. When they passed by Christ Church on Washington Street, gatherings of people were going inside.

"They must be holding a Thanksgiving service here," Dr. Simpson commented.

"Then we should join them, don't you think?" asked Mrs. Simpson.

"Oh, yes, let's do," responded Claire with her typical enthusiasm. The two doctors shrugged their shoulders and followed the women into the church. Gunner pressed against Avery's leg. A few eyebrows went up at the sight of the dog in church, but no one said anything. It never occurred to Avery that Gunner might not be welcomed. Gunner went everywhere with him, and Avery took it for granted.

"This is a very historic church," Mrs. Simpson whispered to Claire. "It's the Church of England and was George Washington's family's church. And before the war, Robert E. Lee also attended services here." Claire was very impressed when Mrs. Simpson pointed out the brass nameplates on the pews.

"This is such a popular and historic place," Mrs. Simpson said, "that every regiment posted in Alexandria receives only one opportunity to attend services here."

"Is that right?" Avery asked. "I didn't know that." He wondered if General Keese's regiment had taken their turn.

Once they were seated, Gunner lay at Avery's feet. Avery and Claire looked all around.

Claire squirmed and whispered to Avery, "I can almost feel his imposing presence here." She gave a little shiver. Avery

didn't know who she was referring to: George Washington, General Lee, or God.

There were many soldiers at this service. Some looked dazed and awed, and Claire knew that they also felt that same presence. She recognized a few of the ambulatory patients from Mansion House Hospital and some of the volunteers with them, all giving thanks for their blessings and praying for the country as their President had asked them to do. Side by side, Claire and Avery bowed their heads. For the first time in quite a while, Avery felt comfortable with himself, as if Alexandria was where he needed to be at this time in his life. He was thankful for that peace.

Following the service, Dr. Simpson asked Avery if he would please escort the nurse home. Avery agreed and, although he didn't mind at all, he wondered if Dr. Simpson realized how capable Claire was of taking care of herself. She smiled at him and slipped her hand around his arm. He liked how she felt on his arm. He found it quite comfortable actually. They walked without talking. One thing he'd noticed about Claire was that she didn't insist on conversation all the time. He liked that about her. Gunner passed him a few confused glances. Avery pretended not to notice. He inhaled a slight fragrance of violets. When they reached the nurses' dormitory, Claire thanked him and said, "See you tomorrow, Avery. Bye, Gunner."

Avery felt a sudden impulse to say something—anything—to keep her there for another minute. "Uh, Claire, uh, I was just wondering, um . . . when is your birthday?" he blurted out.

He felt his face redden. *Oh, why did I say that?* his brain moaned. Gunner rolled his eyes. "I know," he whispered to Gunner. "I know. I did it again."

But Claire looked totally unaffected as if it were a perfectly normal question. "It's the first day of May. Next I'll be eighteen years. Good day now, and thank you for walking with me, Avery. Hasn't it been an altogether fine day?"

"Uh-huh," he said lamely.

Claire went inside. Gunner looked at Avery and cocked his head.

"You think I'm pretty hopeless, don't you, Gunner." Gunner whined his response, and Avery had to laugh. The two hiked back to the Simpsons'.

"I gave thanks today for Claire," he told the dog. "What do you make of that?" Gunner gave a lift of his paw and pranced a little dance around Avery, his tail whipping the air.

"Oh yeah?" He kicked a pinecone, and his happy dog went after it. "You like her, don't you, Gunner?"

They jogged the rest of the way.

CHAPTER THIRTEEN

"NOT HOW IT SHOULD BE, BUT HOW IT IS"

When Avery and Gunner returned to the Simpsons', Avery thanked Mrs. Simpson for the wonderful dinner and had a second piece of rhubarb cobbler. She'd saved an uncooked duck wing for Gunner, knowing that he'd helped to provide it. Avery carried his cobbler into the doctor's study where he found the doctor reading.

"Dr. Simpson," Avery began his prepared speech. "There's something I've wanted to talk to you about. I'm deeply grateful for all that you and Mrs. Simpson have provided for me. But now that I'm receiving my soldiering pay, I'd like to begin to pay for my board and room, if that's not offensive to you. My father always told me it's important that we pay our way in all matters. Could we come up with agreeable terms, sir?"

"You are a tribute to your parents and your roots, my boy. Your grandfather would be proud of you, as I am, also. I understand your need to do this, and I'm gratified. Yes, we certainly can come to terms. Now let's see . . . would one dollar a week for your room and another dollar a week for your meals be justified?"

"Absolutely, sir. That would be just fine. I'll begin to pay with my first soldier pay at the hospital. Thank you, sir." Avery felt as if he might have just grown a bit more beyond the six-foot measure. He and Gunner retired to their room.

A few of the ambulatory patients enjoyed singing together to pass the time. One was especially skilled with shape-note

singing, and he created cards of music so others could learn. Whenever Avery was working nearby or making first-floor rounds, he enjoyed listening to them.

"Whatever it takes to cheer us all up," he commented. "And it looks like music does a pretty good job of that!" Most of their songs were new to Avery, but he especially enjoyed hearing them sing "Shall We Gather at the River." It had a catchy tune, and the men harmonized it so well. He liked the words. *Father would like these words too,* he thought. *I wonder if he's ever heard this?* Avery was humming along. The music helped to keep his mind off home, where there was some troubling news.

The most recent letter from home said that little Phoebe had lost her hearing from measles. Aunt Caroline was frantically checking out a special school for Phoebe in Spartanburg, South Carolina. They were all devastated. In his reply to Aunt Caroline, he told her about Timothy McDougal. He wondered if it might help to talk to the McDougals and see if there might be something done for Timothy at the school too. Was it too late for Timothy to learn how to live with deafness as well as blindness? He wondered if they might be able to comfort and support each other. *Even those who aren't soldiers can be afflicted, and doctors can't help it.* Avery pondered that as he moved among his patients and listened to the singers downstairs.

Avery barely remembered Dr. Simpson handing him the telegram that afternoon. He put it into his pocket, waiting until he could find time to read it. He nearly forgot about it until Gunner nudged his pocket curiously, trying to figure out what was in it.

Avery sat down to read it, and later he remembered only the numbness that encompassed his body as he walked his rounds and wrote his report on each patient. He didn't remember going home with Dr. Simpson, and he didn't remember supper. Had he eaten? His mind, his body, and his soul seemed to be stuck on that moment he read the telegram. He couldn't go back; he couldn't go forward; he didn't want to be in this moment, but here he was—*stuck.*

The news that his father had died in Wheeling was so overwhelming that he simply couldn't digest it. The news seemed to stick everywhere within him, as if the mechanics of his body had suddenly shut down. A large lump stuck in his throat; he couldn't swallow. There was a knot stuck in his stomach; he couldn't digest food. His mind was stuck on that moment, and he couldn't think beyond it. His tears were stuck behind his eyes; his head throbbed, stuck in the vise of sorrow.

This was so sudden, so unexpected. He was stricken with grief so thick—thick as oatmeal—that he couldn't release it. He had the feeling he was in two places at the same time. While his heart was sorrowing with his mother in Kanawha, his feet were stuck in Alexandria, long, difficult miles from home where his father was being buried.

He didn't know how many days this anguish lasted; he lost track of time. He was barely aware of how many times in his lonely sorrow Claire appeared with an encouraging smile and a squeeze of his hand. The Simpsons quietly acknowledged him and encouraged him; he hardly heard them. He didn't know if anyone else noticed, and it didn't matter. His grief consumed him—stuck, just stuck as it was, inside him. He couldn't eat; he couldn't sleep; he couldn't talk; he couldn't think; he couldn't even cry. Would he be stuck like this forever, he wondered, like a wooden soldier? The telegram informed him that a letter would follow. He waited and eventually it came.

Dearest Avery,

You've already received my telegram. I can only imagine how devastating that news was to you. It was a shock and devastation to us all, but we're all here together, and you, dear son, are alone. I pray that you've friends for comfort.

I needn't tell you that your father was a wonderful man. You know that. He enjoyed his life on this earth with us. He was a man of great faith who will reap his heavenly reward.

Dying is a part of living, Avery; you cannot have one without the other. I have taught you that all your life. It is true with puppies, mares, and all those we love. We're all here for an unspecified time, and we can only hope that it was time well spent and pleasing to God.

A good father, husband, and charitable neighbor, your father was honest, hard working, and diligent as a lawyer, a farmer, and a legislator. He was charitable to all, and he had a grateful heart. He was humble. His very life gave praise and glory to God.

You have known these things, of course, loving him as you do. But, oh, how many others knew these things too! I have a basketful of telegrams and letters. Most are from people I don't know, and several are from Boston. But they all express gratitude that he was a part of their lives, and they said he made a difference in theirs. He was a blessing to many people.

The day of his burial was cold, rainy, and windy. The rain threatened all day to become sleet. We buried him on the orchard hill, our favorite place of all. When I looked around me, I could scarcely catch my breath. Buggies and wagons stretched down the road as far as I could see. How word traveled so fast through the valley, I can't guess. The members of congress came in the bad weather from Wheeling, and lawyers, friends, and associates from Parkersburg were also there. Friends from every holler in the Kanawha Valley were there. Everyone he knew came to say goodbye and thank you to our man, paying respect to a life well lived.

What more could anyone ask for in this lifetime, dearest Avery, than to die with no enemy glad to see him gone? To have all the pages of that lifetime filled with goodness? What more?

All who knew him, loved him; all are feeling emptiness, just as you are, in that large space he used to fill. But for him, we must rejoice; the grief is only for ourselves.

He left for Wheeling on a Monday, hearty and hale. He took ill on Tuesday. On Wednesday he sought advice of a doctor. Thursday he went to the hospital, where he died on Friday with the jaundice. He died in Clayton's arms. You, surrounded every moment of every day with the miseries and noise of awful, lingering deaths, can be grateful for his quiet and dignified death.

You must go on with your work there now, dear son, as all of us must do. You must know how very proud your father is of you and your work. Continue on then with a grateful heart that you've been fathered and instructed by such a man. You carry more of him than just his name.

With love and God's blessings,

Mother

When Avery finished reading the letter, he was scarcely breathing. His body was rigid, and his neck ached where the grief had been stuck so firmly for weeks. He felt as if every cell, every tissue, every muscle, every organ of his body would burst. The tears that had been stuck in his eyes poured forth. He bawled buckets of tears. He swallowed the lump that had stuck in his throat, and he sobbed uncontrollably. Tears seemed to issue from every pore of his body and puddle in the creases and wrinkles of his worn, stained clothes.

Gunner came quietly and laid his head on Avery's lap, squeezing between his legs and chin. The steady stream of uncontrolled tears trickled off Gunner's head.

He felt Claire's presence. His shoulders shook with the sobbing, and he felt her strong hands kneading the knots in his neck and shoulders, releasing the tension that had stuck there since

he'd read the telegram. He cried for a long time with no shame or embarrassment until exhausted and drained, he finally ran out of tears. He heard a small voice ripple through his consciousness. It was Mrs. Somebody. *"Not how it should be, but how it is. Not how it should be, but how it is."*

Gunner moved slightly, sensing a change in Avery. Avery turned to look at Claire, but she was gone. He stood up, and tears slid down his rubberized apron, splashing onto the step. Gunner picked something up from the step where Avery had been sitting. It was a handkerchief with a tatted edging. It had tiny embroidered letters in the corner, C.A.M., and was damp with tears. He felt his load of grief shared and lifted. He put the handkerchief into his pocket. It smelled slightly of violets.

"Come, Gunner, let's get back to work." His feet, no longer stuck, moved swiftly. He smiled slightly for the first time in weeks, and Gunner responded with a happy swish of the tail. Avery looked about him and was amazed to discover that the world had continued without him.

On the third floor he saw Claire bathing soldiers with bed bugs, body lice, and sores. "Top of the mornin' to you, Doctor," she said when she saw him. "Where's Gunner this fine mornin'?"

"He must have stayed downstairs to visit, I guess." Sometime he'd have to thank her for her comfort, but it couldn't be now. His wounded heart and soul were healing, but he needed more time. He reached into his pocket and caressed the little handkerchief.

"I'm going to be okay," he told her.

"Yes," she smiled, "you are."

He watched her a little longer, and then he began to hum "Shall We Gather at the River" and walked on. *Yes,* he thought, *I'm going to be okay, and I'll see my father at the river. There'll be a nice brook trout waiting for us, just as it should be. I'll bring the poles, Father.* He smiled slightly, and whistling his new favorite tune he made his morning rounds.

CHAPTER FOURTEEN
ICE AND CANDY

Christmas season in 1863 Alexandria wasn't quite the way folks remembered Alexandrian Christmases. There was no snow. There was rain and sleet. The streets were slippery and dangerous for horses and pedestrians. Supplies coming into the city were slower because the ice blocked the waterways. Iced railroad tracks and roads made all transportation perilous.

Several of the local volunteers had gone to their homes for Christmas Day, leaving the hospital short-handed when they were unable to return because of the ice. Mrs. Simpson had caught a bad cold with a cough and spent the week with a camphor lamp, honey, and Avery's book of poetry.

"Perhaps," suggested Dr. Simpson, "instead of a Christmas dinner, we should begin to plan for a nice picnic in the spring. What would everyone say to that?" Of course, they agreed.

So with their coffee on Christmas morning, Dr. Simpson and Avery said prayers and read Scripture, and then Avery went to the hospital, leaving Dr. Simpson to look after his wife. Claire was already there along with the few nurses who stayed in town and a few volunteers who lived too far away to go home. *How did she get here?* he wondered. He was relieved to see that she was safe.

"Well, since it's Christmas, it's right that we *should* be here. These patients need us to bring them some Christmas joy," announced the reasonable Claire. So as the doctors began their rounds, Claire carried a large candle that she had made. She'd

pressed holly leaves and berries into the warm wax, making a pretty decoration on the candle. She carried it lit and sat it at every bedside while she wished each patient a happy and blessed Christmas. She added her hopes for their recovery and a victory for the war.

"Hear! Hear!" the patients said.

Claire and her nurses sang some carols. They led the ambulatories in Christmas singing and reading from their soldiers' Bibles. The nurses prayed with the weak. The patients all admired the Christmas candle. Everyone felt nostalgic, and both nurses and patients missed home. But Claire's joy overcame any sadness they might have felt. Gunner showed up on the first floor.

"There you are!" Avery said to him. "I should've known you'd be down here having a party with the ambulatories and Claire!"

Claire and Valor Clad, one of the volunteers, tied a little bag around Gunner's neck and sent him around the floor, telling the patients to help themselves to a special treat from Gunner; it would only cost them a pat on the head. Gunner stopped in front of Avery, who reached into the little bag and pulled out a sailing ship. Some of the patients had soldiers, some had animals, ladies, or trains. Each object was amber in color and clear, like glass, with astonishing detail.

"Well, go ahead, taste it," said Val.

"Taste it? We should eat it?"

"It's candy," said Val. He was excited. "Go on, taste it!"

"Looks like a toy," said one of the patients licking his tiny steam engine.

"It's called clear toy candy," he said. "My pa, my brothers, and me, we own a candy factory in Pennsylvania. It's called V. Clad and Sons. My grandpap started it. How do you like it? Good, huh?" The man's eager eyes were shining. All the patients, nurses, doctors, and volunteers were licking, sucking, and smacking. Sugar, a rare treat, had never tasted more pure and satisfying.

"Candy! Imagine that," smacked Avery. "Even the word sounds sweet—candy. How do you make these little shapes, Val?"

"We use molds for them. The molds are made of iron, but the shaping is done in brass. Everyone in Pennsylvania likes them, and Pa thought I ought to introduce them around. He sent them to me at the post office. So . . . do you like them?"

Everyone nodded in astonishment and studied the various detailed shapes. They were in agreement that candy was definitely a nice treat, at Christmas or any other time.

"Well, then," said Val, "here are some cards for everyone, and if you'd like to order candy from us, here is the address. Happy Christmas from the Candy Makers," he cheered. Everyone took a little card and promised to order some candy when they returned home when the war was over.

"May I take a spare candy?" asked Avery.

"Sure," said Val eagerly. "Got a girl?" he winked.

"No, no, I don't." Avery felt a bit embarrassed by the question. "I've got a little cousin who I think might really like one of these. I'm sure she's never had a candy before."

He picked out a little train. He wrapped it carefully in a piece of paper and later would make a packet and mail it to Phoebe.

"An amazing journey for a little train," Avery said, "from Pennsylvania to Virginia to West Virginia in the middle of the war." He imagined Phoebe playing in front of the fire where he had played and read as a child. *When this war is over, I will be there with you, Phoebe.*

The rest of the Christmas Day was spent on the second and third floors replacing dressings, bathing patients, making beds, and examining wounds and surgical sites. *Illnesses and injuries don't care that it's Christmas, but I do. My gift will be doctoring. It's what I want to do . . . at least today.*

Thankfully there were no surgeries or new patients this day, and only two men were buried. Avery was sure there were battles waging somewhere in Virginia or Tennessee or Carolina, but for today Alexandria was coated in ice, and the battlefront was frozen in silence.

The next day the sun came out, and the glistening ice coating began to drip. The icicles dripped into little pools of water, and the ice on the ground began to crack and snap underfoot. The tree branches began to pop, and pieces of ice fell to the ground in little clinks. The wood pile began to drip, and all around was the sound of water trickling down roofs and other inclines. Walking became safer, as long as one remained alert and careful. The air was cold and smelled fresh, and the awful ice storm of 1863 was at last passing in drips and drops.

A few days later Avery was surprised to see General Keese coming across the slushy yard with happy, tail-wagging Gunner at his heel. The General was laughing and playing with the dog as they approached the hospital.

"Good morning, Dr. Bennett," the General cried happily. "Look what I found this morning, an old hound dog!"

"Nice to see you, General," Avery said, meaning every word. It had been quite a while since he'd seen him.

General Keese grinned. He held a little packet in one hand, and with his other hand he saluted Avery. Surprised, Avery quickly shifted the basin he was carrying to return the salute. *This is odd*, he thought. *The General usually isn't so formal with the medical corps.* The General handed a little insignia to Avery.

"Congratulations, Corporal Bennett." Avery looked at the insignia, and it suddenly dawned on him that he'd just been promoted in the army!

He drew himself up to attention and saluted the officer.

Ceremony dispensed with, they laughed and shook hands.

"The world's a better place because of you, Corporal Bennett." His words jolted Avery and echoed in his mind before settling in his heart. It was a sudden realization for Avery. This was his purpose. It was here. And the world was a better place because he was here, trying and doing his best. He gasped deeply.

"Avery?"

"Oh! Oh, thank you, sir. Oh, yes, what did you say? Sorry."

"Would you happen to have a spare bed here?"

"A spare bed? Are you tired?"

"We've got a prisoner in the prison hospital who's decided he'd rather be a Union patient than a Confederate prisoner. He's a bit of healing left to do, but if you can handle him here, we can take his oath of allegiance and bring him here."

"Well, sir, we never have a spare bed, but we can always add a bed or cot or mat, depending on the need."

"He could probably do okay on a cot; he's not sick. I'll bring him by in a little while if that's okay with you. After that there's something personal I'd like to talk to you about, if you can spare a moment of your time, Doctor."

"I can arrange that. This afternoon will be fine. I'll have the volunteers prepare a cot. What is the matter with the man so we'll know where to put him? Wounds? Amputation?"

"It looks like he took a shot in the buttocks. He seems to be recovering well enough. Limps bad. Nervous sort of man though. Maybe it's the war experience. Always looking over his shoulder expecting someone to be after him. Real jumpy."

"Hmm. Likely a bit of anxiety. We'll see to him." And with a new confidence, Avery gave the orders.

CHAPTER FIFTEEN

MA PARKS AND SQUIRREL

The volunteers were preparing a cot on the wound floor when they heard loud voices and commotion down on the first floor. What were the ambulatories up to now, they wondered.

The first-floor patients were lined up along the wall with their hands in the air when one of the nurses appeared and screamed at the sight of a large woman aiming a long rifle at the patients. The nurse's scream alerted the staff who, one by one, hurriedly moved in on this spectacle.

The large woman looked like a man wearing skirts. She wore a leather fringed vest over a man's shirt, men's leather gloves, a scarf around her neck, and a large, floppy felt hat. Her boots were muddy. Her little wire glasses were so covered in dust that it was a wonder she could see through them. She walked and talked like a man. She held a long rifle that she clearly knew how to shoot, and all the patients and staff at the other end of her rifle, with their hands in the air, believed she would.

Gunner came upstairs whining and insisting that Avery follow him. They were just coming down the stairs when they heard the woman's loud booming voice.

"I know he's here, and there ain't no use tryin' to hide him. I'm goin' to find him, and I'll blow his stinkin' head off. And if you don't care to help me find him in this stink hole, then I might just shoot the lot of you as well."

Avery could see the woman from where he stood behind the line of volunteers. He looked around. He could see Claire standing at the end of the bunch of staff and patients who all held their hands up in the air. She had her arms folded across her chest and was obviously annoyed at having her work interrupted. She felt Avery's eyes on her and slowly turned her head to see where he and Gunner were.

"Well, anybody goin' to show me where the polecat's hidin' out?"

One of the orderlies stepped forward.

"Just exactly who are you looking for?"

"I'm lookin' for . . . and *will* find . . . with or without y'all's help . . . the alley cat that stole my share. That low-down snake with the yella' streak down his back. I know he's here. Prob'ly got shot in the backside runnin' away. He's so yella' he'd never put his self in the line o' fire, that much I know. Squirrel is a sneaky, stealin', connivin' gold thief. I taught him everything he knows, and he crossed me, and he ain't gettin' away with it. He figured to hide out in the war. Hah! Well, I'm a-tailin' 'im now," she bellowed.

The orderly gathered his courage.

"I'm afraid we haven't seen anyone matching that description here." Everyone snickered and relaxed a little bit.

"You'll be the first one I shoot, mister smarty pants," she sneered. The room quieted.

Avery slipped through the crowd. He sent Gunner around the other way to Claire's side. He gave Claire a slight nod, and she and Gunner moved slightly in line with the woman. Hoping to keep the woman's attention off Claire and Gunner's movements, he stepped forward in front of the woman.

"May I help you, madame," he said, as if addressing royalty. "I'm Dr. Bennett, surgeon in charge today. Perhaps you'd like to step into my office, and we'll see how we can be of service to you."

The woman gave him a haughty smile. "Well, about time somebody showed some respect here. Where's your office, Doc?"

"I'd like you to release my patients and staff first, so they can get back to work and back to bed. You and I can tend to business then. Okay?"

"Go on," she waved angrily to the room full of people. "Go on, git. I got the Doc here, I don't need y'all, so git to work."

Just as the staff was breaking up and leaving the first floor, General Keese walked in the front door with his Rebel prisoner turned Yankee patient.

The patient was using a crutch, and it appeared to Avery that moving caused him great pain, as his face contorted with every step, and he relied heavily on the crutch. As they opened the door, the big woman turned and saw them. She raised her gun and began to yell.

"There you are, you low-down, sneakin' thief! I knew you was here. I was hopin' those Yankees didn't blow your head off 'til I got here. Your brother told me you was in a hospital in Alexandria. I traveled far and wide to track you down, you snake. You think you were goin' to get away with this? You rotten polecat!"

"Ma!" the prisoner gasped. "How did you find—"

"Ma?" Avery stepped around her and stood in front of his patient where she was pointing her gun. "I have to ask you to put your gun down. This is a hospital. We've no need for guns."

"Well, Doc, now that I found what I was lookin' for, there's no need for you either. So you either move, or I shoot you."

She lifted her gun higher, aimed at Avery, and in the blink of an eye Gunner was in the air crashing into her from the side. The General stuck his foot out, and she toppled over it, hitting the floor hard. Avery grabbed the gun and handed it off to an orderly. The General let go of his patient, who sprinted out the door with no pain and no crutch, running full tilt across the yard. The surprised General looked at Avery.

"You got this one?"

Avery nodded and the General was out the door, Gunner leading the charge, barking, and in hot pursuit. Claire was on top of the woman binding her hands together with bandages.

"Sure hate to waste these good bandages on the likes of her," she mumbled angrily.

The General and Gunner caught up with Squirrel as he tried to hide himself in the shadow of one of the Mansion House chimneys. As soon as he saw the dog racing toward him, he surrendered on the spot, hands in the air. He walked peaceably back to the hospital with no limp and no crutch.

"Please, sir, just take me to the jail. Don't give me up to her. She's a-goin' to shoot me. I just know it."

"Didn't you call her *ma*? Is she *your* ma?"

"Yes siree, she sure is, and this time she means to shoot me. She's threatened me lots of times, but this is the first time she's loaded the gun. Don't give me to her."

"War sure brings them out," General Keese chuckled and shook his head. The orderly went to get the militia, and when the General and Gunner returned with the patient, the militia took charge of the woman and the General's hoodlum patient. The staff and the volunteers listened and watched with interest as the questioning went on and the story unfolded.

Ma, her hands bound tightly behind her with Claire's bandages, stumbled along behind the militia captain who shoved her into the corner.

"So let me guess. You're Ma Parks."

"None of yer business who I am," she snarled. "I'm intendin' to get my stash back from that hare-brained, thievin' son of mine."

"Look who's calling the kettle black," the captain laughed and nudged Avery.

"Need any help here?" General Keese asked the captain. Avery held the woman's rifle pointed to the ground.

"How you know who I am anyway?"

"There's a picture of you at the post office," said the captain. "It says you and your two sons, Claude and Squirrel, are wanted for stealing gold bars in a train robbery in Missouri. Says there's a Federal bounty on you."

"That so, is it? Well, they done got Claude. Last I heard he was in prison in St. Louis. But this here Squirrel, you can just shoot him soon's as I find out what he's gone and done with my share. He's got Claude's share too, but I'm a honest soul, and I only want what's mine."

"Since you stole it in the first place, how do figure it's yours?" the captain asked snidely.

"You lookin' to make a enemy, mister?"

The remark tickled Avery and he nearly choked on his laughter. Regaining his composure, he laid his hand on the captain's shoulder. "Don't you have enough enemies, mister?" he whispered.

The sarcasm wasn't lost on the captain, and General Keese and all the eavesdropping staff broke into laughter. Squirrel's questioning eyes looked totally bewildered. The captain assigned four men to take the woman into custody and notify the Federal marshal of her arrest.

Avery watched the nervous Squirrel twitching, as all eyes now turned toward him. Avery asked one of the nurses to bring him a drink of water. The captain scowled. "Never mind. He's my prisoner."

"He's *my* patient," Avery said calmly and nodded to the nurse to bring the water.

"What's your story, Squirrel?" General Keese asked him.

The man shrugged. "Ma said it was a good idea. We figured out how to rob the train, and we did it real good. Ma always says it's every man thinking fer hisself. When they laid their share out on the ground and went to sleep, I just took it off an buried it. Figured sometime after the war, I'd come back and git it and go live somewhere nice. That's all. I heard Claude was caught, so I joined up the war."

"Then when you thought she was tracking you, you changed sides?"

"Yeah."

The staff and volunteers who'd enjoyed the interrogation giggled and moved back into their routine.

"Avery, I'm so proud of you," Claire said. "And I must say, I think we make a fair team. Wouldn't you say so?"

"You're right. We do make a good team," he answered quietly. "You're pretty brave, you know."

Several days later, General Keese came back. Avery remembered that the General had wanted to discuss something personal with him. They hadn't gotten around to it that day with all the excitement. He couldn't imagine what the General had to say to him that was of a personal nature. The men stepped out into the cold air.

"Avery, I wanted to talk to you about something that has been on my mind for a while. You might remember that a couple of years ago, Dr. Simpson let slip that Caroline had been my first love?"

Avery laughed, "Yes, I do remember that. It was a little awkward there for a few minutes, wasn't it?"

"Well, he was right. She was my first love. She was my only love, and I love her still. When this war is over, I intend to resign from the army and go into business. I want to marry Caroline. I wonder how you feel about that."

"How *I* feel about that? Shouldn't you be wondering how Aunt Caroline feels about that? What difference does it make how I feel about it? I'd be happy for both of you, but—"

"It does matter, to me," the General said thoughtfully. "I can't ask your father, and you're as like him as any man. And I respect your opinion. You'd be happy about it?"

"Of course, I'd be happy," Avery said. "Aunt Caroline would have a fine husband, you'd have a good wife, and Phoebe would have a father. What could be better?"

"Sound reasoning, just like your father. Do you think Caroline loves me?"

Avery lifted his eyebrows in surprise. "Love? I don't know. How would I know? I don't know anything about love. She never said it to me. But I know she's always happy to see you. That's good, isn't it? Did she love you before?"

"Yes, she did love me before."

"Were you, uh, best friends?" He was thinking about his father's advice.

"Best friends?" The General thought about that odd question. "Yes, I believe we were, Avery."

"What happened then? Why didn't you marry her?"

"We planned to be married after I finished at Harvard Business School and she finished up at Wesleyan Women's College. But instead of going to Harvard, I went to West Point. Caroline couldn't abide my being a soldier. My career caused us to go our separate ways. If I had it to do over, I might have made a different choice. I hope I can make that right again."

"God bless you then. I hope you can work it out with Aunt Caroline. It'd be such a good thing for everyone."

"Thanks, Avery. I guess I just needed that encouragement; I'm a little short on self-confidence in this arena," he smiled.

Avery watched him mount Smoke. *Someone like the General can lack self-confidence when it comes to love?* He was astonished at that news. They saluted each other and then waved. Smoke clomped off in the winter slush.

"What do you know about that, Gunner? It's not just me."

Avery watched General Keese ride off, and he saw the ambulances rolling down the slushy road toward the hospital.

"Love? That's what it's about then? We should ask him about that sometime," he said to Gunner. "We might need to know more about that."

He went in to notify the orderlies and nurses that incoming patients were on the way. The ambulances streamed into the yard, and there was no more time to think about love today. Gunner stepped out to greet the horses pulling the ambulances.

CHAPTER SIXTEEN

THE CARL CONUNDRUM

The medical corps had unloaded their patients at the train station and brought them on to the hospital by ambulance wagons. These men were the survivors of the siege of Knoxville. Tennessee wasn't on Avery's map of battles yet. He made an addition to his large Virginia map which already included Pennsylvania and the Carolinas.

These soldiers were in pitiful condition, and Avery's temper was boiling. The Knoxville hospital tents were completely overflowing. The Union turned some of their prisoners free to make more room in prison tents for their wounded men. They spent days burying their dead in the frozen ground, while the wounded languished in the cold damp with few doctors and surgeons and low supplies. Many of these incoming were amputees whose bandages hadn't been changed. Some had untreated wounds. Most of the injured wore squares of muslin pinned to their shirts. Their names were printed on the muslin. Some had torn off, and some soldiers couldn't remember who they were.

The staff efficiently erected additional cots and laid more mats on the floors. Orderlies and volunteers carried men to the third floor if they were coughing, bleeding, or vomiting. Men who were able to move around, and seemed well enough to manage, made themselves comfortable on the first floor. All the others went to the second floor for evaluation. The Mansion House Hospital was a model of efficiency using Avery's reorganization plan. Avery

was in surgery with Dr. Simpson and another surgeon until after dark. Many limbs were filling the wagons under the windows.

The doctors had depleted their supplies. Everything from bandages to chloroform and from soap to clean water was running low. Nurses were heating snow. The camphor for the lamps was nearly gone. The staff was exhausted. Dr. Simpson said he would send a message to the Sanitary Commission to try to get more supplies and some more nurses. Maybe they could borrow another surgeon. Avery sent an orderly to see if Matt could be spared from his hospital.

Late into the night the staff worked by lantern, bathing, bandaging, comforting, and trying to relieve the suffering. In the morning the orderlies would do the burying.

It was shortly before midnight when Claire came to find Avery. Gunner came with her. Avery greeted his dog, wondering where he'd been all day. They were all very tired.

"Dr. Bennett, may I see you privately for a moment?"

"Of course, Claire." They stepped to a corner. "What is it?"

"It's about one of our soldiers. I was bathing him and preparing to look at the wounds which hadn't yet been addressed. The patient has been impaled in the rib cage." She was whispering, and Avery wondered why she didn't want anyone else to hear. The wounds couldn't be any worse than the others.

"And what's wrong?"

"The soldier's a girl."

"A *girl*? Are you sure?"

Claire snapped her head up and scowled at him oddly.

"I don't think I could be mistaken on that count, Doctor."

Avery squirmed. "No, no, of course, I, I didn't mean . . . I was just surprised. That's all. How do you suppose—"

"I just wanted to tell you. Second floor, bed thirteen. Says her name is Carl Burns. I'm guessing she's about twelve years old. I just wanted you to know." She turned and huffed back to the patients.

The next day Avery sent for General Keese. *He'll know what to do about this girl*, he thought. The General couldn't come

for another two days, and by the time he arrived no one thought too much about the situation anymore. Carl's wound was clean and healing okay, and the tall freckle-faced girl with the boyish haircut looked like any other skinny farm boy. Her secret seemed safe for the time being.

General Keese made the rounds with Avery, encouraging the patients and helping them write letters home. When they arrived at Carl's bed, Avery said, "Carl, this is Major General Keese, come to visit with you. How are you feeling today?"

"Fine, just fine. I could get back to duty soon, I think," the young soldier said bravely. Avery winked at the General and moved on, leaving him at Carl's bedside to try to sort the young girl out.

"So you were in Knoxville, I hear. Pretty bad, huh?"

"Yes, sir. It was all that. I sure wish we could've won that one, sir." Gunner came to the side of the cot and nudged the patient.

"Hey, looky here," said the delighted girl. "I got me one good hound dog at home too."

"His name is Gunner," the General said. "He's Dr. Bennett's dog. He's always around bringing cheer to the patients."

The patient laughed and petted the smiling dog. Gunner nuzzled her ears and put his feet on the bed, getting very close to the girl.

"I know, we've already met," she laughed. The General remembered that Avery joked about Gunner being a lady's man. Gunner made himself comfortable across the girl's lap. *Yes*, the General thought smugly, *it would seem to be true. And Gunner already knows the truth.*

"I've got some time, Carl. Could I help you write a letter home?"

"Oh, thanks, sir, but I can read and write just fine, so I can tend to that myself. But thanks."

The General was disappointed in that answer, as he hoped to learn who the girl's family was.

"Where are you from, soldier?"

"Mountains."

"How old are you?"

"Old enough to serve my country." He wasn't getting much information from Carl.

"Is your father's name Carl, too?"

"No, it's only my name. I'm not named for anyone."

"Anyone you'd like us to notify about you being here?"

"No, sir, I can write them myself."

"Well, Carl, you have a pleasant day. I hope you recover well," the General said, and he got up and moved to the next bed. He was disappointed and thought the girl was quite wily for one so young.

Carl laid back and smiled smugly. Gunner nuzzled her and snuggled down on her bed beside her for a nap.

"Well, General, do we have some information about Carl?" Avery asked him later.

"I'm sorry, Avery, uh, Doctor, I got nothing from him, uh, her. I wonder if one of the nurses might have better luck."

"Yes, sir, you're probably right. If anyone could, it would be our nurse Claire."

Avery asked Claire if she could spend some time with Carl and try to get some information from her the next day.

"Good morning, Carl. How are you feeling today?" Claire said cheerfully.

"Oh, I'm real good, Nurse." Carl eyed the wash basin. "I got up early and gave myself a bath today, so you won't have to bother with me none."

"Well, wasn't that smart of you," said Claire. "Then we can have some visiting time, can't we?"

"Well, I probably need to take a nap real soon. Doctor said I needed rest."

"I see. I guess, Carl, that you don't want me to ask you too many questions. Is that it?"

Carl was caught completely by surprise. "Huh? Well, no, I mean, I just don't want you to waste time on me when others might need you more, see?"

Claire sat down hard on the edge of the cot, causing the patient to bounce and wince. She put her face close to Carl and whispered loudly into her ear.

"Listen here, young lady, I know what you're up to. I admitted you to this bed, and I know your little secret. I'm going to give you paper and ink pen, and you'll show me how well you can write. I want your name and address and your parents' names on this paper right now or your secret is out. Do you understand me then?"

Claire got up and in her cheerful normal demeanor said, "Okey dokey, Carl, you're looking really good today. Here is a little something to entertain you. I'll see you later today. Would you like a little more drinking water?" she asked sweetly.

Carl grumped in the bed. Arms crossed over her chest, she scowled at the nurse.

Claire came back later that day and asked cheerfully, "Do you have a bit of something for me, Carl?"

The girl sat in the bed with her arms still folded across her chest, rolled her eyes, and didn't speak or look at Claire. She sighed loudly and reached one hand under the blanket and brought out the paper and pen. She handed it to Claire without looking at her.

Claire glanced at it and was satisfied. "Thank you, Carl," she said lightly and moved on with the evidence tucked in her apron pocket. Meeting up with Avery later, she produced the paper. The writing was neat, precise, and somewhat fancy.

"Her name is Carlotta Burnside. She's thirteen years old. Her parents are James and Lola Burnside. General Burnside is her uncle. She only wanted to do her duty, Avery. You can't blame her for that at all. She lives in Jonesboro, Tennessee. She was wounded when she fell over a barricade structure, and she impaled her side on the post."

"Nice work, Nurse," Avery smiled.

"Anytime, Doctor. And just so you know, I think the lass is a heroine." She quickly moved on.

Avery smiled and watched her go.

"I guess you're right," he said. "Hero, heroine, I've seen it in everyone here."

The staff watched Carl's wound carefully. With no infection present, it was healing. Everyone was mindful of the patient's privacy, and no one let on that they knew, although by now, everyone did. Carl was moved to the first floor with the ambulatories, and Avery sent for General Keese.

Avery gave the General the information on Carl and told him that the patient was ready to be discharged. It was now his responsibility to send Carl back to the front . . . or whatever he decided.

General Keese decided to hold a little ceremony for Carl on the first floor. Avery asked some of the staff to attend. Gunner, of course, arrived first and sat in front in case it was an occasion for refreshments.

General Keese looked formal and announced, "Private Carl Burns, having fulfilled his enlistment, is discharged from the army with honorable citation for bravery at Knoxville on behalf of a grateful nation. The army has arranged an escort to see Private Burns safely back home to his home in Jonesboro, Tennessee."

Everyone applauded and whistled, happy for Private Burns who had healed and was going home. They all wished they were going too. The war was over for Carl Burns.

So on this evening, everyone who was well was in a gay mood and had two things to be grateful for. First of all, one soldier was well and going home. Secondly, the year 1863 was coming to an end. Tomorrow would be 1864. This could be the year they'd waited for—the year the war would finally end. Maybe this would be the year that they'd all go home, like Carl. They hoped.

PART TWO

RAINBOWS AND CANNON FIRE

1864

CHAPTER SEVENTEEN

HEALING ART

Avery lay in his bed. The light was just peeking in around the chintz curtains in his room. "The first day of the first month," he said to himself. "Again. This is the fourth January of the war and my fourth birthday during the war. What about that, Gunner?"

He stretched lazily, thinking about the years he'd been in Alexandria living with Dr. Simpson and his wife. He thought of all the men who'd died or had life-changing injuries because of the war. He thought about the families who'd left the cities because of the war—some because their homes were confiscated, and some because their homes were destroyed. Some left to avoid the war; some left to get into it.

He thought of his own family in West Virginia and how many changes had taken place there since he left home in 1861. The state of West Virginia had been created—a brand new state, and his father had helped to write the new state constitution. His brother had become a lawyer, his mother had founded a school, and he'd become a surgeon. His baby cousin had become deaf, and Claire's brother Timothy had lost both his hearing and his sight. His mother's school was making changes in the lives of the farm families. Aunt Caroline had brought freedmen to the valley, and some of the peaceable people had to adjust their thinking. His father had died. He'd gotten to know Claire, and he had some strange and confusing feelings for her.

He was paying his own way at the Simpsons' now, and he was a degreed surgeon at seventeen years old. He'd measured over six feet tall last summer, a little taller than his father and a lot larger than most other men. But the one thing that he had most wanted had not happened. Everyone in the entire country had wanted it to happen. The war had not ended. It was getting harder for anyone to believe that it would ever end. All of America was tired of the war.

Avery stretched his long legs, rolled over, and slid out of bed. The legs of his long woolen drawers climbed up his legs. Were his clothes shrinking? He hurried through his morning routine and met the doctor outside. Avery, Dr. Simpson, and Gunner climbed into the doctor's buggy to go to work. Fan whinnied goodbye, always sad that she wasn't going along. She stayed behind with Leon in the stable. Gunner sat tall sniffing the fresh air, and as they pulled out of the barn into the falling snow, he snapped at the snowflakes. They could always count on Gunner to start their mornings with laughter. Dr. Simpson clucked, and the horse picked up his feet. They were off to the hospital to start a new year.

Many of the soldiers still at the Mansion House Hospital had been wounded in the fall of 1863 and were wintering here at the hospital, hoping to recover before getting sick with dysentery or pneumonia. One of the soldiers that Avery was particularly interested in was a young soldier from a New York regiment. He had lost both of his legs in the battle of Fredericksburg and hadn't uttered a word. Avery believed the terror and the trauma of the battle had caused his muteness.

"How's our patient Pioli from New York? Any improvement?"

Avery shook his head. "Not really, Dr. Simpson. But you know, despite not talking, he tells us more about the war than any words could tell; he's an artist. Day after day he sketches. At night when he can't sleep, he draws the horrible things he's seen. I've told the nurses to let him draw anywhere he wants. I think it's the best therapy for him."

Dr. Simpson nodded in agreement.

"To tell you the truth, Doctor, from the looks of his drawings . . . well, I don't know if anyone could recover from such sights. I'm beginning to wonder if I will." Avery shuddered.

One morning the nurses were shocked to find Pioli's bed sheet entirely covered with ghastly, intricately drawn scenes from the war.

Nurse Dorothy, who'd been educated at a New York finishing school, studied the soldier's anguished face, and then she asked him softly, "Can you tell me about the pictures?"

The nurse and the soldier locked eyes. With her hands down low by her apron, she motioned for the other nurses to move away.

"You've seen Dante's *Inferno*," Dorothy said again, her eyes locked on his. "Can you talk about it?"

His eyes followed her, and they brimmed with tears. He dropped his head, and the tears splashed down on his hands. The nurse knelt at his bedside.

"It's okay. You can tell your story this way. Here. Here's another bed sheet. You tell your stories. You tell them so everyone will understand what the war was like for you." The other nurses watched her; they all moved quietly away to their next patients. Dorothy turned to leave.

"No. Come back." The nurses all froze in their footsteps. They were his first spoken words. They looked at Dorothy; she turned and went back to his bedside.

"Stay," he pleaded. The other nurses whispered and went on, knowing that what Dorothy was doing was important for this soldier's recovery. All that morning the soldier sketched while Dorothy watched and encouraged him to draw. As he drew, she asked him questions, and he nodded his answers. By the time the noon meal arrived, the soldier had drawn all over his bed, on the floor around the bed, and even on his arms. He was getting more and more excited about what he was drawing and sharing with Dorothy.

By supper he was signing his work. He remembered that his first name was Anthony. Later he remembered Pioli. He signed his work *Anthony Pioli*. Dorothy stayed with Anthony and helped him get ready for the night.

"Stay," he said. She sat with him into the evening and all through the night. He slept on ticking covered with his sketches. The drawings were so powerful, so real, that everyone who saw them gasped and stared in silence. The drawings were clearer pictures of the horrors of war than words could ever render. When Anthony fell asleep, he was holding Dorothy's hand tightly, fearing the nightmares. Before leaving for the night, Avery covered Dorothy with an army blanket.

In the morning Dorothy was asleep in a chair at Anthony's bedside. The patient took a piece of paper from his drawing case and sketched her as she slept. He put a title on the sketch: "My Angel of Peace" by Anthony Pioli. It was the first thing Dorothy saw when she awoke to the sounds of the morning activity in the hospital.

She smiled at Anthony and asked if he'd slept well. He nodded and smiled that he had. He smiled! Another important first; Dorothy knew that was important. He gave her the sketch.

"Thank you." She studied his face and saw that the tormented look on his face had vanished.

Anthony drew pictures and sketches for everyone that day. He seemed to have been drained of the dreadful battle experiences. He drew portraits of the staff, pictures of horses in pastures and horse auctions, pleasure riders on horseback, and exciting horse races. He drew a picture of a foal in a barn. He drew rainbows over meadows, and, even though he always drew in gray lead pencil, everyone saw them in brilliant colors. Dorothy learned from his drawings that his family raised thoroughbred race horses in Saratoga, New York, and had built a thoroughbred race track there in 1863. He was already fighting in the war and hadn't yet seen the race track. Anthony drew pictures of children playing and of a county fair. Anthony was recovering, and everyone knew it was because Dorothy had understood that where he had been was

more important than where he was. Both Anthony and Dorothy lived in New York state, both had attended college in the Northeast, and they were the same age. They had a lot to share.

"Sometimes what our patients need doesn't come in a medical bag," said Dr. Simpson. "Sometimes the cure lies in the heart and soul of someone who cares."

"I think that's a good thing for all doctors to remember," Avery added.

"We can't ever forget, Avery, that we are only the hands, only the instruments. It's a greater power that handles the healing."

Avery felt the doctor's words burrowing into his heart. He watched Dorothy fussing over Anthony, smoothing his bedclothes, trying to make him more comfortable. *I've been forgetting that part. That's important and I can't forget it again.*

"You are right, Dr. Simpson. You are right."

Claire suggested that they frame "My Angel of Peace" and hang it in the hospital as a reminder to everyone of that important truth. Avery brought her a hammer and a tack and admired her skill with the hammer.

CHAPTER EIGHTEEN

MYSTERIOUS SCAFFOLD

As he moved through the hospital on this particular day, Avery was so preoccupied that when a volunteer handed him a note, he put it in his shirt pocket and didn't remember it until much later. The note in his pocket was from the acting mayor of the city of Alexandria.

"We have an acting mayor?" Avery asked aloud in surprise.

"Sort of," answered a local volunteer who thought Avery was asking him. "Our real mayor went off with the Confeds when the Union came to occupy Alexandria in '61. This guy, ol' Phineas P. Profitt, steps out from the city planning board and volunteers to be acting mayor. Nobody else was fool enough to want the job, so there he is. He's been totally ineffective, and no one pays him any mind, except to call him names like Puffer Belly Profitt. When Alexandria went under martial law in '62, he kind of lost his job. Nobody else cared. But, oh, he does. He's eager to be seen and recognized so he doesn't get forgotten. He wants to win when we hold mayoral elections again, you see. So he occasionally does something really outrageous to draw attention to himself and the fine job *he* thinks he's doing. Lately, he's been promising the city a grand reception at his daughter's wedding, where the entire town can come and feast. As if there were banquet fixings available. Ha! He's a public joke. Why do you ask?"

"He wants me to call on his daughter, Penelope. He doesn't say what's wrong with her. Do you know if she's sick? Why would she need a house call?"

"That woman is big trouble, if you'll excuse my saying so."

"Hmm. Perhaps it's a breathing problem," diagnosed Avery. "Well, I'll go by there on my way out this afternoon. Where does this mayor live?"

The volunteer pointed the way, and when Avery left that afternoon with Gunner and Fan, he carried his doctor's bag to the home of the acting mayor.

"Well, this is a fine house, isn't it, Gunner?" Avery knocked with the large, brass pineapple door knocker.

"Door's open," called the loud response.

The acting mayor apparently has no household staff, Avery thought to himself. *Probably the war.* He let himself in. Inside, the elegant home smelled dirty and musty, and it was dark and gloomy. Heavy, dusty draperies hung over the windows, their elegance faded into mildew.

"Unhealthy air," Avery diagnosed.

"Hello?"

"In here," came the loud reply. He followed Gunner into the darkened parlor.

There sat the largest woman Avery had ever seen. He couldn't tell what she was sitting on—a chair, an ottoman, a sofa. Whatever the perch was, her corpulent body smothered it. She wore a pink, satin dressing gown and a lot of jewelry. Avery was overwhelmed and thought she looked like a sparkling pink snow bank.

"How do you do? Are you Miss Penelope Profitt?"

"Are you Avery?" she cooed in sweet reply.

"Uh . . . I'm Dr. Bennett. Your father sent for me. What seems to be your problem? Are you feeling ill?" he asked nervously.

"No, I'm not sick. My father is looking for a suitor for me. And you look like you'll do just fine."

"A suitor? I'm a doctor, Miss Profitt. If you're not in need of my service, I'll just be on my way."

As he turned to leave, the parlor door slammed shut, and the lock clicked. Gunner ran to the door and began to paw and whine.

"Who did that?" Avery asked with annoyance.

"Doesn't matter who did it. You're here, and we might's well get to know one another, as that's the proper way for a courtship to begin. Sit down," she ordered.

"Miss Profitt, I'm not interested in courtship. If you've no need of medical service, I wish to leave now. Please open the door." He hoped he sounded like he was in command. Gunner sat at the door and whined.

"Listen, Avery, give us a chance. We could be quite a pair, you a famous doctor and me a wealthy socialite. The city would have a wonderful banquet, and the hungry would be fed. See what a service you'd be doing? And I hate to tell you what your other choice will be. If I were you, I'd support my father's plan. Now c'mere and sit down." The syrupy sweetness in her voice was melting fast. Avery didn't move.

"All right then, but don't say I didn't warn you. You've chosen the alternate plan." With that she let out a blood curdling scream. The door flew open. Two men jumped into the room and tackled Avery, nearly mashing Gunner in the process. Gunner barked, and Avery worried for his safety.

"Gunner, go home!" He struggled with the men, who dragged him to his feet and tied his hands behind him. "Gunner, go! Get help!"

Gunner ran past the men, through the open door, down the hall, and out the front door. He ran pell-mell across the city streets, through the town, across the church square, and up the hill to the Simpsons'. He raced up the porch steps barking. He pawed at the door, scratched and whined.

"What on earth? Such a racket . . ." said Dr. Simpson. He got up from the supper table and went to the door. Mrs. Simpson sat at the table next to Avery's empty place. She heard Gunner and looked concerned. The doctor opened the door, and Gunner

ran straight into the dining room where he barked and wheeled in circles.

"I believe he's trying to tell us something."

"Gunner, where's Avery?" said Mrs. Simpson. Gunner ran to the door and spun around, looked at them, and barked. He jumped up excitedly.

"I'll get the buggy." Dr. Simpson had trouble following Gunner because the dog was running a straight beeline, and the buggy had to stay on the road. Gunner, in his frustration, ran in circles to keep Dr. Simpson headed toward him.

At last they reached the large house on Magnolia Turn. Dr. Simpson looked at the house.

"Puffer Belly Profitt's house . . . what would Avery be doing here?"

Gunner ran up the steps, pawed the door, whined, and begged the doctor to follow. Dr. Simpson rapped the door knocker. The door was promptly opened by the butler.

"Dr. Simpson to see Mr. Profitt, please," the doctor said.

"I am sorry, sir, but Mr. Profitt isn't in. Would you care to leave a calling card?"

"I'm looking for a friend of mine, Dr. Avery Bennett. I've reason to believe that he's here, or was here earlier. Is someone ill here?"

"No, sir, no one is ill. I don't know Dr. Bennett. I don't believe he is here."

"Is anyone here?" the doctor asked in desperation.

"Yes, Miss Profitt is in. But I believe the lady is in for the evening and isn't receiving callers at this hour. It's a bit late to be calling, Dr. Simpson," the butler chided.

"Yes, well, thank you. Good evening." The doctor turned to go. Gunner wasn't convinced; he wouldn't leave the porch. The doctor watched the dog pacing, pawing, and whining at the door.

"Something's wrong here, very wrong." He called the dog to the buggy seat, but Gunner was reluctant. He kept turning and looking back at the door.

"Let's find him." He clucked his horse and headed to the outskirts of town toward General Keese's encampment.

"Halt!" called the sentry. "Who goes there?"

The doctor identified himself and asked to see General Keese. A runner was sent, and before long the General was approaching the picket. The sentry was talking to Gunner and renewing their friendship.

"Dr. Simpson? Gunner? What's this? What's wrong?"

"I don't know, Geoffrey, but I don't like it, not one bit. Something's very wrong." He told his friend that Avery was missing and under unusual circumstances and that Gunner was telling them that something was wrong.

"I'd never second-guess Gunner," the General said, looking grave. The doctor told him about the incident at the Profitt's house and that Gunner had taken him there.

"That pompous old phony," the officer said. "One of my men had a bad experience in that house. The soldier says he was forcibly kidnapped, but Profitt says he was there courting his daughter. My man says Profitt is counting on a big wedding affair to ingratiate himself with the city and get reelected as mayor. We finally got our soldier back, but Profitt was making it pretty ugly. My private says he never saw the woman before two thugs dragged him in off the street and locked him in. I believed him, but the military governor sided with Profitt. I think we should send some watchmen over to that house, and if anything looks at all suspicious, they'll get a read on it. I don't think they'll hurt Avery, but I'll bet he's not happy. The private called that Profitt woman a dragon."

"Well, thanks, Geoffrey. I knew I could count on you. I'll go back home, in case he shows up there. Keep me posted."

"Uh, Dr. Simpson, just a thought—would you consider leaving Gunner with us? If anyone could find Avery, it'd be Gunner."

"Good idea, Geoffrey."

"Come, Gunner."

Gunner made himself at home in the encampment, visiting his old army buddies. But he kept looking away toward the city and whining. General Keese positioned some of his men around the Profitt house out of sight. He sent another small detail to the city square to watch for anything unusual there. Gunner went with them.

Shortly before dawn the city watchmen returned to camp and reported that during the night a large structure had been built in the town square. The watchmen had seen the hammering going on all night. Someone had erected some kind of platform. Some of the gossip was that it would be for a wedding.

"Put four fresh watchmen on it," the General ordered. "You men get some rest."

As the volunteers and staff for the day began to arrive at the hospital, the gossip was all about the mysterious scaffolding that had appeared overnight in the town square. Someone said they'd seen Phineas Profitt there this morning.

"Oh, do tell," someone teased. "It's a wedding platform for the long-awaited wedding—the party of the century. Think there'll be food?" Everyone laughed; the fair Penelope's wedding of the century had been the joke of the city for months.

"Dr. Simpson," called Claire, "I wondered if you'd seen Dr. Bennett this morning. Did he arrive with you?"

"Uh, no. No, Claire. He didn't."

Claire studied the doctor's worried face, and she felt a shadow creeping over her.

"I haven't seen him or Gunner yet this morning, and we were planning to try a new leg brace on one of the patients this morning; Ezra Sanders is expecting us this morning. I've been waiting for Av . . . uh, Dr. Bennett."

Claire told the doctor the truth, but she didn't tell him all of it. She had a strange foreboding this morning. A little knot was drawing tighter in her middle. Something was wrong. This wasn't like Avery, and she worried. The pickets hidden in the square heard the town crier about nine o'clock that morning.

"Hear ye! Hear ye! A traitor of the Union will, in one hour, be hanged to death in the town square! The fine citizen, Phineas P. Profitt, invites all patriots to turn out for this auspicious occasion. Hear ye! Hear ye!"

"A hanging!" The pickets took off for camp with the news that the mysterious platform was for a hanging, not a wedding, and it was for a traitor.

"A traitor?" the General bellowed. "How would we not know about this? This isn't right. Something is suspicious. Take Gunner and get back to town. No one is to be hanged, and that is my order. I'll put together a small cavalry unit. Send someone to notify the governor's watch."

At a quarter to ten the townspeople began to loiter around the platform, eyeing the scaffolding with interest.

"You'd think this town hadn't seen enough killing in three years that they have to come out for this spectacle," one of the soldiers commented dryly.

At ten o'clock, when a slow drumbeat began, the crowd hushed and whispered.

"A traitor they say."

"Deserves death, he does."

"Consorting with the enemy, while our own sons die fighting."

"I'd like to hang that traitor myself." The pickets, overhearing all this, looked at each other in astonishment.

"Are we fighting for such a place as this where a man no longer goes to trial?"

"So much for Lincoln's government for the people."

The drum cadence got louder as it approached the square, and the crowd grew anxious. A prisoner dressed in a long black gown with a black hood over his head and hands tied behind his back was led through the crowd. The crowd began to boo and hiss at the alleged traitor. The two guards, one on each side, led him to the steps of the platform. Suddenly, breaking through the crowd came pie-eyed, puffed up, portly Profitt in his finest clothing,

doffing his hat to the ladies and congratulating himself on his patriotism.

"No need to thank me, folks," he said humbly, "just doing my patriotic, proud duty to protect this city."

A few people applauded him.

The prisoner stumbled as he was going up the steps to the platform and had to be helped back up. The acting mayor stood in front of him on the top step to appear tallest.

"Well, traitor, what do you say for yourself?"

The prisoner remained silent.

"There, you see?" Profitt said to the crowd. "Guilty! Can't say a word in his own defense."

The crowd murmured in agreement.

"I caught him red-handed, sneaking strict military secrets from my house to give to the Confederates. He's a traitorous spy."

"Ooooohhh," said the crowd.

"Get on with it then."

"Show him what this town thinks of traitors."

"Alexandria knows what to do with spies."

One of the General's men vaulted onto the stage and was already there when the guards dragged the prisoner up the steps.

"And what strict military secrets might you have at your house then, Profitt?" the soldier asked loudly, so everyone could hear him. "Since when does the acting mayor have access to military secrets?"

The crowd was impressed with the soldier in his Union blue uniform. They whispered and looked interested.

"Hurry it up!" Profitt hissed to the guards. "Get this done." His henchmen shoved the prisoner to the scaffold.

"There is to be NO hanging today by the military order of Major General Geoffrey Keese, Army of the Potomac, United States Army. Stop what you are doing right now." The soldier made sure that everyone in the crowd heard this announcement.

"No hanging?" The crowd began murmuring and hissing their disappointment.

Gunner's nose was on the ground, and he was working through the crowd, stopping periodically to sniff the air. He was weaving through the crowd headed toward the platform. The watchman in charge of Gunner lost him in the crowd.

On the platform the hangmen were putting the noose over the prisoner's head when, from the other side of the platform, three nurses came charging toward them shrieking and honking like mother geese after a fox. One brandished a broom, one stabbed the air with a crutch, while the other carried a bucket of water that sloshed as she ran. They raced across the stage.

From the front of the platform Gunner was now bounding up the steps. He threw himself into the first hangman and knocked him off his feet, and as the man lay there on the platform, the nurse doused him with the water bucket. Claire rammed the crutch into the gut of the surprised second hangman and rolled him off the platform into the crowd. She dropped the crutch and reached the prisoner at the same time Gunner reached him. A soldier snagged Phineas P. Profitt as he was running through the crowd to make his escape.

The sound of horses announced the arrival of a small cavalry unit who found Profitt and the two hangmen already bound and ready to be taken into custody. The crowd watched as the nurses cut the prisoner's hands free and pulled off his hood. They gasped at the sight of the prisoner's mouth stuffed with rags and bound tight.

"No wonder he didn't speak to defend himself," they buzzed to each other.

Then the nurses pulled off his black gown, and someone in the crowd yelled out, "It's not a traitor; it's the hospital doctor and his dog!"

Gunner was there licking Avery and dancing all over the place, tail wagging in jubilation.

"Oh, Avery, I was so worri—" Avery's eyes met the brave Claire's in astonishment as she swooned and folded into a heap on the floor in front of him.

"Claire! Mercy, Avery, she's . . . she's fainted!" cried the nurse with the bucket.

"And she's going to be mad as a wet hen when she wakes up." He smiled at the nurses, who readily agreed.

"Not like her at all, at all," they said giggling.

They collected Claire, and Avery stepped to the center of the platform. In his loudest voice, he announced to the crowd, "Ladies and gentlemen, if there is anyone among you who is hungry or in need of some kitchen staples, I want to assure you that Phineas P. Profitt has, at his home, several bedrooms full of staples and food. We know how civic-minded he is, and I'm sure he'd want you to have this."

The crowd began to yell insults to Profitt, and the hungriest took off running for his house.

"Profitt has pulled his last stunt in this town," a voice in the crowd shouted angrily.

"But, but, it's for the wedding, and for my reelection party," Profitt sniveled. "I only wanted it for the wedding for my daughter and for my election, and if you'd only cooperated none of this would've happened," he blubbered to Avery.

"General Keese, my medical bag is at the Profitt's home; could one of your men get it for me, please, before this crowd knocks his house over?"

The General sent the cavalry unit over to the Profitt house to oversee the dispensing of food so no one would be trampled, and one of the men returned with Avery's medical bag. The nurses had wrapped Claire against the cold in Avery's black prisoner's gown. Avery knew she'd be mad as a hornet about fainting, and he was carefully practicing what he should say to her. He pulled a small bottle out of his bag. One whiff and Claire would be sitting up, and he hoped he'd say the right thing. Gunner nuzzled her face, trying to wake her. The doctor put a little of the spirits by her nose. She inhaled, sputtered, and sat up quickly.

She looked around, and, gathering her wits, she buried her face in her hands and moaned.

"I fainted in front of the entire city. I'm so embarrassed. Oh, what is wrong with me? I've never fainted before in all my life."

"Thank you for coming to my rescue." It wasn't what he'd planned to say.

"Avery, I have never, never fainted before. It's such a silly, sissy, girlish thing to do!"

"Well, medically speaking, Claire, fainting isn't something we have a lot of control over." He knew that was the wrong thing to say as soon as it was out of his mouth. And he'd planned his speech so carefully. She scowled at him.

"It's okay, Claire. You're not a sissy—anything but a sissy."

"Oh, Avery, I was so frightened for you. I was afraid I wouldn't be in time. What if they . . . What if you . . . Are you all right then? I was so afraid for you."

"Yes, I'm fine, thanks to you and our friends. Do you feel strong enough to get back to the hospital? It's cold. You should get inside."

"Yes, I believe I'm okay now. Oh, I'm so angry with myself. I never faint. But I was just so relieved to see you. I was so worried—"

"It's okay, Claire. I understand. It doesn't matter. Thank you." Her lips were still pale. Avery draped the prisoner gown over her shoulders and wrapped his arm around her to hold it in place and to give her some additional warmth and support. They walked briskly back to the hospital. *Well, I seem to be getting better at this.*

Gunner pranced and sniffed at the clumps of snow that alternated with the clumps of grass and trash. His tail waved merrily all the way to the hospital.

"Fan! How did you get here?"

"Fan brought herself, Avery; I saw her coming all by herself. That's how I knew for certain you were in trouble."

"Well, what do you know? Hello, Fan, it's good to see you." He patted his horse and watered her. He'd imagined a difficult search to find her and feared she'd be stolen. This was good news.

Mysterious Scaffold

It was beginning to snow, a late March snowfall. By morning thick snow blanketed the city. The blooming daffodils tried to shake it off, but the weight of the snow prevailed. Spring would have to wait a few more days.

CHAPTER NINETEEN

GROWING PAINS

At the end of a spring working day, Avery asked Claire if he might escort her to the nurses' residence. She was surprised but seemed pleased.

"I'll get my wraps and be right with you." She wore a warm shawl and was tying on her bonnet when she returned. She wondered if Dr. Simpson had suggested this escort or if it was Avery's idea. The early spring air was fresh, but it was still quite chilly. They walked a while in comfortable silence. In the distance, above the tree line, they could see the artillery smoke of today's battles, lingering like a shroud over the landscape. They both knew there'd be some fresh wounds in the morning. But for now they didn't have to talk about it. Gunner checked out every tree and bush along the way, happy to be outside with Avery and Claire. The slushy snow and the warming breeze promised that the heavy surprise snowfall in March would soon be gone.

"Claire," Avery began, and then hesitated. *Why is it still so hard for me to talk to her?*

"Yes, Avery?" She answered very quickly and nervously. He wondered if it was hard for her too. He'd never thought of that before. But her embarrassment over fainting last week had surprised him, and now he knew that she also at times felt vulnerable and unsure. *I wonder. Maybe I should try to make it easier for her to talk to me instead of worrying so much about me talking to her. Maybe I should practice it that way.*

"Claire, I was just wondering something. How did you know that the traitor in the hood was me? How did you know where I was? When my father died and I was overcome with grief, you were there with me. How do you always know where to find me at the hospital?" He spewed it all out at once, speaking faster and faster with each question. This wasn't how he'd practiced it.

"Well, now, you want answers to all that? Which shall I answer first? Maybe I can't remember all those questions."

They stopped and looked at each other, and then they both looked down at the path and continued their walk.

"You know what I mean, Claire."

"I didn't mean to be impudent, Avery. How did I know? I just guessed it. I would recognize you in any kind of costume."

"So you recognized me once you were there. But how did you know where I was?"

"Oh, that . . . well, I guess Gunner showed me."

"No, Claire, Gunner wasn't with you. Gunner was with the General's men. You always know where I am in the hospital when others are looking for me. You know what I need in surgery before I ask."

"I guess I'm a good guesser."

"I think there's more to it than that. Whenever I need a hand, there you are. . . . Where do you come from? Do you just spy on me all day? I know, it doesn't make sense, but you always seem to know everything about me."

"Well, I can hardly say what makes sense to you and what doesn't now, can I?"

He knew she was being evasive and more than a little flippant. His frustration was sounding more like annoyance.

She looked at him. She wanted to say something about how many questions he was asking and make a light conversation about it, but she knew it was too late for that. They walked on in silence.

"Avery . . . this might be very hard for you to understand."

"I'll try."

"You might think me rather forward."

"I already know you are. So go on."

"I care about you, Avery. Do you remember the first day I was here? Don't you remember what I told you? Or have you forgotten why I came?"

"Maybe."

"I told you then I would work at your side one year and maybe . . . I said I'd never mention it again. I haven't . . . till now."

"I guess I remember it some. You were just a silly girl, Claire. I didn't pay much attention. You were annoying then and forward."

Claire stopped walking and blinked at him.

"Well, then, that's fair notice to me, isn't it. This lass will not be takin' more of the doctor's time with her silliness."

"Stop it, Claire. I was younger. We both were."

She looked up at him. She was overwhelmed with sadness and looked away. "I'm too forward for the likes of you, and you are too practical for the likes of me. It's okay, Avery. I understand. This changes everything. I'll leave you alone. I can go the rest of the way on my own."

She walked away from him in a hurry, head down; tears clouded her vision and she stumbled. Collecting her composure, she hurried on down the path.

He stood there watching her run away, wondering why she was upset. *Did I say something? Why is she so sad? She looks like the world has come to an end. I just said . . .* Suddenly he understood.

"Oh, no . . . she thinks—Claire! Wait!" He ran to catch up with her, and they walked in silence the rest of the way. Claire sniffed and wiped her angry, hurt tears. Avery chewed his lip, wondering what to do next. Gunner walked tensely between them.

When they reached the nurses' residence, Claire walked up the steps and didn't say goodbye. When she reached the top step, Avery spoke over a large lump in his throat. His voice squawked.

"Claire, wait! I never meant to hurt your feelings; but I'm sure that I have. I can feel your hurt; I can see it. I'm so sorry. Please. Don't go."

He didn't know what else to say; he hadn't practiced anything. He'd probably make the situation worse, but he couldn't let her leave like this. He climbed the steps and forged ahead.

"I think you're amazing, Claire. Everything about you is wonderful. The way you smile, the way you care about people, the way you can say honestly what's on your mind, how you always want to learn new things, the way you look at me, the way you can laugh when things are hard . . . the strange way I feel when I'm with you. You're a wonderful nurse; you're smart and you're competent; everyone looks up to you, and you're a good friend. And I think you're just . . . just perfect. I don't really understand all the feelings I have for you, but I'm learning that some things don't need to be understood. You know—like rain, like birthing, like snow, like rainbows, like healing and prayer. All things wonderful don't have to be explained, do they? Do you know that I care for you, Claire? I am so, so sorry that I've upset you and hurt you and made you cry. I never want to hurt you. Not ever. I understand now why you fainted. I know how it feels when you think you might lose someone that you . . . care about."

Gunner stared at him, mouth drooping open, tongue dangling. Claire blinked. With one hand on Avery's arm, she allowed her tears to escape.

"That's beautiful, Avery." She could think of nothing else to say. She was stunned by all those words! Her tears trickled down her cheek. Avery took her grandmother's handkerchief out of his pocket, and he dried her tears. When she looked up, he was smiling down at her.

"It's okay, then, isn't it?" She held his hand with the handkerchief against her cheek.

"It's okay," he smiled. He whistled for his dog, and then he whistled all the way home. Avery and Gunner raced through the darkening streets breathing in the cold, fresh air of the early spring. He sensed his heart telling his mind something. He wasn't sure what, but he hoped that his mind would have the good sense to listen. Gunner sloshed through the melted puddles in good spirits.

"Okay, it's easy for you, Gunner. Your mind always listens to your heart. A dog's mind and heart might be the same thing."

Avery sloshed merrily through the puddle behind his dog.

CHAPTER TWENTY

BASEBALL AND BEES

As the battles of war moved ever closer to the two capitals, the hospitals bulged at the seams with more wounded and sick men. More houses and warehouses had been sequestered to become hospitals. Spring on the way meant more battles. Trains brought more cots, more bandages, more volunteers, and more patients.

"Springtime used to mean everything new and fresh on our farm," Avery said to Dr. Simpson one day on the way home from the hospital. "I'm not sure this spring in Alexandria means that."

Dr. Simpson nodded sadly in agreement.

"I wish we had some good news for some of the patients," the doctor said. "It's hard enough to be sidelined from the action, but harder still to hear that they're still losing the battles."

"Do you suppose it's possible that the Union can lose all the battles and still win the war?"

"I wonder, Avery, I wonder. And I pray it will be over before it comes to that." When the few blades of grass left in the hospital yard struggled through the last bit of melting snow, and the spring breezes began to warm, the ambulatory patients returned to the outdoors. Being outside renewed their spirits.

Avery remembered the old beekeeper in Richmond and sent for a beekeeper to bring a hive and put it in the side yard near the tree line at the back of the property. The hospital used a lot of

honey to treat wounds and burns. Avery stopped at the feed and seed store and picked up a handful of sweet clover seed to throw down in the yard to make the bees feel welcome. "Grow clober," he commanded.

The Alexandria beekeeper, a stout lady with a net over her hat, provided an afternoon of entertainment for the patients and their caregivers who were enjoying the spring air and exercising. They watched her at work in the yard as she put her little hive together with hammer and nails. She brought the trays out of the box in the back of her wagon. Bees hummed around the wagon and followed her to the side yard, where she slid the trays into place.

She wasn't very friendly and was as quiet as Elmo was talkative, but she was efficient, and soon the hive would be making a new store of honey for the hospital.

"Can't have too much honey on hand," commented Avery, trying to be friendly.

"Hmpf," she grumbled.

"For the war effort," he assured her.

"Hmpf," was all she said. She bounced down the road in her wagon back to her honeybee farm.

One day a stranger walked up to the side yard. The patients eyed his general's stripes. Those who could do so, saluted. Avery went out to meet him.

"General Doubleday?"

"That's right!"

"Welcome, sir. I got the telegram that you would be here waiting for your new detachment."

"It'll be a day or two until they arrive. Can I make myself useful here while I wait? I can sleep in the buckboard I'm driving, and I have my own provisions. But I can cheer some of the men, if that's allowed."

"Allowed and encouraged. We can use all the hands we can find—even the generals!" joked Avery. "Come on in."

"Hello, men; carry on, soldiers. General Doubleday here. How are you, son? How are things going, soldier? Anything I can

do for you fellows today?" He wrote a few letters, read some letters, and shared news of the war.

"They say Richmond's collapse is imminent. We get to that capital and we've got the Confederacy locked down," he promised.

The soldiers cheered.

"How would you fellows like to learn a new game?" he asked the ambulatories.

One of the soldiers asked, "Do I recall your name, General Doubleday? Are you General *Abner* Doubleday from New York?"

"Guilty!" laughed General Doubleday.

"Then I recall it was you who got off the first retaliatory shot for the Union at Fort Sumter in '61, when the Rebs started this whole shootin' match. Do I remember that right?"

"Guilty as charged! However did you remember such an obscure fact as that, soldier?"

"You've a bit of an unusual name, sir, and I've been keeping a journal of the war since the very beginning. I guess I read it somewhere and wrote it down. It's an honor to meet you, sir."

"The honor is mine, soldier." The soldier made an attempt at a salute, but General Doubleday reached out and shook his hand instead. "The honor is mine. Now then, let's play some ball!"

He took out a small leather ball and showed it to everyone. The men rubbed it, smelled it, and tossed it around to each other. Then Doubleday brought out a wooden bat and everyone who had an arm took a practice swing with it.

He explained the rules: simply throw the ball, hit the ball, run around to the three *X*'s marked in the dirt, and score. He told them that some cities had teams made up to play against each other in this game called Bases and Balls. If a soldier couldn't run, someone could run for him. If he could run or walk the bases but not bat, someone could bat for him. It would be grand exercise for sidelined soldiers. More and more of the volunteers began to drift out the door into the yard.

Avery was missing some of his staff, and Claire was wondering where all the nurses had gone. The two of them showed up on the porch just in time to see one of the nurses blast the ball's cover off with the bat, lift up her skirts, and run the bases. Her team was cheering and whistling, and General Doubleday was announcing the score. The nurse dusted off her skirts, took a bow, and headed indoors, where she met Dr. Bennett and Nurse Claire on the porch. She bit her lip, nipped her head, and said, "Excuse me," as she passed through the door, feeling embarrassed.

"Well done," said Avery. The nurse turned around and smiled at him and went back to work.

Avery had a word with Doubleday and suggested that especially the paid staff be excluded from the games during work hours. So the following Sunday afternoon, everyone who wasn't working was invited to a meadow outside town for a real baseball game. Anyone who wished to learn to play was invited. Dorothy and Claire thought it would be fun to take some of the ambulatory patients along. Dr. Simpson said they could use the hospital wagon.

Throughout the hospitals and around the town the word about the baseball game spread like wildfire . . . or disease, some said. Everyone in town was planning to come to cheer for the wounded soldiers, bat for them, and run for them. Town folk offered wagons to take the patients to the ballgame. Maybe they'd get in a swing or two themselves. The competitive spirit of the patients was aroused, and everyone wanted to practice so they might win. So every afternoon that week, instead of taking their afternoon rest, the ambulatories and the volunteers gathered in the hospital's side yard to practice the pitch and swing, skills they now knew were necessary for victory.

"I think their attitude is, if we can't win on the battlefield, we'll win on the playing field," Avery joked to Dr. Simpson. General Doubleday was amiable, and the soldiers enjoyed his visits. He told Avery he would only be around for a few more days. His regiment was on the move.

"It seems that most regiments are on the move these days," Avery commented.

The bases and ball practice was going well, everyone taking turns, with the volunteers coming and going. Dr. Simpson took his staff to task. The paid staff was not to play ball during working hours. He would prefer the volunteers to do their share of the workload, but volunteers could come and go as they pleased. These days, it seemed to please them to play ball.

On Saturday before the big game, a few of the weekend volunteers were organizing the practice with the ambulatories while the indoor patients rested. One of the volunteers managed a perfect pitch across the target marked with the *X*, and the batter managed a perfect swing. The bat met the ball and cracked loudly as the ball and both halves of the bat went sailing to the tree line.

The volunteer in the field raced toward the ball to make the catch. Looking at the ball, he ran directly into the little beehive at exactly the same moment that the ball slammed into the hive, splintering the corner of the box, making a second loud crack.

The runner fell backwards over the hive, and the angry bees swarmed out on the offensive. Another army on the move! The bees covered the volunteer, who was yelling, rolling, calling, and trying to get up. He tried to run, covering his face and swatting all at the same time. All the other volunteers ran toward the hospital. The first one in the door brought some of the honeybees inside on his shirt, and others flew in after him.

"Shut the doors and shut the windows, quickly! Bring water, bring sheets," he shouted and he ran back outside. Windows began slamming shut before anyone knew why. Some whispered it must be a fire. Others wondered if the enemy had made it to Alexandria.

It wasn't long before the bees started dropping into view inside the hospital. Avery was on the second floor when he looked out the closed window and saw the volunteer struggling on the ground, his face swollen, his arms swatting, and every now and then receiving another sting. Avery stared at the man, wondering why he didn't get up.

"The man's hardly breathing," he said, and he took off down the stairs at a run. With bees buzzing around their heads, two volunteers were dragging the man toward the hospital.

"Get his clothes off," ordered Avery. He ran to the side yard where nurses were trying to get the ambulatories moving away from the angry bees. Avery yelled to try to get them far enough away from the hive that the bees wouldn't think them a threat. He didn't want to bring them inside, because all the bees would then be inside with patients who weren't strong enough to live through such an attack, some of whom would be defenseless.

Claire and all her nurses came running toward them with bed sheets, which were dripping water. They threw the wet sheets all around the patients as Avery and the others tried to move them.

Just inside the door, volunteers stripped the bee-infested clothing off the man and threw it out the door. They tried to cool his mottled, swollen body with water, and the man struggled to breathe.

"I'm getting the doctor," one of them said. He slipped out the door, swatting the bees off. As he ran, he called to Dr. Bennett, "*Emergency!*" Avery knew what the emergency would be and hoped he had enough tonic and elixir in his emergency kit to help this man. He stumbled through the door, falling over the man lying on the floor. The man was covered with hundreds of welts. Avery ran into the office where he kept his medicines and quickly returned. His hands shook, and he needed to take a deep breath. Suddenly Claire stood beside him, steadying his hand. She held the man's head up while Avery poured the herbal elixir down the man's swollen throat. And then covering him with a wet sheet, they waited, and they both prayed. Avery mixed quantities of a paste to put on the welts.

The nurses began to bring in the others, saying that the bees appeared to have returned to guard the area around their hive. The ambulatories, the nurses, and volunteers all had many stings. On nearly every window and wall the bees tried to fight their way to freedom and back to their hive.

Avery gave everyone instructions to capture, not kill, the bees that had found their way in. The idea of trying to save the bees didn't appeal to them, but Dr. Bennett was adamant; the bees were needed. Some of the nurses had collected several of the agitated honeybees in cups upstairs. When things quieted down they'd be able to release them, Dr. Bennett told them, and the bees would return to their hive.

One by one, the patients, volunteers, and staff treated each other's stings, using Avery's salves and pastes sparingly. As far as he could tell, none of the bedridden patients on the second or third floor had been stung. Dr. Simpson was making rounds now to verify that.

Avery looked around for Claire and found her treating one of the volunteers who'd carried the sick man into the hospital. When she finished, Avery took her by the hand and pulled her aside.

"Sit down, Nurse Claire. Let the doctor have a look at you." She obeyed, looking very tired. He pushed her hair away from her face and began salving all the welts on her face and neck. He checked her arms and legs. "You nurses look like speckled puppies," Avery told her. Their tired eyes met and Avery's heart leapt. He bent down and placed a tender kiss on her damp forehead.

"Thank you, Avery," she said.

"You're welcome. Thank you and your nurses for all your help."

By supper time, the man on the floor seemed to be recovering. *Another dose of tonic*, Avery thought, *and he should be breathing okay.* They dressed him in a hospital night shirt and continued to salve his stings. Someone started to count his welts, but either he couldn't count that high or he forgot where he was in the counting.

More bees were captured and released. There were still too many flying around outside to open the windows, even though it was stuffy and stinking inside. Avery asked around to find out who knew where the beekeeper lived, and finally one of the volunteers responded.

"It was me, Doctor, who went for the lady beekeeper the last time. Do you want her to come back?"

"Yes. Would you mind getting her for me? Ask her to come tomorrow if she can, or if not, as soon as possible. Thanks."

Avery told everyone to wait until dusk to leave when the bees would likely quiet down on their own. One at a time, the staff slipped out the door as the evening light dimmed. They slipped out and headed to the other side of the building, away from the side yard and the bees.

The volunteer with the bee stings would remain as a patient overnight at Avery's request. Avery told Dr. Simpson he'd stay overnight at the hospital too, just in case the man's condition changed. Dr. Simpson called Gunner and invited him to ride home with him, but Gunner preferred to stay with Avery.

In the quiet of the night, while Avery was lying on a cot saying his night prayers, he reached down to pet Gunner, who winced a bit. While petting him, Avery discovered welts on Gunner's body. He lit a lantern and looked at his dog, discovering that Gunner had several bee stings, including a very swollen one on his nose.

"Where were you when all this was going on, Gunner? I don't recall seeing you." He applied a little ointment to his dog's welts and to some of his own as well. He invited Gunner to join him on his cot, and this is where they spent a quiet and, thankfully, uneventful night.

When Avery awakened at dawn the next morning on the cot in the records office, the early sunrise was streaking through the closed window. On the desk were the tiny bottles that held the medicines Avery used every day. The sunlight shone through the little bottles. Amber, clear, cobalt blue, and emerald green glass reflected on the wall.

"A little rainbow," said Avery, who was still saying his morning prayers. "Thank you for rainbows."

He went to check on his bee-stung patient and found him breathing easily and sleeping soundly. The little rainbow on the office wall reminded Avery that this was Sunday and that he'd miss going to church with the Simpsons and Claire this morning. He'd

miss watching Claire pray and sing, praying beside her, while the colored windows, like little rainbows, reflected on her hands.

"Thank you for this rainbow and all the promises it holds for me," Avery prayed. "The promise of medicine bottles that hold miracles and cures that I can't explain; the promise of the sun rising every day, a miracle I don't understand; the promise of love, which I can't define; the promise of Claire I'm only now beginning to appreciate. Thank you for all these rainbows. Amen."

Late that afternoon, the lady beekeeper arrived. She wore a net over her broad-brimmed hat, her shirt sleeves tied tightly at the wrists, and her pants tied at her ankles. Her too-big gloves kept slipping off her hands. Moving in hurried steps and her lips pursed angrily, she didn't say a word to Avery or anyone else. It was clear that she was most disgruntled about the state of her hive. She put the new hive a little farther away and a bit closer to the trees. Avery promised her there would be no more ball playing on this side yard of the hospital. She kept on working and didn't answer him.

"Hmpf."

"We're all really sorry about this."

"Hmpf."

"We tried to capture and release as many bees as we could from inside."

"Hmpf."

The woman was as mad as her bees, and there was no point in trying to talk to her.

"Thank you for coming out today. I appreciate that it's Sunday. I will pay you whatever it costs."

"Hmpf."

Avery went inside and the beekeeper continued her sulk until the work was finished. She put the broken hive in her wagon and headed on down the road. Every now and then, a stray bee tapped against a window and then flew off to the new hive to honor his new queen, visit the spring crop of clover, and get the hospital's honey factory back up to production.

When the bees had returned to their new hive, and the sun had gone down, the staff opened the windows.

CHAPTER TWENTY-ONE
MAY DAY

"Tomorrow is the first day of May, Gunner. It's Claire's birthday." Avery admired a paper May basket at the Apothecary and Stationer's Shop in Alexandria. It was a lace-paper cone with a ribbon handle attached.

"What would a girl use this for?" he asked the clerk. "Doesn't seem too practical."

"I'm sure I don't know," said the clerk. "But the gals sure do like them."

"Well, okay." He picked out the green one with the white paper lace. It had several ribbon streamers flying out of the cone and off the handle.

"She might think of some use for it. It should do for a birthday surprise."

He bought two peppermints wrapped in shiny paper and dropped them into the paper cone basket. Later he made a small jar of hand cream and put it in too.

"Mrs. Simpson, would you mind if I cut just a few little flowers from your garden?"

"Not at all, Avery. There are some violets in the shade behind the stable." Avery took a little tour of Mrs. Simpson's garden. He cut some parsley, chives, and a sprig of mint. *All useful plants*, he thought. He snapped a little branch off the flowering quince. He found some dandelions, chicory, and the violets. Claire had

given him violets the first time she spoke to him; perhaps she liked violets. He trimmed them all to fit into the little cone May basket.

"Pretty good! I wonder what girls do with these things? It just doesn't seem terribly useful, does it?" Gunner sniffed the basket and whipped his tail in approval. "Maybe she won't like it. She's a practical sort, I think." Gunner whined. Avery took the flowers out of the May basket and put them into a cup of water for the night. In the morning he put them back in the basket and took it to the hospital to surprise Claire on her May Day birthday. *While everything around us looks charred and barren, this little basket does look cheerful. I hope she'll like it.*

"Good morning, Nurse Claire," he said, when he saw her come in the door.

"Top o' the mornin' to you, Dr. Bennett." She put on her best Irish.

"Happy birthday," he said quietly, with his hands behind his back.

"Avery—Dr. Bennett, you remembered it was my birthday?"

"And happy May Day also." He handed her the little May Day basket with the ribbons hanging down, bursting with spring flowers.

Claire was speechless. Her cheeks flushed, her mouth opened, but no words came out.

"Oh, my goodness, I don't know what to say," she said at last. "This is the prettiest May Day basket I've ever seen and I—oh—'tis altogether lovely . . . I just don't know what to say."

Well, he thought, *I'm not the only one who sometimes doesn't know what to say.*

"You could say thank you, and then I'd know what to say next."

"Oh, of course, Avery, thank you. Oh, I do mean thank you."

"Then, you're welcome." The two friends locked eyes and smiled. They both blushed and went off to begin the work of

healing broken bodies and spirits. Avery looked around and hoped no one else had noticed the whole basket and flower scene.

"Gunner, that was close. I thought she was going to jump up on her toes and try to kiss me. Violets may bring that out in her."

Claire showed her pretty basket to all the nurses and volunteers who were envious of the May basket. She showed it to the patients, who felt a bit of joy at seeing the pretty flower-filled basket.

"Just like at home," one soldier said.

"My mother makes May Day baskets."

"My sisters always liked getting those from their beaus."

One of the soldiers pulled out his mouth harp, and his buddy on the next cot began to sing a folk tune called "Seventeen Come Sunday."

As I walked out on a May morning, on a May morning so early,
I overtook a pretty fair maid just as the day was a-dawning.
With a rue-rum-ray, fol-the-diddle-day.
Whack-fol-lare-diddle-I-doh.

How old are you, my pretty fair maid? How old are you, my honey?
She answered me right cheerfully, I'm eighteen years, come Sunday.
With a rue-rum-ray, fol-the-diddle-day
Whack-fol-lare-diddle-I-doh.

The patients played and sang *eighteen* years instead of seventeen, and Claire danced a little Irish step, holding her basket high. Her eyes sparkled all day, and Avery was glad he'd bought the little basket. It seemed to give her much pleasure, and her pleasure made him happy.

CHAPTER TWENTY-TWO
LEGLESS HORSEMAN

Claire and Dorothy posted Anthony Pioli's drawings all around the hospital where everyone could enjoy them. Since many of the soldiers were farmers, they enjoyed seeing the farm and animal pictures. Gunner often lay on the cot with Anthony. Since the man had no legs, Gunner found himself with lots of room on this cot, and it was getting to be a favorite nap place.

Avery watched as the nurses moved the soldier around and helped him balance on his stumps. Claire mentioned that before too long he could join the ambulatories outside. Avery was pleased with how the man's legs had healed.

Claire had a plan, and she spoke to Dr. Simpson. He laughed, shook his head, and said she had his blessing. So she went to Avery to make her request.

"You want me to bring Fan to the hospital?" he asked. "Why?"

"Would you, please?" He looked at her smile and knew he'd give her whatever she wanted, even his beloved Fan.

"Sure," he said. "I'll bring her tomorrow. I can't wait to see what you've planned for our amusement this time."

"You'll see," she promised with a wink.

She was waiting on the porch of the hospital when he arrived on Fan's back. Gunner trotted alongside. Fan and Gunner

had their gaits so well timed that one of them never touched the other, but they trotted as if their legs were tied together.

"We're here as promised."

"Thank you, Avery . . . Dr. Bennett," Claire said. Avery dismounted, wrapped Fan's rein around the porch rail, and went in to start his rounds. Claire petted and nuzzled the horse and passed Fan a bit of wrinkled apple. Gunner watched, waiting to see if she had anything for him too. She pulled from her pocket a tiny bit of cracker, which Gunner licked from her fingers, using his best manners.

Claire and Dorothy brought Anthony Pioli to the porch. After several weeks of practicing, Anthony was moving around learning to do more for himself. This would be his first attempt at stairs. He sat down with his stumps out in front of him, and using his hands to lift himself, he lowered his body, one step at a time. Perspiring with the effort, Anthony smiled proudly. "What you think, girls? How'd I do?"

"Wonderful!" they both rejoiced. At the bottom of the stairs, Claire instructed him to wait. She'd seen Avery get Fan to lie down on the ground, but she hadn't tried this before; she wasn't exactly sure how to do it. She tried a couple of times, and the horse moved away from her to one side and then the other. Anthony laughed.

"What exactly do you want from the horse?" he asked. Claire explained she wanted Fan to lie down on the ground. Anthony picked up Fan's reins and spoke to her. She dropped her head to him, where he petted and caressed her ears and talked to her, horseman to horse. Fan was totally enraptured with her new friend.

"You speak horse language, Anthony," Dorothy said with admiration.

The soldier wrapped his hands around the reins firmly and used them to pull himself up to a stand. The horse whinnied and bobbed her head up and down. He talked to her and finally took her bridle. He whispered something to her and she moved,

nearly pulling the tottering man over. He took a little half step and held his position upright.

"Oh, good for you, Anthony, good for you," cheered Dorothy.

Claire sighed, "Oh thank you, God! This man will recover and be able to have a life. Great balance, Anthony, hurrah!"

Fan was folding her knees and dropping her body to the ground. Anthony moved to her side, and with no assistance from either nurse he slid his body onto the saddle. He sat there for a few minutes talking and petting before indicating to Fan to rise. When Fan started to stand, both nurses gasped. They could see the man sliding from side to side with no legs to straddle and support him in the saddle. He leaned forward, hugged himself to the horse's neck, and miraculously held on while Fan finished the maneuver to get four legs under her. His nurses watched with nervous awe.

"Good for you, Anthony! Well done!" The nurses looked at each other. Now what? Neither knew what they'd do next. The soldier didn't hesitate. He sat up straight and clucked, and the horse began to walk around the side yard. The ambulatories whistled and whooped and applauded the soldier, encouraging him and congratulating him. Claire and Dorothy walked on either side of the horse. The soldier kept Fan in a slow, steady gait.

"I know you'd like to step out, Fan. You're a fine gaiter, but this is as much as I'm up for at the moment, old girl. Be patient with me," Anthony said.

Avery was on the second floor when he heard his horse whinny. He looked out the window down into the side yard and saw the animated ambulatories leaning on their crutches, cheering and clapping. Then Fan came into view, carrying the legless soldier. Fan's stirrups were empty, no knees directing her. When the soldier leaned forward and showed Fan his appreciation, Avery was touched.

"He's truly a horseman," he said aloud to no one. Avery felt a lump of gratitude growing in his throat. "What a wonderful idea she had," he marveled. "This man can continue his life in the

company of his beloved horses; not the same as before, but the best way he can. *Not how it should be, but how it is.* This man can soon be going home to his family and his horses. Not the same as before, but how he is."

The patient whose bandages Avery was changing nodded slowly. "That's how it is for ever'body these days, Doc. Most things aren't how they should be anymore, just how they are."

A slight breeze blew across the water basin sitting next to the window sill. The light caught the water, and a little rainbow flashed across the table, spilling light into the window. Claire caught the flash of light and looked up to the window, where she saw Avery. She smiled and waved.

She does have a lot of wonderful ideas. I'll speak to General Keese and Dr. Simpson. Perhaps it's time for the horseman to go home to New York and leave this war behind.

CHAPTER TWENTY-THREE
NO END IN SIGHT

Claire had stopped at the post office on her way back to the hospital. She'd picked up mail held at the post office for Anthony Pioli and a few other soldiers. She had a large envelope for Avery. She found him in the staff office eating his cold meat and cheese left over from last night's supper.

"Wonderful news, Doctor, a letter for you from Kanawha Valley, West Virginia." She waved the envelope in the air.

Avery smiled and took the letter. He had no time to read it right now. He and Claire went up to the second floor to begin afternoon rounds. That evening he took the letter out.

Dearest Avery,

It seems forever since you left here and so much has happened, yet compared to the rest of Virginia, not much at all. We have been spared much bloodshed. The newspapers have told us all we really want to hear of the terrors of this war. Our farm feels like a garden of paradise compared to the devastation elsewhere.

Banjo has done a fine job of plowing with our one lonesome draft horse. He also plowed a portion for his family. Our summer crops have come in well, and the weather has been favorable. Maize and I will be preserving most of the summer. We should have a good supply of food laid by for winter. We've traded

the McDougals some corn for potatoes. Their potato farm is prospering.

Molly McDougal wonders if you might have run across their daughter who is also working at a hospital as a nurse somewhere in Alexandria. It would be nice for both of you to know someone from home. She's about your age; perhaps you remember seeing her when you were children.

Caroline, Phoebe, and Timothy McDougal have gone by train to Spartanburg, South Carolina. There's a special school there for the blind, mute, and deaf. Caroline will learn to teach the afflicted. She says little Phoebe is very fond of Timothy, and the two of them are companions learning sign language together. It is very hot in Carolina, and Caroline says the weather there gives her a terrible rash. She's missing the shady hollers of the Kanawha Valley.

My pupils are doing very well. Our school is so crowded now that I'm trying to hire another teacher. We have discussed forming a school board and building a bigger school. We're bursting at the seams as it is.

Perhaps Clayton has written you already, and I hope I'm not spoiling his news. He's met a young lady in Boston of whom he is very fond. Her name is Elizabeth Jane Claymore. He writes that he is contemplating marriage. Isn't that exciting news?

I miss you very much. I pray for you daily. Please write whenever you can. When this ugly war is over, we'll be together again.

Love, Mother

Avery read the letter a couple of times. Had he never told his mother about Claire? Had Claire mentioned him to her mother? Clayton was getting married. Well, well. Avery hoped that Father had given Clayton the same guidelines he'd given him. Did Clayton and Elizabeth pray together? He wondered if Clayton's mind had listened to his heart, as his father had instructed, or did he just know? How did he know he loved Elizabeth? Maybe he'd write to him and ask. It was good to hear about the green fields and the good crops at home.

"Good morning, Doctor," said cheerful Claire. "Did you enjoy your letter from home yesterday?"

"Yes, I did; lots of news."

"Any that I might like to hear? Not meaning to be in your business, I don't mean to be. Just thought . . . you know, Kanawha Valley and all."

Avery looked up at the sound of arriving guards on horseback bringing paperwork.

"Incoming ambulances," he called. He shoved his letter from home into his shirt pocket as Claire hurried off to the receiving area. The staff scurried to make room and make way for the injured from Petersburg. How many were coming today? Where would they put them?

Avery wondered what the city of Petersburg looked like. It was mentioned in every newspaper. He knew it was on the Appomattox River and was only about twenty miles from Richmond. He read everything in the papers about it, trying to figure out why Petersburg was so important to both the Union and the Confederacy. He studied the battles.

The ambulatory patients watched while he drew Petersburg on his big wall map and decorated it with little bursts of cannon fire. The men clapped and showed fists while murmuring in agreement. Petersburg was next. The Union would take Petersburg; they just knew it. The newspaper printed more bad news for the injured and disappointed soldiers; another dismal battle for the Union.

"The siege of Petersburg is going to last all through the heat of the summer, looks like to me." The soldier leaned on his crutch and peered over Avery's shoulder at the big map on the wall.

"Doesn't seem to be the kind of siege I read about in history and ancient classics or even in the American Revolution," Avery responded. "This is more of a trench war; you're right, it could go on for a long time."

"It's already gone on too long," the soldier muttered.

Avery watched the cloud of gloom hovering over his patients.

In July one of the volunteers came in with a wild tale that a regiment of General Burnside's Union forces, who were coal miners from Pennsylvania, mined a tunnel more than five hundred feet long under the Confederate lines. Avery pointed out Pennsylvania on the map, but he wondered if the volunteer was making this up.

"On the last day of July, the miners detonated the explosives they'd buried in the tunnel. BOOM!" he bellowed. "They made a crater a hundred thirty-five feet wide. Blew up about three hundred Johnny Rebs." He did a little dance and the soldiers cheered.

Avery drew a mine and a stick of dynamite on his map. *I wonder if he's making this up to cheer the patients?*

"Woo hoo!" shouted the soldiers. "That's showing them."

If he is, it's working.

The volunteer rested his muddy boot on a patient's cot. Claire slapped his leg with a towel as she passed by; he stood straight up and saluted her, causing the other patients to giggle.

"But that's not the end of the story," said another volunteer who'd been listening. "Tell the rest of it."

Avery could tell by the tone of the man's voice this wouldn't be a happy ending.

"You tell it," the first man grumped as he sauntered away. He hadn't wanted to tell that part.

"Union troops ran down into the crater. While they struggled to climb up the steep sides of the crater, the Confeder-

ates slaughtered them. Like sitting ducks, they were. They're saying over five thousand Union casualties, and for no advantage."

"Will this madness ever end? Where are we going to put them all," Avery grumbled. "I'm really getting disgusted with this whole sickening war."

"Yeah, me too," whispered a hoarse voice behind him.

Avery looked over his shoulder and saw the bandaged, mutilated body of one of his amputees.

"Me too, Doc."

Avery's face burned and he wanted to hide. "I'm sorry. I didn't mean . . . I'm ashamed," he said. "I'm honored to be your doctor."

"I get your meaning, Doc," the soldier said.

In August as the siege continued, Lee's army was out of food. Petersburg was in Union hands, but Richmond had still not been taken. Every day the patients asked for the news, hoping it would be good.

"How these men cope with the constant disappointment is a wonder to me," Avery said to Matt Mason one afternoon. Dr. Mason had been Avery's best friend from the first day he'd arrived at Mansion House Hospital and one of the few Avery shared his inner thoughts with. "How do they continue in their battle when they keep losing? Some days I feel depressed just thinking about those men. Sometimes I wonder if God is listening to their prayers."

"I know exactly what you are saying," Matt answered quietly. "I've seen some of them in the last moments of their lives. I didn't hear complaint or remorse. They only wanted to go home; they were sorry that they didn't win the war."

Avery grew quiet and thoughtful. *Am I losing faith?* He wondered about that. "I don't think I can keep this up, Matt. It's not what I want to do anymore."

"That's how I feel too, Avery. But here we are. And they need us. That's the thing. To be working where you're needed. There's the blessing."

Avery digested that. "I hadn't thought about my work being a blessing. I'm just so sick and tired of this war."

"Well, you sure aren't alone there, Doctor."

The leaves fell and the daylight hours grew shorter. Both sides were digging in for the long winter ahead.

What if spring never comes? Will they live in winter quarters forever? Will this war never end? God, are you listening? Are you planning to help me out with this?

CHAPTER TWENTY-FOUR
PIECES OF RAINBOW

After Lincoln's proclamation last year, Thanksgiving Day had already become an American tradition. Food, still harder to come by this year, would sit on the tables of all Americans, no matter how meager. All Americans would offer their prayers of thanks. Families would gather as best they could, and some would set empty places for their missing members. They would put up their decorations and put on a grateful face. Americans anticipated their unique holiday.

"Avery," called Mrs. Simpson, as he and Dr. Simpson were leaving for the hospital. "You doctors!" she waved and called. "One of you, at least, or both of you, please request the company of the lovely Claire for Thanksgiving Day. And if you can find the elusive General Keese, ask him as well please. We'll have a fine time of it, won't we?"

They waved. Avery couldn't quite identify the feeling that bit of news gave him.

The first few times that Mrs. Simpson had invited Claire he'd felt slightly annoyed, knowing he'd be expected to talk to the girl and would suffer the humiliation of being totally tongue-tied. Then the next few times, he had felt nervous about it but had enjoyed being with her. Now? What was this he was feeling now? His face felt flushed as he thought about how he'd invite her. *What if she doesn't want to come? She likes Mrs. Simpson, and she likes Gunner.* He decided he was looking forward to spending the

day with his best friends. *Maybe this time I'll look at her across the table instead of looking at my plate of food. Maybe this time it will be my own idea to walk her home instead of Dr. Simpson asking me to. But what if she doesn't come? Gunner will be disappointed.* His heart and his mind were in agreement. He wanted her to come, he admitted to himself. And he'd invite her himself. He bravely looked forward to her company. If the General had overcome his insecurities about Aunt Caroline, he could too.

He was partly finished with his rounds before he saw Claire that morning. She was smiling and joking with Dorothy and Anthony. She was packing the supplies for Anthony and giving him lots of silly advice, hence the laughter. Anthony was going home; General Keese had assigned a volunteer to accompany him. In a week or two he'd be home in Saratoga, New York, far away from the battlefields of Virginia.

"Dr. Bennett, may I have a private word with you?" Pioli asked. The surprised nurses shrugged and walked away.

"Congratulations, Anthony. I'm so happy for you. You're going home. And I'm even happier with your recovery. It's been complete. Thanks be to God," Avery said, patting the man's shoulder and shaking his hand. "Good luck to you."

"Yes, and thanks to you," said Anthony. "Doctor, I wanted to ask you a personal thing. I'd like to take the nurse Dorothy with me to New York and marry her. Do you think I've any right to ask a girl to marry me when I'm only half a man? Do you think I can provide a home for her?"

"Anthony, don't ever think of yourself as half a man. You're alive; you're whole, married or single. You'll be a fine husband. Don't you worry." Avery smiled and shook his hand firmly. "You'll be just fine, Anthony."

Anthony wiped his eyes with the back of his hand. As Avery moved away, Dorothy and Claire started back, and Avery intercepted Claire. He took her by the elbow and walked the surprised girl in the other direction. She started to protest, but Avery held her elbow firmly.

"They need some time alone," he whispered.

"What?" she whispered in surprise.

They heard a little squeal and turned around to see Anthony Pioli on the floor beside his bed. Dorothy was seated on the bed with her hands over her mouth. She dropped onto the floor beside him and the two embraced.

"You were right!" said the astonished Claire. "I never even guessed that."

"Claire, Mrs. Simpson requests the honor of your company on Thanksgiving Day. Will you come?"

"Well now, is it only Mrs. Simpson who wishes my company?"

"Well, I think Gunner might be sadly disappointed if you didn't come."

"Tell Gunner and Mrs. Simpson that I should be altogether delighted to attend the dinner."

He wasn't aware of doing it, but both his hands reached for her hands. "And, Claire . . . I want you to be there too."

She was beaming. Had he really said that?

"Dr. Bennett! Claire! I'm going to be married, and I'm going to New York," called Dorothy excitedly. "I'm going to be Anthony's wife and live on the horse farm. And my own family is also in New York. I'm so blessed and so happy!"

Claire hugged her friend. "I'm so happy for you, Dorothy. Anthony is a fine, strong man of good character. You'll have a good life; I'm so happy for both of you."

"What's all this?" asked Dr. Simpson coming upon the celebration.

"Our nurse Dorothy is marrying our handsome patient Anthony, so she is resigning to go to New York! Isn't this wonderful?" Claire said joyously.

"Well now, that is wonderful news. For everyone but the hospital, that is. We'll miss you my dear; you've been a blessing to us. Congratulations to you both. Good luck and best wishes to both of you. Dorothy, you find me at midday meal, and I'll see about your pay. You'll be wanting that, won't you?" He shook hands with Anthony.

"Thank you, Doctor, and thank you everyone. Oh, this is so exciting!" She went back to Anthony who was standing next to his cot, beaming with joy.

"I've just the horse for you, Dorothy. She's a beauty. She's Queen of Alfonzo; I call her Allie. And I'll teach you to ride her." The nurse and the two doctors watched the two happily begin making plans for the rest of their lives.

"Guess we can cancel the traveling volunteer," Dr. Simpson noted. "He has himself a permanent escort now. Oh, Claire, before I forget, Mrs. Simpson would like to have you come to dinner for Thanksgiving. How about that?"

"Yes, thank you, Dr. Simpson. Avery, um, Dr. Bennett, that is, invited me already, and I've most certainly accepted."

Dr. Simpson looked surprised and amused and he cast a sidelong look at Avery. *Well maybe the young man is opening his eyes . . . and maybe his heart.*

Avery smiled at the doctor, and to Dr. Simpson's amazement, Avery wasn't blushing.

Dr. Simpson hired the livery wagon to go to the nurses' residence to collect Dorothy and her trunk and then to the hospital for Anthony and his few belongings. The staff gathered in the side yard, and everyone waved and shouted their good lucks and goodbyes. The happy couple was off to the train. The battlefield was only a memory for both of them now. They were heading north to begin their new life together.

When the wagon pulled away, Avery and Claire looked off into the distant landscape. The heavy smoke hung low. Above the smoke in the pale sky, broken fragments of rainbow shimmered off the high ice crystals between the sun and the earth.

"Look, Avery," pointed Claire, "pieces of rainbow."

Everyone in the yard looked up far into the horizon above the artillery smoke, and they all saw pieces of broken rainbow high above, splashing color onto a colorless sky.

"It's a good sign altogether, don't you think, Avery?"

"Yes. Yes, I think it is. Rainbows."

CHAPTER TWENTY-FIVE
GRATEFUL HEARTS

Both armies established their winter quarters—within miles of each other. Avery commented one cold morning that the armies could probably each see the breath of their enemy. *What a strange war this has turned out to be,* he thought.

Claire wrote a note to General Keese about an idea she had for Thanksgiving. She put a notice in the newspaper about sharing Thanksgiving with our troops on the front. Everyone would make one extra pie and bring it to an address on Worth Street on the Tuesday before Thanksgiving Day. This address was the former home of a wealthy Alexandrian banker. But now it was a headquarters office of the Army of the Potomac.

After work on Tuesday, Claire went to Worth Street and discovered that so many pies had turned up that they were sitting outside, covered with old newspapers, guarded by a picket. The office had run out of space. She and the clerks in the headquarters packed the pies in crates on wagons, being careful not to mash them. This took until after dark. When Claire was satisfied that her pies would be safely delivered, she wrapped herself in her warm cloak and started out into the dark night.

"Nine o'clock and all's well," the lamplighter called out.

Thanksgiving Day brought rain and cold wind. Dr. Simpson sent Avery with the buggy to call for Claire at the nurses' residence. He felt awkward when one of the nurses let him in.

"Dr. Bennett?"

She seems surprised, and rightfully, thought Avery. He asked for Claire and realized by the look on the nurse's face that the gossips were going to have a great time with this.

"Uh, um . . . she is the guest of Dr. and Mrs. Simpson today. I've been asked to come for her because of the bad weather. Dr. Simpson sent me here."

"Oh, I see." The nurse was obviously disappointed. "I'll get her for you."

Avery settled Claire in the doctor's buggy and spread an oilcloth over her lap to protect her from splashing rain.

General Keese arrived for dinner but couldn't stay long. He wanted to visit his troops who were in winter quarters. Several were in the trenches at Petersburg. He'd be there himself in another week.

"Well, those men will be enjoying pie today, General Keese," said Claire excitedly. "Thank you so much for your help in arranging the transportation. You'd be amazed at all the pies that were brought in. There were pies of all kinds. I saw potato, chicken, sweet potato, pumpkin, apple, vegetable, cherry, pecan, creams, berry, shoofly pie, rice pudding pie, minced meat, and some I never saw before. Mrs. Simpson sent a rhubarb pie. People were all so generous, even though no one has much. Some might have given all they had. I'm sure it was a surprise and a treat for those men to have a piece of pie."

"I'm sure you're right about that. Thank you for your thoughtful kindness, my dear. It was the Army's pleasure to provide the delivery to the front for your wonderful idea."

Avery stared at her, fascinated with her enthusiasm, her good ideas, and her self-confidence. *I can't imagine a Thanksgiving dinner without her.*

They caught up on all the gossip in the hospital, news from Kanawha Valley, and the updates on the siege. General Keese couldn't stay, but they all enjoyed a lovely dinner. After he left, Avery wanted Claire to go to the stable to see his gypsy horse. She was intrigued.

"You have a gypsy horse? Where did you get a gypsy horse? You are certainly full of surprises, Avery Bennett."

"I'll tell you about it. Get your warm wraps. Leon will have a nice little fire in his stove, but it'll still be chilly out there."

"Avery, take this plate of hot food out to Leon. He'll be happy for it." Mrs. Simpson held up the plate as they passed through the kitchen.

"Here, I'll carry it," offered Claire.

Avery put on his coat and hat and escorted Claire out the back door, past the kitchen, and into the barn. Gunner led the way.

"Oh, Avery, she's beautiful. How did you get her? She's unusual, isn't she?"

Avery captivated her with his story of the deserter thieves and how he came to have the gypsy horse named Rose.

Leon told them stories of his "good ol' days" and enjoyed the plate of hot food.

Sitting next to Claire in the fresh hay, laughing and talking with Leon, enjoying the little potbelly stove, seemed to Avery to be the most natural things in the world.

This is where we belong, isn't it? In a barn with the air scented with fresh hay and animal smells. We're farmers, and this feels like home. Yet here we are a doctor and his nurse. That feels right too.

They lingered far longer than Avery planned, and before he knew it, he was driving her home in Dr. Simpson's buggy in the dark.

"It's been a wonderful Thanksgiving Day, Avery. Thank you."

He watched her enter the building; he turned the buggy around and drove home. Gunner sat tall and proud on the buggy seat and waved his tail merrily.

CHAPTER TWENTY-SIX

KITCHEN PROJECT

Most of the emergencies they were seeing now were dysentery or influenza. The lull of the war and the softly falling snow cast a hush over the normal din of the hospital. The nurses and the volunteers were trying to get their patients into the Christmas spirit. They tried singing Christmas songs with the patients, but the songs sounded mournful. Keeping the patients warm was an even bigger challenge. They boiled water and offered it to the soldiers. They called it cider or tea or broth, whichever the patient preferred. But it was all hot water.

One of the local volunteers had shredded a red taffeta dress that she had once worn to a ball, in the days of balls and banquets before the war. She had a stack of inch-wide red taffeta ribbons and was ready to decorate anything and everything from cots to doorknobs. She had so many ribbons from the enormous skirts of the layered ball gown that she took some to the other hospitals. She gave red ribbons to anyone who asked. Avery asked shyly if he might have one, and Claire asked if she might have a couple. It seemed likely that everyone's gift would have a red taffeta ribbon attached this year.

Avery purchased a packet of writing linen from the stationer's shop and mailed it to his mother with a Christmas letter. Then he began the task of finding just the right things for his friends. He bought some scented water for Mrs. Simpson, a leather bookmark for Dr. Simpson, and for Gunner a big soup

bone, which he packed in the snow until Christmas Day so it wouldn't spoil. Even the bones of the meat were a treasure these days. He wrapped the little gift for Claire in a piece of rice paper that he bought at the stationer's shop. He had used his red ribbon on the Simpsons' packages, so he tied Claire's gift with a piece of Mrs. Simpson's embroidery thread. It looked pretty enough, and maybe she could use the embroidery string for something, the pragmatic doctor thought. He hoped she would like his gift; he thought it was quite special.

Feeling confident after reading reports in the newspaper concerning her Thanksgiving pie project, Claire hatched a new plan for Christmas. She wrote a note to Mrs. Simpson.

When she read it, Mrs. Simpson chuckled and shook her head. "That girl is such a joy; what'll she think of next?"

Mrs. Simpson wrote a reply and gave it to Avery to deliver when he next saw Claire. He was curious; what was she up to now?

One evening after supper the week before Christmas, Mrs. Simpson didn't retire to her room. Instead she was busily setting out bowls, spoons, and cups in the kitchen. Gunner was very interested in this unusual kitchen activity, but then, he liked activity in the kitchen anytime.

Mrs. Simpson's kitchen was unusual because Mr. Simpson had connected the kitchen to the rest of the house with a tunnel-like walkway, so she didn't have to go outside to get to it. The kitchen had a heavy door which could be closed off in the event of a kitchen fire, to keep it from spreading to the rest of the house. It was a very modern idea and quite unusual. Gunner sidestepped around the kitchen, watching Mrs. Simpson's every move. Avery watched from the parlor, wondering what she was going to do. He was seated in a large easy chair in front of the fire, preparing to read.

The door knocker rapped and the bell rang. Dr. Simpson opened the door to the sound of female chattering and laughter. On the porch some of the nurses stamped the snow off their feet and entered the warm foyer.

"Good evening, ladies," said the cordial Dr. Simpson. "Where's your general?"

"She's right behind us; she and Anna are pulling all the supplies in a little sled they've rigged up."

Avery sat still in the parlor chair with the book in his lap, feeling the heat from the fireplace warming his face.

"Here I am!"

Avery recognized Claire's voice. *What is she doing here?* Some of the girls stepped out onto the porch and carried in bundles that Claire was handing to them. Dr. Simpson pointed them the way to the kitchen.

"Hello, girls," called Mrs. Simpson. "Welcome, one and all. I'm glad you're all here. I think this is a wonderful idea, and I'm happy to lend you my kitchen."

Avery sat still, knowing that no one had seen him and hoping they wouldn't. He liked all these nurses at work, but he sure didn't want to talk to them here in the Simpsons' parlor, social-like. *What are they doing here?* He wondered if he looked different here at home.

"Let me take your wraps for you," said the helpful Dr. Simpson.

What if I had a fine home like this one day and these nurses showed up? Would I take their wraps? Father was always gracious to visitors and talked easily to ladies. What is wrong with me? Oh, please don't look in here and see me. What are they doing?

"Could I get you some hot cider, ladies, or some tea?"

"That would be lovely, Dr. Simpson," one of them answered.

"I would love some cider, thank you." He recognized Anna's voice.

"Would you like me to help you get the drinks, Dr. Simpson?"

Claire's voice caused a flutter in his stomach. The fire embers glowed, but it didn't lighten his anxiety. It seemed to take forever, but eventually every last one of them had moved through the hallway, past the parlor, and out to the kitchen. Apparently no

one had seen him. He'd heard Dr. Simpson take his leave, and he knew the doctor was comfortably ensconced in his bedroom reading by his cozy fire. *That's what I should do. But what are they doing out there? How long are they planning to stay? Where's Gunner? Oh sure, Gunner the ladies' man. I know where he is.*

It wasn't too long before the house began to smell deliciously like ginger, clove, cinnamon, and every nice thing that Avery could think of. He'd smelled this smell before, but he couldn't remember where or what it was.

"Maybe I'll just stay here and read a little bit longer. The fire is getting low, so I'll go to bed soon. What is that smell? What are they doing out there?" He was muttering to himself. Things in the kitchen were getting noticeably quieter. He was feeling drowsy and decided to take himself off to bed. Gunner must have been getting bored in the quiet kitchen, because as Avery stood up to go to his room, Gunner came looking for him.

"Good that one of us has some social manners," he said jealously to the dog. "Let's go to bed."

In the morning he grabbed his watery coffee and one of Mrs. Simpson's warm biscuits, noticing that the nice smell was just barely lingering. The kitchen was cleaned and orderly and he saw no sign of last evening's activities. *Very odd. How long had they stayed? What were they doing?* Avery and Gunner stepped out into the fresh snow, and Avery noticed that all the footprints in the snow from last night's visitors were already covered.

No surgeries were planned today, only wound treatment and regular patient care. There were no pneumonia patients at the moment. That could all change by the end of the day. They had so many pneumonia patients at the post office hospital that a volunteer had come to borrow one of their camphor lamps to use there.

He hoped for a quiet day today, and he hoped that last night's volunteers would have thought to bring in a load of firewood before the snow fell. Doctors and farmers, Avery mused, must think of a lot of things that have naught to do with their jobs, like bringing in the water before it freezes and hauling in the

wood before it's buried in snow and ice. It's all the same everywhere for doctors and farmers.

"One of these days, Gunner, we'll be back on the farm."

CHAPTER TWENTY-SEVEN

RAINBOW FOR CHRISTMAS

Claire and Mrs. Simpson let the two doctors know that they planned to attend church on Christmas Eve at midnight.

"Midnight!" Avery was astounded at the thought. "Midnight? You go to church at midnight? Do you fall asleep there?"

"Well, it's a tradition, isn't it?"

He knew she was making a statement, not asking a question, so he didn't respond.

"Oh, Avery, you can manage it just fine," clucked Mrs. Simpson. "And Dr. Simpson, you don't say a word now," she warned.

Avery and Dr. Simpson shrugged and the plan was official. They called for Claire late Christmas Eve and pulled up shortly before midnight to a candlelit church, overflowing with people. Gunner had stayed on Avery's bed and couldn't be convinced that it was time to get up.

Avery looked at the church lit all around with candles and full to the brim with standing worshippers, having arrived, like themselves, too late to find a seat. Many soldiers were among them. Candles lined the walkway up to the church. The choir sang Christmas carols, and everyone joined in. Holly clipped from sturdy trees was draped over the ends of the pews; incense filled the air. Avery was overcome with the beauty of it all. The service took a long time, but every time he glanced her way, Claire

was staring at him. Surrounded by the crowd of worshippers, he felt his neck and ears getting red. He winked at her and smiled, then reached for her hand and held it. Her stunned look nearly caused him to choke, but he looked away into the crowd of praying people. She stared in disbelief. He glanced at her shocked expression. He was amused and pretended not to notice. Dr. and Mrs. Simpson looked surprised at first, but then nodded knowingly to each other.

The buggy took them through the cold winter night under bright stars to the home of Dr. and Mrs. Simpson. Mrs. Simpson fixed a breakfast, and they gathered in the parlor. Gunner got up, looked at the darkness still outside the windows, and went back to sleep.

Avery hadn't figured out yet what Claire thought of his behavior. She hadn't said a word, but kept looking at him as if she wanted to say something. She looked a bit flustered, totally unlike Claire. Finally she took his hand in hers and gave it a squeeze.

Mrs. Simpson brought out her little basket of gifts and passed them around. Claire had a little gift for each of them, and Avery gave them his gifts. His sleeping dog would have to wait until morning to get his bone from the snow. Mrs. Simpson noticed the shy reticence on the part of Claire and Avery to present their gifts to each other. She suggested to Dr. Simpson that he come with her to prepare their coffees.

When the two were alone, Claire reached behind her and handed Avery a square package wrapped in brown butcher paper with the red taffeta ribbon tied around it. He took it and saw that she was biting her lip nervously. *She worries I might not like this.* He was surprised and touched at that thought. *Maybe her feelings are sometimes just like mine.*

She smiled a nervous smile and said, "Open it up, Avery. I hope you like it."

He opened the paper and turned it over. It was a framed picture of Gunner, completely embroidered. It took his breath away. In the corner in tiny letters was embroidered *C.A.M.*

"Claire! You made this? You made this yourself? How did you? It's wonderful! You've learned to embroider? How long did this take you? It's more than beautiful." He was astonished that the stitchery looked just like the head of his dog.

"Just like you, Avery, too many questions. Yes, yes, and yes. Mrs. Simpson taught me how. Anthony Pioli made the drawing. Mrs. Simpson helped me turn his drawing into a pattern. I've been at it for many months and only finished it last week. I hope you like it; I thought you might. And I used the special little scissors you gave me last Christmas too."

He leaned across the settee and kissed her softly on her cheek. "I really, really do like it."

She knew he meant that. Avery was filled with gratitude. It was something she'd thought of, something she'd made. It took a lot of time, and it was something special for him.

"Thank you. Here, this is for you. I hope you like it." It was a heavy, odd-shaped little package, wrapped in unusual paper and tied with embroidery thread. She smiled a little as she pulled the string, guessing that Avery thought the string was useful. She unrolled the item from its cocoon of paper, and the heavy, colorless glass object lay in the palm of her hand. She studied it, turned it over, and wondered what it was.

"Look. Watch." Avery held it up by its little gold cap. It was like a large teardrop made of glass with many facets and many colors. He held it by its cap and the light from the fire shown through it. As he turned it slowly by its little top, a rainbow of colors appeared on the opposite wall and swirled about. Rainbow on top of rainbow filled the room. Claire was captivated.

He hoped she liked it; she wasn't saying anything, so he charged ahead. "It's called a prism. It'll always make rainbows for you," he said. "And that's what I wanted to give you—rainbows, always."

He was suddenly overcome with an attack of shy uncertainty. She took it from his hand and kissed the hand that held the prism; the hands of a very good doctor, a humble and kind man, whom she loved with all her heart.

"Thank you, Avery. Rainbows are very special gifts indeed."

The rainbows sparkled and danced on the walls of the parlor. The Simpsons returned with the tray of "almost coffees" and were delighted to see the dancing rainbows on their walls.

"I declare, it makes me want to dance," laughed the old doctor. He lovingly grabbed his wife by the elbow and swung her around the room with the rainbows crisscrossing over them while they moved. Claire hummed a little dance tune, while Avery laughed. Gunner looked up from his paws and sleepily opened one eye.

After the whirlwind dance and coffee, Mrs. Simpson suggested a nap before the doctors and their nurse needed to get off to the hospital. She brought a blanket and put Claire to bed on the settee, where she fell asleep feeling like a child, playing with her prism in the waning firelight.

When they got into the buggy later that morning, Avery was surprised to see many boxes stacked on the floor of the back seat. Claire got in carefully and instructed the sniffing Gunner to leave them alone. At the hospital Claire handed the boxes down to the two doctors. The nurses came chattering to greet them and carried the boxes inside. Avery recognized the gingery, cinnamony aroma from Mrs. Simpson's kitchen escaping from the boxes. Gunner was greeting each nurse hopefully. Each nurse picked up an opened box and started through the wards. The patients were all getting something from the box. Avery and Gunner watched with curiosity.

"Dr. Bennett," asked Claire "would you like one of Mrs. Mikesell's Moravian ginger cookies?"

Avery took one of the cookies from the box and grinned. *This is the familiar smell. This is what they'd been baking in the kitchen.* A flame of homesickness flickered within him.

"The people in Kanawha Valley will be eating these today. Cookies like these will be decorating the little Christmas tree at the meeting house. The war cannot change everything," he said

stubbornly, "not everything. This is really nice. Thank you, and thanks to the nurses."

The patients were proclaiming the cookies to be the best in the world.

"The people of Kanawha Valley, Mrs. Mikesell's neighbors, have always known that," Avery told them. Gunner quickly licked the crumbs off their beds.

Later Avery prayed gratefully, "Thank you, God, for all these people, for Gunner, for Claire, for all the rainbows in our lives, and for the promise of another year. Bless us all."

He hung Gunner's embroidered picture in the office, where he could see it often. He was amazed by its detail. The entire head was made of tiny, even stitches. All the colors of Gunner, even the light in his eye, were captured in these stitches. Claire passed his office and was pleased to see him admiring her embroidery.

"You might be interested to know, Avery, that the day Anthony was drawing Gunner sitting on his bed was the day the bees came. When the bees got into the hospital, Anthony slipped under his bed. Gunner lay with him, covering him up, snapping at any bees who tried to get to his patient. Anthony was so amazed at Gunner that he gave the drawing to me free of charge. He said he would've had lots more stings if it weren't for Gunner's protection. Isn't that just like the protective ol' hound?" she exclaimed. "I'm glad you like the picture."

"So that's where you were, Gunner. What do you know? I should've guessed that you had a job to do when the bees came. Of course, you would have."

He hugged his dog and closed his eyes. *Kanawha Valley. I wonder what Mother is doing this day?* The homesickness washed over him. His mind eased westward, lost in a daydream.

In the peaceable Kanawha Valley, the neighbors will gather in the meetinghouse to share their Christmas greetings, their prayers for peace, and their gratitude for another year of health, crops, and friendships. They'll give thanks, share their meal, and sing Christmas carols. They will share news, good and bad—whose sons are home,

whose sons have left, whose sons aren't returning. They'll pray for all their sons. Mother will be praying for me.

Mother won't be the only woman who is alone this year. Some men, like Father, have died naturally; others have been killed, as thousands have. Families are smaller as the children grow and go their own way, as Clayton and I have done. The two eldest McDougals are missing this Christmas too.

Avery imagined Mother in her familiar bonnet waving to her friends and neighbors, clucking to Father's horse, and trotting across the valley to the farm. The route was so familiar to him he could imagine her rolling past the farmhouses, rattling across the bridges, and coming into their own holler.

If I were there, I'd be putting up the horse. Snow would be on the horse's eyelashes, and frost around his muzzle. The snow would blanket the fields of our farm, and the low afternoon light would be casting long shadows across the yard, where my old swing hangs from the walnut tree. I can smell the hay in the barn.

Mother will pause by the pond, like she has always done, and admire the mallards' colorful reflection making a little rainbow swimming beside them on the quiet, lonely pond, under the long shadows of blue and gray.

"We'll be there soon, Gunner. When this war . . . soon."

CHAPTER TWENTY-EIGHT

NEW YEAR'S SOCIAL

"It was Claire's idea," Nurse Anna explained to Avery.

"Of course it was," Avery laughed. "I think it's a fine idea. Have you talked to Dr. Simpson?"

"I did, and he said since you would be in charge here that evening that it'd be up to you."

"Oh, I see." He rubbed his chin to cover his amusement. "Well, I can imagine that it would be a fine thing for the ambulatories and perhaps some of those recovering on the second floor. It'd be a little too disruptive to the third-floor patients. Suppose you keep it on the first floor, and we can bring some of the second-floor patients down to you? Would that suit you?"

"Oh yes, Dr. Bennett, yes. that'd be perfect!" The young nurse threw her arms around Avery's neck, kissed him, and flew away. "We all just love you, Dr. Bennett," she squealed.

Claire came around the corner looking surprised at what she'd just seen. Avery turned scarlet, and she laughed. "Did you just propose to that nurse?" The nurse was her roommate Anna, a freedwoman from Baltimore. She was one of Claire's closest friends, and she was in love with Matt Mason.

"No. I just approved your plan."

"Well, in that case I guess I owe you a kiss too!" She blew him a kiss off her hand and hurried on down the hall.

"Oh, Dr. Bennett?" she called over her shoulder, "Thank you!" Sensing excitement in the air, Gunner padded along behind her, wanting to be close to the source.

"You're welcome," he smiled. So the plans were underway for a New Year's Eve social at the hospital for all the recovering and rehabilitating veterans of the war. The notices were posted in the town where townspeople would see them as they went about their business. The volunteers and staff all announced it to their various church congregations. Donations of cider, cookies, and candles were solicited.

"Here is a chance to thank our soldiers for their sacrifice and to wish them good cheer in the new year," the notice at the post office informed everyone.

"Do you think anyone will come?" worried one of the nurses.

"Well, if no one else comes, we're still here; we've still had the fun of doing it, and the soldiers will still enjoy it, right?" answered the undaunted Claire.

"That's right, Claire, and that's a good way to look at it," replied Anna.

Volunteers scrubbed the floors. They cut leaves and twigs from the scant shrubbery. They pushed candles into the ground, marking the walkway; orderlies carried chairs and benches from churches. Rabbit, one of the volunteers, laid a big bonfire in the side yard. They hoped the weather would be clear and still; there was no room inside the hospital for a social.

The week following Christmas, a package arrived at the post office from Clad and Sons Candy Company in Philadelphia. Avery remembered the little candies from last year when Val Clad was a volunteer here. He opened the box and saw once again, the clear, amber-colored candies. Avery studied a little ship with its mast and sails and a little donkey with a mane, tail, and sleepy eyes, like little toys made of glass. In the box was a note wishing the staff and all the recovering patients a nice holiday, signed, "Your Friend, Val Clad."

These will be perfect for Claire's little social, Avery decided.

The afternoon of December 31, the sun was out, there was no wind, and the sky was dotted with white fluffy clouds. The horizon was clearing since there hadn't been much artillery fire for a few days. It was shaping up to be the perfect last day of the year.

About four o'clock in the afternoon people were winding their way through the town, heading for the Mansion House Hospital. Some were bringing bags; some were carrying trays. Some carried bundles that turned out to be musical instruments.

All afternoon and into the evening the patients were treated to the music of different choirs from different churches, mostly women. With a backdrop of fiddle playing, visitors passed their trays of cookies and bread and butter sandwiches and thanked the patients for fighting for the Union. Pats on the back, hand shaking, and lots of "God bless yous" were the order of the day.

Rabbit played his fiddle, and people joined in singing hymns and Christmas carols. A lady from the town brought a small harp and played some pretty Irish melodies. A quiet Amish man, who arrived alone in his buggy and watched from a distance, handed Anna a large hoop of cheese.

"I made this for the nourishment of the body. I'll not fight brethren, but I respect those who've done so. Perhaps they've ensured the union of states for us all. I thank them for that." He nodded his head and walked back to his buggy.

Claire walked to Anna and put her arm around her shoulders.

"That was so nice," whispered Anna. Claire nodded and together they carried the heavy hoop of cheese into the hospital where they sliced pieces for the men.

The social lasted a lot longer than anyone had imagined. The patients were exhausted but thoroughly pleased.

"Happy New Year," they greeted each other. "Perhaps this'll be the year we all go home."

PART THREE

GOING HOME

1865

CHAPTER TWENTY-NINE

EVENING TO REMEMBER

Gunner pawed the bed. Avery yawned and rolled over. Gunner whined. Avery opened his eyes. Gunner jumped up on the bed.

"What are you doing, Gunner? What's going on? What time is it? Is it time to get up? What day is this?" Avery's head ached, and he felt strangely confused.

Gunner cocked his head and pricked up his ears, giving Avery a quizzical look.

"Come here my loyal friend," he laughed and pulled his dog close to him. He slipped out of bed and pulled open the chintz curtains in his room. The intensity of the sunlight told him that he'd overslept for sure. He quickly washed, dressed, and entered the dining room only to find it quiet and deserted.

"Where is everyone, Gunner?"

He went into the kitchen where it was obvious to him that breakfast had been served a while ago. There was barely warm coffee in the urn, cooled tea in the teapot, and cold biscuits on the platter. A few thin slices of meat were curling and drying on the plate. Did Dr. Simpson leave early today? Had Mrs. Simpson already left to roll bandages with the auxiliary?

"What kind of a day is this, Gunner?" He looked for the bowl of food that Mrs. Simpson saved for Gunner, and he found the bowl empty on the floor.

"So you've already had breakfast too?"

Avery had returned home very late the night before. It had been a wonderful evening of music, riddles, poetry, and rare treats to eat. The social didn't end until late, and Avery had no idea what time everyone actually left, but he was so tired, he knew it was late. In spite of having lived in the city since 1861, Avery still told the time like the farmer he was. He rose with the sunrise, went to bed when the sun set, ate his midday meal when the sun was overhead. Last night's social was very late for him, and sleeping in just wasn't something he did.

The last song that Avery remembered hearing was "The Battle Hymn of the Republic." All the voices had blended together like a huge choir. Rabbit had played his fiddle, and tears streamed down people's faces, inside and outside the hospital, as everyone sang from their hearts. Avery had been caught up in the moment.

Through the crowd, he had seen Claire lending her singing voice to the chorus. He had moved through the crowd to stand beside her, singing along with the northerners, the southerners, the wealthy and the poor, the hearty and the weak, people of all colors—all Americans—who wanted this war to be over.

"Here," he had whispered in her ear, "is America as God wishes it to be."

When the song ended, he had turned to Claire and, with urgency, said to her, "We must never forget this moment, Claire." He'd wrapped both arms around her, bent down, and kissed her. She looked up at him and answered, "As long as we both shall live, Avery."

He vaguely remembered hearing people calling "happy new year" to each other and hearing "thank you, Doctor," and hearing farewells. He remembered seeing people walking away with the lighted candles. Now it was like a dream with everything all jumbled. Where had she gone? He hadn't seen her moving around in the crowd. She had simply vanished. He didn't remember how, or when, he arrived home. But here he was; he'd overslept; he was obviously too late for breakfast, and very late for work.

"Gunner, let me tell you something, boy. Don't let your heart get mixed up with a girl. It'll make you very confused. Look at that sun; we're late. Farmers never oversleep." His aching head was swimming.

He saddled Fan, and they hurried off to the hospital, pretending that it was just another ordinary day. He wondered what Claire would say to him. Maybe she wouldn't want to say anything to him—ever.

"Why did I do that, Gunner? I didn't think; I just did it." He was angry and disappointed in himself. "I don't know if I'll ever get all my feelings sorted out. But this much I *have* figured out. I can hardly go an hour without thinking about that girl. It used to annoy me to find her standing next to me, dropping in out of nowhere. Now I look forward to finding her beside me. I like her in my thoughts. I used to think she was forward and bossy, but she's really smart, Gunner, don't you think? I used to think she crowded my life. Now my life would be empty without her. Something has changed. Did she change? Or did I? And now I've kissed her. I think I did—maybe I dreamed it. But if I did, that'll change a lot of things. I wish I could talk to Father about this, Gunner." His dog trotted alongside and listened attentively.

He rode into the side yard and dismounted. He tried to walk casually, normally. Maybe no one would know that he'd kissed their nurse and that his life had turned upside down. Some of the ambulatories were bundled up against the cold and were walking around aided by some volunteers. He didn't see any of the nurses. They were probably still washing patients and changing bandages.

"What would we do without these nurses," he blurted to one of the patients. "They do it all, don't they?" He made his rounds, and as he passed from patient to patient, his eyes scanned the rooms. He didn't see Claire. He didn't see Dr. Simpson either. This was such a strange day. He hadn't been there very long when midday bread and beans was served, and he realized he'd missed almost a half day of work.

How did that happen? This isn't like me. He shook his head in disbelief.

The patients were still talking about the New Year's Eve party of last night. It had meant a lot to them, and many were writing letters home today to tell about the wonderful party. Volunteers had their work cut out for them today. Avery saw many of them writing for the disabled or illiterate soldiers.

Hmm, thought Avery. *I guess it was a party, wasn't it? It started out as a social, but I think they're right, it was a party. But that isn't an excuse for my sleeping late this morning. There's never an excuse for that. Now I sound just like my father!* Gunner fixed a stare, shook his head, flapped his hound-dog ears, and went off on his own rounds.

"I know, Gunner, you never feel guilty about sleeping in."

By mid afternoon a little knot of nurses was gathered on the stoop. He hoped one of them was Claire. He worked his way through the sickly, through the wounded, through the amputees, down to the ambulatories. No one was talking much to him today, and everyone seemed a bit distracted as if they were deliberately avoiding him. *Maybe I embarrassed them if they saw me kiss their nurse last night.* He tried to act normal. *Maybe they're all disgusted with me.*

As he turned to the next patient, everyone in the room called his name and cheered.

"We wish you a happy birthday, and a happy new year."

Most of his staff and Dr. Simpson were scattered about the big room. The ambulatory patients were cheering and singing. Claire held up a small, lopsided cake with the remnant of one of last night's candles smoking in the middle of it.

"Happy birthday, Dr. Bennett!"

"Many returns of the day, Doc!"

"Hey, three cheers for the good doctor! Hip hip hooray! Hip hip hooray! Hip hip hooray!"

All around him he heard cheerful voices wishing him a good day. *So no one's angry with me? No one saw me kiss their nurse? I didn't embarrass anyone but myself?*

Claire stood facing him, smiling, with the birthday cake. *She didn't mind that I kissed her? Maybe I really didn't; maybe I just dreamed it.* His thoughts whirled like a cyclone.

One of the nurses handed him a little card. It unfolded to become a very big card. The nurses had made it.

"It's from all of us, Dr. Bennett, from the staff and the volunteers and all the patients too. It's from all of us. We all love you," explained Anna.

He unfolded it and saw everyone had written their name or made their sign on the card. It had a familiar red taffeta ribbon, cut from a ball gown, run through it, holding it all together.

"Thank you," he said. "Thank you everyone, very much." He couldn't think of anything else to say. He'd even forgotten that today was his birthday.

Claire and Avery stood awkwardly face to face in the middle of the bustling room. Even with the crowd of workers and the patients and the chaos of the normal routine, when their eyes met, they were, for a moment, alone.

"Happy birthday," Claire said as she handed him the little cake. "And, Avery, about last night . . . about what you said? I'll never forget that moment—not ever." She smiled and tied on her apron. She pulled her red curls into the scarf, tied it up, and went about her business of healing and comforting.

"So it happened just as I remembered, huh, Gunner?" Gunner was admiring the little cake and drooling.

"How old are ya, Doc?" asked one of his patients.

"Huh? Oh, thank you, I'm eighteen."

"Eighteen? I'd have guessed twenties."

Avery smiled and looked down at him. "Yes, I hear that a lot."

CHAPTER THIRTY
SOLDIER'S DISEASE

General Keese came by later that day to check on three of his soldiers. His regiment would be leaving in a day or so. Would those three men be traveling with him, staying in the hospital, or be invalided? It turned out he had one of each.

All three were in the ward of ambulatories. Avery gave all three a thorough examination, and Nurse Claire assisted.

"I believe you've recovered from the pneumonia," he said to the first soldier. "Your lungs sound clear, and you aren't coughing; the nurses say you are eating and sleeping well; no sore throat, no fever. Soldier, I believe we've done all we can do for you."

The soldier shouted for joy when Dr. Bennett released him to General Keese. "I'm going to be in Richmond when it falls!"

"How you doing, Ezra?" Avery asked Ezra Sanders. "I see you are learning to walk on your new leg brace quite well. I'm glad this contraption is working out for you." Claire and Avery had designed this new leg brace, and the blacksmith in town had helped them create it. They'd needed to make several adjustments and changes for his comfort.

"It's a one of a kind, you know. I got the idea from the cover of a baseball. With the help of the saddler in town, you're now walking on a little saddle that looks like a baseball cover."

"Is that so?" Ezra and Avery had a good laugh together.

This is the good part of doctoring. This is why I'm here.

"You've had no infection, and you're mostly without pain; you're balancing well and learning to manipulate this heavy brace. I think with a little more time you could be out on your own." Avery read the disappointment in Ezra's eyes.

"It won't be much longer," he reassured Ezra. The General shook Ezra's hand and left without him. Claire put her arm around the sad man and assured him that he'd soon be marching.

The third patient had been a puzzle to Avery for several weeks. This was the talkative John Parker.

"He seems to turn up on every floor," complained Avery.

"Most recently he was brought down here to keep him from jumping out the upstairs window and to prevent him from bothering the upstairs patients who need rest," the orderly explained. "How serious is his wound, Dr. Bennett?"

"Very. And it won't stop bleeding."

"He's prattled for days about getting on the next train back to the battleground. We even tied him to the bed," the orderly said.

Avery winced and said, "I suspect he's being given too much pain medicine. It keeps him from resting and healing. I've sutured, re-sutured, and fought infection around the clock. An infection in this wound would mean death. I don't want him to return to battle. Would you find Dr. Simpson and ask him to meet me and General Keese in the office for a conference? Thank you."

The orderly went to find the surgeon.

"He's a danger to himself, and he'd be a danger to you and your men. His behavior is erratic, and he has a lack of judgment," was Avery's opinion. Dr. Simpson agreed that he shouldn't return to battle, but felt he should be sent home. Avery was hesitant.

"Perhaps another week, with no pain medicine, to see what he does and to be sure the bleeding doesn't start up again?"

The surgeon went along with that. General Keese wrote the invalided papers. He collected his one happy soldier, said goodbye to the disappointed one, and freed himself from the drugged and witless John Parker; then he was gone.

John Parker reached out and yanked Claire's skirt as she walked past his bed. She tripped and fell, and her basins scattered and clanged across the wooden floor.

Avery and Dr. Simpson ran to her and helped her up. She wasn't hurt, but she shot the patient an angry glance. She took Avery and Dr. Simpson by their arms and stomped angrily away from the patient.

"He did that deliberate," she said through pursed lips. "He reached out and grabbed my skirt deliberate. I did not trip. Anymore of that and I'll tell my nurses to avoid him." She picked up her basins and shot a warning glare at Parker. Avery and Dr. Simpson went into conference with another surgeon.

"You think painkiller is Parker's problem?" asked Dr. Simpson.

"I'm sure of it. The man should be in pain. But he's getting so much medicine he's out of his senses most of the time—but not in any pain. He needs a little pain to keep him quiet so he can heal. Without feeling any pain, he thinks he's well, moves around, opens his wound and bleeds again. We need to get him off the pain relievers." So the doctors agreed on a new plan they would share with all the staff in the morning.

During the night, when most of the staff had gone home and the patients were mostly asleep, one of the volunteers went to the office to get her shawl. There she found the patient, John Parker, going through the medicine cabinets. He was taking some of everything and dropping it into his knapsack which was already bulging. The morphine shelf was empty.

She turned quickly to find one of the male orderlies to help her, but Parker saw her. He pushed her and sent her sprawling across the floor and several medicine vials along with her. When his knapsack would hold no more, he slipped out the side door and disappeared into the dark of the night.

Avery left home earlier than usual so he could prepare some of his remedies before starting his rounds and arrived to find the unconscious volunteer on the office floor. When she awoke with a large purple bump on her forehead, she told the chilling

story of the crazed man John Parker, with his bloody bandages holding him together, stealing the medicines. He was gone and much of their supply with him.

Avery clenched his teeth and fought with his temper. "We need that medicine. Gunner," he called. The dog appeared.

"Gunner, find it," he said, pointing at the floor. The dog sniffed the floor; he sniffed the medicine vials broken on the floor. He sniffed the medicine cabinet. He sniffed the woman's skirt; he sniffed the door, the hall, then he followed his nose to the side door. Avery opened the door as Gunner pawed it.

"Find him, Gunner." Gunner's nose was down, and he was moving swiftly across the side yard. He crossed the road and trotted between two buildings. His nose was on the ground, and his tail was in the air. He passed the livery; he sniffed to the road crossing and down the railroad tracks. He followed the railroad bed to the switches.

He began to move faster, and his tail whipped the fog in the early morning air. Avery jogged to keep up with him. Gunner began to bellow, and Avery couldn't keep up as the dog broke into a run. He waved to a couple of surprised railroad workers and yelled to them to come and help. Gunner was outside a railroad switchman's shanty, pawing, and growling. The three railroad men came panting breathlessly, while Gunner put on his show of viciousness.

They caught their breath while Avery informed them there might be a thief inside the shanty. The first railroad worker picked up the big sledge hammer switchmen use. The second one picked up a large rock from the rail bed. Avery eyed them.

"He's a badly injured man. I don't think he'll put up much of a fight." Gunner was pacing, impatient to discover his quarry.

"Let's get 'im outta there," said the first railroader. He pulled the latch and opened the door. Gunner charged in. The shanty wasn't very big, and Gunner was on top of his quarry. Avery called him off. The second railroader nudged the thief with his foot.

"Git outta here."

The man didn't move.

Avery dropped down to check him. The bandages were soaked with blood and hung loose. Wet blood pooled on the floor. He checked his pulse. He looked up at the railroad men.

"He's feeling no pain."

As the staff and volunteers arrived that morning, Avery gathered them and explained what had happened. He restocked the medicine supply from the man's knapsack and locked it away in his cabinet. He wondered how many patients they'd sent home, healed from their wounds, only to be afflicted with this new Soldier's Disease, an illness that would bring trouble to their entire family. John Parker wouldn't be one of those.

CHAPTER THIRTY-ONE
RICHMOND FALLS

"What you lookin' at, Doc?" asked the orderly.

"It's a map here in the monthly. It shows how the Union's general, Sherman's his name, is marching from Tennessee across Georgia. See here how it goes? They're calling it the 'March to the Sea.' The story says towns and cities, fields, factories, and farms are all being destroyed by the Confederates before the Yankees approach. What's still standing when the Union soldiers arrive, they loot." Avery spoke softly, and the orderly shook his head.

"Ain't going to have much to go home to, are we," stated the orderly. He and Avery studied the map and looked at the sketches in *Harper's Weekly*. Avery added Georgia to his big Virginia map on the wall.

"I ain't learnt much about the maps and such. But I can see it's a big country. I'm from Tennessee. You got that on yer map?"

"It's here," Avery pointed. "This reporter says the march looks like a locust storm."

"Uh-oh. Locust storms, them's bad. I remember one year when I was a little boy, there was a locust storm on our plateau. The locusts moved across them fields like a storm cloud, divin' down into the corn and devourin' every plant. The farm families, we all ran for home, but some of the locusts came down the chimneys. Them locusts ate the sod roofs off some of our homes and ate

all the animal feed in the barns. We heard them critters marching on the roof, chawin' up everything."

Avery stared at the storyteller. "That had to have been a terrifying experience." Avery could envision the devastation left when the locust army moved on. "This army of locusts is wearing blue and gray uniforms, and I'll bet it's just as terrifying for anyone in the way on this 'March to the Sea'." He showed the orderly a sketch in *Harper's Weekly*. Avery knew the orderly couldn't read, so he told him what the captions said. The staff and the patients crowded around to look at the pictures and read the articles. It was quiet on every floor except for a few agonized moans of patients in pain who weren't yet aware of the latest of the bad news. It was a terrible price for a victory.

Avery was praying for General Keese. He hadn't found anything specific about General Keese's regiment in the newspapers, but Avery felt sure that by now they'd reached Richmond with the rest of the Army of the Potomac. Everyone was anxious and on edge.

Dr. Simpson hurried into the room waving a telegram in his hand.

"Avery! All of you! Look here," he said. "It's from the war department. It's official. Richmond has fallen. The Union now occupies the capital of the Confederacy!" He looked around the room at the anxious eyes. He made the announcement on every floor and in every room of the hospital. This was the long-awaited good news. On the third floor some of the sick, who were awake, smiled or raised an arm in victory or said "hooray" in weak whispers. On the second floor they shouted hip hoorays and applauded. On the first floor and in the side yard they hollered, rejoiced, and pounded their crutches jubilantly on the blood-stained floor.

The man who delivered the telegram was bursting with news and excitement; it took little convincing for him to tell all he knew of Richmond's collapse. He'd seen many official telegrams, he told them. "Why, I know as much as most of the newspaper reporters, maybe more," he boasted.

"General Lee sent the first telegram to Jefferson Davis. He's president of the Confederacy," he said, as if they might not know that. "Davis got it while he was sittin' in church on Sunday morning. He issued the first orders for the Confederate government to begin evacuation. It was all very secretive." He lowered his voice, and his audience moved in closer.

"The people in Richmond saw little fires burning in the street in front of the government offices where officials were burning documents. People asked what was going on, but no one knew; no one was telling the people." His audience of patients and staff listened intently, trying to visualize his story.

"No one knew? Everyone's been talking about it for months or years. Shouldn't have been a surprise," Avery said.

The delivery man shrugged and shook his head. "People heard rumors about official papers being burned, so they gathered to see what was going on. The streets got crowded with people asking questions, starting to panic. I've seen some of the telegrams coming and going, and I'm telling you, it must've been something to see." He shook his head. "The morning broadside says all night long on horseback, cart, wagon, buggy, train, barges, boats, anything at all to carry and haul, the prom-in-ent citizens and the war o-ffi-cials left the city. At eleven o'clock last night, Jefferson Davis snuck out of the city under cover of darkness. Yes, sir, he did. He boarded the train and left Richmond to the Yankees. Yee haw!"

"The coward," shouted out one of the patients in disgust. "And left the people who paid so dear for him?"

"He should've gone down with his ship," yelled a sailor.

The telegram man picked up his story, speaking louder over the murmurs. "Now the people of Richmond knew they had to leave, and they worked all night long to prepare. But when they saw the soldiers leaving, they really believed the soldiers would come back for them to defend the city and take it back from the Yankees."

"Really?" The orderly scratched his head in disbelief. "Strangest war I ever saw."

"Yes, and it gets even stranger. The few city officials who'd been left behind knew the Yankee soldiers were coming. So they

tried to pour all the whiskey and liquor left in the city into the gutters, so the Yankee soldiers couldn't get it. But when the men of Richmond saw this, they ran into the street and tried to drink it up. They filled their shoes and hats and lay down on their bellies and guzzled 'er right up from the street gutters."

His audience laughed.

"And then what?" someone asked him, interrupting the amused laughter and comments.

"Hush, listen. Let him tell it."

"Just wait! Next they ordered all the cotton and the tobacco to be moved into warehouses that would burn quickly, and they set the warehouses on fire."

"Why on earth?"

"To keep the Yanks from gettin' it. No other reason."

Everyone shook their heads in disbelief.

"But that isn't the worst of it!" the delivery man continued excitedly. "Next they ordered all the food to be destroyed. Now understand," he explained, "the people of Richmond have been without food, shoes, and all kinds of necessities for a few years now. They've held starvation balls to raise money for food, and they've gone without so the soldiers would have food."

"What food could that be, then?" asked Avery, remembering Phineas Profitt. "I remember the shortages in Richmond from my year there. It was bad even then."

"The people of Richmond discovered there were huge stashes of food and commodities stored all over the city in warehouses and in large homes. Blockade runners, pirates, speculators all took advantage of the situation and hoarded these goods, waiting for the prices to go up to make them richer."

"No!" Everyone was in disbelief. "How could they do this to their own people?"

"So these people, who were barefoot and hungry, practically wearing rags, saw all the smoked meats, flour, sugar, coffee . . . well, you can only imagine what happened then."

"Reminds me of the Bread Riot in Richmond when I was there," Avery murmured to no one in particular. Avery's fingers

caressed Gunner's neck, rejecting the urge to become fists. He was shocked by what he was hearing.

"And by then the center of the city was in flames. The fires burned out of control, so they were forced to evacuate."

"What of Chimborazo Hospital? Do you know if it's okay?"

"No, Dr. Bennett, I don't know. If I hear anything, I'll let you know though."

"Thank you." He was thinking of people he knew while he was a student.

The telegram man looked at his captive audience and resumed his story.

"The wind picked up, and embers from the document burnings blew into the business district." His audience gasped. "The ironworks, the big Tredegar Iron Works, caught fire, and then all those loaded shells exploded and demolished that entire area of Richmond."

"That probably did more damage than the Army of the Potomac could've ever done," commented one of the veterans.

Avery gulped. He knew this area well. He and Gunner had fished there by the river. The telegram man paused to let them imagine the blaze.

"Musta' looked like the fires of hell, like the judgment day had come," imagined another.

"Yes, sir, I imagine some of them thought that. I reckon they did. You won't believe what I'm going to tell you now. The Confederate Navy set their ironclad ships on fire out in the river. To keep the Yankees from taking them, of course," he answered before anyone could pose the question. "When the ships' arsenals exploded, the explosions broke windows for two miles around Richmond. It knocked over tombstones in the cemeteries, tore doors off the hinges, and blew people over in the street."

The horrors were unimaginable. Avery was picturing the two-mile radius around the city and figured the college was missing some windows, and his old dormitory probably had considerable damage. The audience of patients, volunteers, and staff

remained speechless and still as statues. Avery's stomach tied itself into a knot. Dr. Simpson looked pale and his head hung down. Claire was drying her eyes. One of the nurses chewed her fingernails. Some of the veterans looked sorrowful.

"We've probably heard enough upsetting news for today," Avery said quietly to the telegram man, and he stood to indicate the story was over. Anna looked up, but the man continued.

"Anyway, then when the Union Army entered the city, many of their troops were black. Soldiers claim that some diehard Confederates took their own lives, rather than surrender to a black soldier. Can you imagine that? But for those who'd been held in slavery in Richmond, it was a glorious thing to behold. They saw the dawning of freedom." The messenger was enjoying his moment of drama. "I saw the telegram come in at 8:30 this morning. It read: 'U-nited States flag flies over Virginy capital.' There you go, a happy ending, Doc."

A few sucked in little breaths; some breathed out audibly. Avery caught the reference to the black soldiers and wondered if they were General Keese's men from Ohio.

"It's over," someone whispered. A few tears escaped and a few noses sniffled; Anna and Claire hugged each other.

"Thank you for telling us," Avery said to the telegram deliverer. He looked around the room. *What an odd thing. Everyone in this room has been waiting for five years to hear this news. Everyone expected jubilation, cheers, and handkerchiefs tossed in the air. We all expected to dance for joy. But here we are in a hushed reverence. Richmond, the brave capital of the Confederacy, has fallen, at the hands of those who were protecting her.*

"It's been a strange war," Avery sighed. "I wonder how history books will tell this story?"

"God help us all," murmured Dr. Simpson. He wiped his sleeve across his eyes and went home to tell his wife that Richmond had fallen. The war would soon be over.

Avery crossed the room and stood next to Claire. He just felt like having her close to his side for a moment. He hoped she wouldn't mind. He didn't care if anyone saw him.

CHAPTER THIRTY-TWO

"LET 'EM UP EASY"

Volunteers and staff tried to buy newspapers on the way to work the next day, but all the papers in the city were sold out by early morning. People crowded around the morning broadside. The broadside said that the fire in Richmond had burned out of control for five hours and that fifty-four city blocks were destroyed.

The papers also reported on the irony of all that. "The Richmond fires," the papers said, "were all set ablaze by the men who were there to protect the city. It was saved from total destruction by soldiers of the United States, who had come to invade the city."

"Ironical," the newspapers said.

"Ironical," the readers said.

Later that week Avery read a small notice of tribute concerning Chimborazo Hospital in Richmond and his friend Director McCaw. Avery tore the article out to show it to Dr. Simpson, who was a longtime friend and colleague of McCaw.

> **The transfer of Chimborazo Hospital to the blue-coated Federal troops was performed with dignity, and much credit was due to Medical Director James McCaw and his staff. The size of this great military hospital, the number of soldiers admitted, treated and furloughed, discharged and buried, its successful work**

for nearly four years with perfect discipline, order, and harmony with comparatively low mortality, is to the credit of James McCaw, the medical students, alumni and faculty of the Medical College of Virginia.

When Avery showed the article to Dr. Simpson, their eyes met briefly, but neither of them said anything. There seemed no need to comment. Avery pasted the article in his journal. He'd been a part of that piece of history.

On the day President Lincoln toured Richmond, the official order was telegraphed across the country: at noon all military installations should fire a one-hundred-gun salute. The salute was to honor the long five-year struggle to return the Confederacy to the Union. At noon that day in Alexandria all the church bells rang one hundred times. Avery and his dog stood still and listened reverently. Every patient who was able to do so, stood. The hospital was quiet while the bells tolled. In the distance they heard the thunder of the cannon firing the salute. Claire suddenly appeared beside Avery. She slipped her hand into his, and he squeezed her hand lightly.

"This might be the last time we hear the cannon fire, Avery."

"Praise God."

They were standing in the middle of the third floor. It was hot, and it was quiet. They could hear the heavy breathing of the sedated, and the camphor lamps hissed. One soldier wheezed and gasped, struggling with his deflated, collapsed lungs. Avery knew the man would not live to see the sunrise of another day; the soldier was glad he'd lived to see this one. He looked at Avery and forced a short smile and raised his clasped hands together. Yes, he was glad he'd lived to see this day.

One newspaper reporter said the former slaves were so grateful for freedom that they dropped down on their knees in front of the president when he toured Richmond. The reporter

said President Lincoln told them, "Don't kneel to me. You must kneel to God only and thank Him for your freedom."

Another reporter said he witnessed a black man removing his hat and bowing to President Lincoln. Tears were rolling down the man's cheeks as he said, "May the good Lord bless you." Then Mr. Lincoln removed his hat and bowed to the man. Without a word, he erased centuries of slave laws and customs.

"The greatest leaders lead by example," Avery commented when he read that. "My father always told me that."

"And your father was right," said Matt.

"I agree, Avery. And I think you must be like him," added Claire.

Five more days of hard fighting followed, but only a few casualties came into the Mansion House Hospital. Without a capital to protect, the heart had gone out of the Confederacy. But elsewhere, the war continued. Avery made rounds at the prison hospital and talked to the Confederate prisoners there.

"I guess we'll all soon be going home," he told them. "I learned today that General Robert E. Lee surrendered his troops to General Ulysses S. Grant at Appomattox Courthouse. The American Civil War—at least in Virginia, that is—is over, gentlemen." He watched their despondent faces, and their tears flowed. They worried they'd not be allowed to go home. They feared the treatment they'd receive; perhaps they'd be held in prison forever or be hanged as traitors. Avery wanted them to relax and get well.

"You needn't worry. The commander of the Federal troops asked the president how they should treat the surrendered Confederate troops," Avery told them. The fearful soldiers looked at him and waited for more bad news.

"The president told him, 'If I were in your place, I'd let 'em up easy, let 'em up easy.' "

"He said that?"

"Are you sure? You mean he intends for us to go home?"

"General Grant ordered that all the officers and men in Lee's army are to be allowed to return to their homes."

"What?" The prisoners were amazed. Their stunned looks turned to cheering. Tears of relief flowed down their cheeks. "We won't be hanged as traitors?"

"Hey, Doc, how long we got to stay put?" One of them smiled a nearly toothless smile. "I got me a young'un at home born while I's away. Ain't seen it yet."

"You won't be disturbed by the U.S. authorities as long as you observe your paroles, cease fighting, and obey the laws in force where you live. According to the broadside I saw hanging at the post office, President Lincoln has made that clear." Avery was proud of their president and happy to be the bearer of such good news for these worn-out men.

"Grant says if you have horses, you're to keep your animals. He's arranging for the hungry Confederate soldiers to be fed."

"Well, I'll be. Guess we never seen that one comin'. That's right civil of him. Ahm 'preciative," said a stunned prisoner.

"Wish't I still had my horse. We done ate him."

Grant instructed all the Federals that they weren't to fire their guns in celebration or exult or gloat when the Confederates surrendered.

"The Civil War in Virginia is over," he told them. "We're all countrymen once again."

In Alexandria the prisons and hospitals opened their doors, and the defeated countrymen limped out, looked around, and headed home.

The solemn and dignified celebrations continued. All the regiments around Alexandria paraded through the center of town to the joyful shouts of all the proud people who ran to shake the soldiers' hands, pat their horses, and say thank you, as the soldiers who'd camped nearby prepared to leave for Washington, D.C. Their war was over. As the last soldiers pulled out of Alexandria, the people cheered and applauded for their job well done. Patients who were able to move on their own waved goodbye and went home.

CHAPTER THIRTY-THREE

LAID TO REST

Patients were being put to bed, and most staff had gone home for the night. A few volunteers remained with Avery at the hospital on the evening of Good Friday, April 14, 1865. *Surely it won't be long now, and we can all go home. Maybe I won't be giving these men any more bad news.*

But in the morning a newsboy ran out to Dr. Simpson's wagon. "Extra edition, Doc. Better get one!"

"Don't care if I ever read another one," Dr. Simpson said, handing a coin to the boy. "Time for some good news." He clucked to his horse and continued on his way. At the hospital he tossed the paper to a weary Avery who was ready to turn the wards over to Dr. Simpson.

Avery unfolded the paper and glanced at it. He grabbed Dr. Simpson's arm. "Stop."

"You feeling ill? You're looking pale, Avery."

Avery couldn't speak. He handed the paper back to the puzzled surgeon. He pointed to the headline.

PRESIDENT LINCOLN ASSASSINATED

Avery's hand shook, and the paper rattled. Dr. Simpson steadied the paper, and the two read in silence.

The President and First Lady were enjoying an evening performance at the Ford Theatre . . .

Dr. Simpson began to read aloud. "At ten o'clock last night a shot rang out in the theatre. The President slumped over in his chair, unconscious. At 7:22 a.m., Saturday, April 15, 1865, this morning, the President, who had reunited the war-torn nation, died."

The color had drained from Avery's face; his jaw hung open. Dr. Simpson's hand was across his heart. His lips were pale. Newsboys in every city of the nation peddled special editions up and down the streets.

"Extra! Extra!" they called. People across the nation read their papers and shared the shock and disbelief. They wept in public, and the worried Americans, who'd just endured five years of hardship, wondered openly what would become of the wounded nation now. Would it ever recover?

"What now?" whispered the dazed Avery.

Claire and the nurses were sobbing. Avery held the newspaper crumpled in his hand. Dr. Simpson's eyes brimmed with tears, and his chin was set, but he comforted the nurses. Dr. Simpson tried to reassure them that he was confident, in spite of the unthinkable tragedy, the country would heal. They all put on brave faces for the patients, who were just learning about the latest tragedy. Moans and groans came from every cot.

"Assassination?" sobbed Claire. "Whoever heard of such a thing?"

On Easter Sunday clergymen around the country praised Lincoln in their sermons. Claire, Avery, and the Simpsons prayed for the president, his family, and the nation. Throughout the large church quiet sobs echoed.

The news of the president's death filled the South with fear, because the Southerners knew most of Washington's bureaucrats desired harsher policies toward the South than Lincoln had in mind. Many politicians weren't looking to "let 'em up easy."

Some of the hospital volunteers who lived near the Washington, D.C., area left earlier than planned so they could view the funeral procession. They watched along with millions as a caisson pulled the coffin, accompanied by a drummer and a few horses,

down the center of the street in the nation's capital. Dr. Simpson, Claire, and Avery thanked each volunteer for their dedicated service and said goodbye to friends and coworkers. Gunner made his goodbyes to each one. In the midwest the war that was still raging began to lose momentum.

"He was a good father and a good man," murmured Avery. "Just like my father. I'm glad his son will be buried with him."

"This is all just too much to absorb, isn't it? Where is the joy in this victory? Has it been laid to rest, too?" Claire asked quietly. "Do you think they know about this in Kanawha Valley?"

"I don't know, Claire. I think this war might be something else we aren't going to understand. My old friend would say this isn't how it should be, but it's how it is. We have to carry on the best we know."

On May 10, Confederate President Jefferson Davis was captured in Georgia, the government of the Confederacy dissolved, and it too was laid to rest. The soldiers cheered.

General Keese and the Army of the Potomac marched down Pennsylvania Avenue in Washington, D.C., thirteen days later. The mourning of the president gave way to joy as dignitaries, including the new president, Andrew Johnson, brought out the crowds; and the sorrow, for a little while, was also laid to rest.

General Sherman's army held their parade the next day, followed by Grant's army.

"This isn't to be a Roman parade of triumph," Grant told all the soldiers. "We're not exhibiting trophies and gloating. This isn't a victory celebration. We'll not wipe our boots on the men of the Confederacy. This is a celebration of the dawn of peace; a reestablishment of the Union." And with those words, Grant laid his Civil War in Virginia to rest.

Avery read the account to the patients gathered around.

"The man is every bit decent then, isn't that so, Avery?" Claire declared.

"Boy, I'll say!" answered one of the men. "More decent than most of us would be, I dare say."

Avery nodded in agreement. He wondered if that was easy for Grant or if Grant agreed with his father that the right thing to do was often the hardest.

"Extra! Extra!" The newsboys shouted on the streets again on May 26. "The Confederate troops west of the Mississippi River have surrendered. Read all about it!"

Avery ran up the steps to the hospital, the newspaper shredding in his fist. "Claire! Claire! Has anyone seen Claire?" He charged up two flights of stairs and found her dressing wounds.

"Claire. It's over. It's over." He embraced her while the patients whistled and cheered. "The war is over, everyone," he announced to all of them. "The Union is restored; the United States is united again. Thanks to all of you. We're all going home," he shouted, staring at Claire whose tears were merrily dripping to her chin. Some of the ambulatories cheerfully gathered their few belongings, knowing that their discharge was imminent. The patients on the second floor were jubilant, but wondering how they would get home and how they'd manage when they got there. What would their new life be like? What would they find if they did manage to get home? The patients on the third floor, quietly absorbing the good cheer around them, wondered if they would recover enough—would they live long enough—to go home?

Matt Mason ran to Mansion House Hospital and found Avery shaking hands with the ambulatories. "Did you hear? It's over, Avery. Praise God, it's over! We've got work to do to get these poor soldiers discharged and out of here, but I just had to see you." He and Avery embraced and pounded each other's shoulders heartily, laughing and wondering if this could really be true or if it was only a dream.

"We'll keep in touch, Matt," Avery said. "The war is over, but our friendship will last forever."

"Amen to that, Avery. I've got to see Anna." He ran up the stairs to look for her.

Avery gathered his staff, and they made plans for evacuation and discharge procedures. The news was good, but their work wasn't over yet.

CHAPTER THIRTY-FOUR

HEARTS AT A CROSSROAD

Officers from different regiments had been in and out of the hospitals in the past few days making preparations for their hospitalized sick or invalided men. But several of the men who'd been transported here to Alexandria from great distances seemed to have been forgotten. Dr. Simpson and Claire organized lists of those men by name and regiment and arranged for their army discharge and transfers to civilian hospitals near their homes. Avery sent many telegrams to families. Citizens of Alexandria were lending their wagons to transport the patients to the crowded train station.

The evacuation of all the hospitals and prisons was moving smoothly, although slower than everyone would like. Everyone was in a happy, cooperative mood, finally believing the terrors of the war were behind them. Soldiers and volunteers worked together happily, and Rabbit could be heard singing in the busy hospital rooms.

With all the momentous happenings of the past couple of weeks, Avery had little time with Claire. Now, with the business of discharging thousands of patients throughout the city, all the medical personnel continued to be overworked and exhausted.

In the midst of this chaos Avery asked Claire if he might escort her to her residence at the close of the day. Claire tried to contain her joy, but Avery could tell she was pleased. Spring was all around them, the war was over, and he would walk Claire

home this evening. He was elated. When the sun lowered and the evening birds began to whistle, Avery, Gunner, and Claire ended their busy week at the hospital and walked to the nurses' residence.

He found this escorting business to be easier and more enjoyable; he was able to converse with her without his ears turning red. He still fussed at himself a lot for saying the wrong thing at the wrong time, but he enjoyed being with her anyway, and it seemed to him that she enjoyed being with him. She was almost skipping; Avery felt her happiness, and he couldn't stop smiling.

"I've wanted to ask you something. I'm just curious about this. Have you ever written your mother about . . . me?" Avery asked. "I mean, have you mentioned that we're friends or work together?"

"What a funny question. Why are you asking?"

"Because sometime ago in a letter my mother wondered if I'd run across Molly and Sam McDougal's daughter who's a nurse."

Claire giggled, and Avery thought she was blushing.

"No, Avery, I've not mentioned that. It seems like . . . well, kind of my own private . . . well, something. I just don't feel like sharing you, I suppose." She was definitely blushing. "Did you . . . did you answer your mother?"

"No!" he answered quickly. "No, not yet."

Their eyes met and they laughed.

"I guess it's our secret then, isn't it?"

"Gunner, don't you tell!"

They both laughed. They held hands and walked on to the nurses' residence.

"You remember that time, Claire, that I hurt your feelings? I thought I'd lost you over that." He stopped walking and looked at her. "I couldn't bear that thought."

"And at your near lynching? I feared I'd lost you. And I fainted!"

They laughed at their shared memories.

"I wonder, Avery, if it means we are meant to stay together?"

"Seems like a real possibility, doesn't it?"

Mrs. Simpson was planning one more dinner party.

"Dr. Simpson, Avery! You two!" She called to them as they were leaving for the hospital with Gunner perched on the buggy seat between them. "Don't be late today, please. We're having a little dinner party this evening. And bring Claire along, please," she instructed them. "Gunner, don't let them forget."

"Having a dinner party are we?" laughed the doctor, shaking his head. "Well, whatever Mrs. Simpson says. We won't miss it, will we."

It was a statement, not a question, and Avery smiled, remembering how many times he'd seen Dr. Simpson defer to his wife. It brought to mind a memory of his father drying the dishes for his mother because it pleased her. "No, we won't miss that, will we, Gunner?"

Dr. Simpson chuckled. He clucked to his horse, and they were off, jostling down the rutted road.

"How many times do you suppose we've bounced along on this road between your home and the hospital?" Avery questioned.

But Dr. Simpson either didn't hear him or ignored it. "Now that our work at the Mansion House Hospital is coming to an end, have you given any thought to your future?"

Avery was startled at the question. "My future? No, I guess not. I think I'm not very good at planning ahead. For a while I was conflicted about medicine. I wasn't sure I wanted to be a doctor after all. I thought I was more cut out to be a farmer. Now that the war is over . . . I'm not real sure what my plan will be."

"I'm not trying to pry or interfere, but will Nurse Claire fit in to your plan in some way?"

Avery was quiet. How did she fit in? All he knew was that in recent days, watching everyone preparing to leave, he knew he didn't want her to leave.

"Well, I, uh . . . I don't know exactly. I mean, I really haven't planned for much, I guess. We've been pretty busy."

Gunner stared at him with interest.

"Avery, my boy, though you're a young man, you're wise beyond your years. In knowledge and in common sense you're much older than you believe yourself to be. However, being a humble and unassuming man, you may not have realized that lovely little lady has a big heart reserved for only you."

Avery stared open-mouthed at Dr. Simpson. "Really? You think that? You know that? I mean, *how* do you know that? Did she tell you? What should I do about that?"

Dr. Simpson was used to Avery's multiquestion statements and just chuckled. "What do you *want* to do about it?"

"Well, I don't know. What can I do? What should I do?"

"Why don't you ask the young lady herself what you should do? I'll bet she's got a plan!"

Avery was quiet for a moment. "Now that you mention it, she did have a plan when she showed up here in '62. She told it to me," he said quietly, while slowly remembering. "I guess she's been waiting for me to figure out my part of that plan." He was working it out even as he spoke. "Yes, I forgot about her plan."

"Uh-huh," chuckled the doctor. "I figured as much. That young woman is just full of good ideas and plans!"

"The thing is, Dr. Simpson, she confuses me. I don't always understand her. She just confounds me so."

"Avery, my boy, that's just the way it is. It's the way it's always been since Adam and Eve, and the way it'll be till kingdom come. When you've been married to a wonderful lady for as many years as I have, then you'll realize that you'll never figure her out. I still don't understand my wife. But I sure do enjoy her. I don't worry about being confounded anymore. Don't wait until you understand the girl, Avery, because it's never going to happen."

"Thank you, sir. I'll remember that." In a few minutes they reached the hospital ready for another long day.

Avery felt jittery all day trying to absorb the doctor's advice while looking forward to spending the evening with Claire. He hardly saw her all day, they were so busy. But his confidence grew as the day wore on. *Maybe we'll have a plan soon*. Gunner had

been in and out seeing off patients and greeting officers coming in with discharge papers. Avery thought Gunner looked a little jittery too. Gunner could tell things were different; things were changing.

At the end of the day Avery gathered all his courage and found Claire. He announced in his most confident voice that he'd be escorting her to the Simpsons' for dinner.

Surprised to see her shy friend looking and sounding so assertive, she smiled and gathered her things. She sat between the doctors on the buggy seat with Gunner's head in her lap. She was chatty as usual, but Avery wasn't really concentrating on what she was saying.

She was surprised that when their eyes met, he didn't look away and blush. Instead he continued to watch her. He smiled a lot and didn't look so serious or nervous. At dinner he hardly looked down at his dinner plate at all. He looked across the table and scarcely took his eyes off her. She was beginning to squirm under his close inspection.

"So, Claire, have you any plans for when the hospital doors close in a few weeks? Do you know what you'll do next?" Mrs. Simpson asked.

Gunner looked up at Claire from his nap on the floor. He seemed to be waiting for her answer too.

"I do have some decisions to make," she said rather quietly. "I'm not sure just now what the opportunities will be. No, I've not made any decisions." Head down, she chewed slowly.

Avery watched her, noting that she seemed a bit sad. Gunner lay back down on his paws and eyed Avery.

"How about you, Avery, any plans?" Mrs. Simpson was speaking to him.

Gunner raised his head and listened for the answer. Claire hesitated and listened for the answer. She didn't look at Avery.

"Well, not really. I'm a degreed surgeon and an experienced farmer. I have some property in the wilderness. Some of the men are talking about California. I don't know how I'd be at that, but I guess I need to figure it out."

Claire ate her meal slowly and looked down at her plate, uncharacteristically quiet.

Mrs. Simpson brought out the coffee and the cobbler; they all retired to the parlor.

"Mrs. Simpson," Claire said quietly, "may I ask you a question?"

"Of course, dear." She glanced at her husband and raised an eyebrow.

"Avery, looks like it's time for us to make ourselves scarce," the doctor chuckled and ushered Avery out of the room. Avery looked puzzled. "Girl talk," the doctor whispered. "We're not included." They sat and talked in the doctor's study.

"Dr. Simpson, what you said this morning—I've been thinking about it. I have really strong feelings for Claire. So strong that they sometimes get all knotted up inside, and I think I'm going to explode. I don't want her to leave. I think about her all the time until I'm totally distracted and can't think straight. I want to be with her, whether it's on the plain or in Kanawha Valley or anywhere she wants to go. I don't know where I want to go or what I want to do, only that I want her to be a part of it. I've always been able to think things through—except with her. Now my mind is a jumble, and my stomach is tied in knots. I don't know what to do. I've never felt so confused."

"The diagnosis is simple: You love this girl. Your feelings are very normal, Avery."

"Really?" Avery was surprised. "I'm normal? This is love?"

"It seems to me that you only have one choice to make."

"Only one? What?"

"Marry the girl," said the doctor. "Marry the girl."

Avery stared, breathless.

"Mrs. Simpson," the doctor called out, "Let's you and me wash the dishes together, dear."

"I thought so," whispered Mrs. Simpson to Claire as Avery entered the parlor looking pale, his eyes slightly glazed over.

Avery and Claire were alone in the parlor. After a few awkward moments, they both began to speak at the same time. They laughed and tried again.

"Ladies first."

"Okay then. I've only one really important thing to say, and Mrs. Simpson says I must say it out loud or burst. Avery, I love you with all my heart, and I want to be with you wherever you go, whatever you want to do. And that's the only important decision I've made."

"You do? You have? Well, that's what I was going to say to you. I was going to say I love you, Claire, with all my heart. I want to be with you, praying beside you, loving you always. Anywhere you want to go, whatever you want to do, I want to do it with you. And if it would please you, I want to ask you . . . would you . . . marry me?"

Claire beamed. "It's more than okay. I will go with you wherever you want to go, and I'll be at your side always."

His father was right. She was his best friend, and her love was a beautiful gift. He was ready to burst with joy. Gunner sat at their feet, panting excitedly. Avery was frozen in place, grinning from ear to ear.

"Avery? Don't you think it's okay to kiss me now?"

CHAPTER THIRTY-FIVE

VIOLETS IN HER HAIR

On June 16, 1865, Mansion House Hospital for Union Soldiers closed its doors forever. Claire was one of the last nurses left in the nurses' residence, which would close as a dormitory by the end of the month. Her belongings were packed. Most of what she owned fit in one carpet bag. She had only one bonnet box. Her nurse's pay was in her little purse. *Not much to show for three years of toil*, she thought. She was wearing a new dress that she and Mrs. Simpson's dressmaker had made from an old party frock left over from Mrs. Simpson's younger days.

Mrs. Simpson was busy with her own preparations. She was setting a festive table for later with flowers on the table. When Claire and Avery came in, Mrs. Simpson settled a little wreath of violets on the girl's shining curls. Mrs. Simpson looked very nice, wearing her old, but finest, church clothes. Avery was wearing his graduation suit, sleeves and legs shorter than when he'd worn it at his college graduation. Claire declared him to be the finest-looking man in the city. He could tell in her eyes that she really believed that. He thought she looked breathtaking in her new dress with violets in her hair.

"Where is Dr. Simpson today?" Claire asked.

"He's just gone off for a quick errand," Mrs. Simpson answered. "He'll be along shortly."

Gunner barked, and the wagon rolled to the barn behind the house.

"Looks like the doctor has picked up some riders," Avery said.

The doctor didn't come in right away, and Avery worried that if he got caught up in a conversation they might be late. He was nervous enough without arriving late.

"Well, I believe we're all ready now," announced Dr. Simpson, coming into the parlor. "We should probably be going now, don't you agree?"

They all got up to leave, when Mrs. Simpson swung open the kitchen door, and in walked Major General Geoffrey Keese. Avery hardly recognized him in his civilian suit looking so handsome. Beside him on one side was Aunt Caroline, smiling and looking beautiful. Hanging on the General's leg on the other side was Phoebe. Holding Caroline's free arm was Claire's red-haired brother, Timothy McDougal.

Claire shrieked, "Timothy!" Caroline quickly picked up Timothy's hand and wrote a sign on his hand. He grinned, looked blankly ahead at the wall and held out his arms to receive his sister.

"Claaare," he said.

Avery shook hands with the General, hugged Aunt Caroline, and bent down to kiss little Phoebe. He took her tiny hand and wrote "hello" on it. He'd practiced this many times. She looked at him and blinked.

"Hello, Avery," she said.

"We need to get going," Mrs. Simpson said, bustling around the room. They all went out the front door to be greeted by Leon, dressed up in a nice vest, coat, and a top hat. The wagon was spread with quilts and decorated with greenery, flowers, and ribbons. Leon had braided flowers and ribbons into Rose's tail and mane.

Everyone exclaimed, "How beautiful," and Leon was very pleased. Avery shook his hand and thanked him. They all climbed up on the wagon. All along the way people stopped, pointed, and waved, admiring the gypsy horse pulling the festive wagon, little bells jingling.

When they arrived at the church, their friends Anna and Matthew were already there to serve as their witnesses. Claire and Avery walked up to the altar. The candles gleamed, and the aroma of incense filled the air. The sun streamed through the stained glass windows, washing them all in shimmering colors.

"Raybow," said Phoebe, as she touched it and tried to pick it up.

Gunner lay in the aisle beside Mrs. Simpson. His tail thumped in unison with Avery's pounding heart.

Avery and Claire recited their prayers and their vows before their friends and family, dog and God, promising to love, cherish, and protect each other all the days of their lives. The sunlight spilled in through the windows, bathing them in the rainbow. Avery kissed his bride. Caroline signed to Timothy on his hand. He smiled, imagining how beautiful it must look.

Everyone rode along in the wagon to the celebration at the Simpsons' home. Mrs. Simpson produced a wedding cake with fresh plum jam between the layers and flowers on the top.

Dr. Simpson made a toast: "To Doctor and Mrs. Avery Bennett for a long and happy life and a safe journey to wherever their home will be. God bless you."

Later that afternoon, Leon drove Avery, Claire, and Gunner to the train station. They had Claire's carpet bag and hat box, Avery's carpet bag, an old knapsack carrying his grandfather's surgical instruments, a box of books, and a deed of wilderness land. They had a beautiful cradle carved with tiny roses, and Rose, the black and white gypsy horse. They had Fan with a McClellan saddle and Gunner with a leather leash, never used. And they had each other.

Avery paused on the step into the train car. He was flushed with memories. *This entire journey started when I was only fourteen. This is the last leg of the journey. It's been a journey of a lifetime.*

CHAPTER THIRTY-SIX
GOING HOME

They settled into their crowded train compartment with their animals secured in the stable car. They were going home together. The train was full of celebrating soldiers who were going home and solemn families moving westward because they no longer had homes. There were freed slaves and their families hoping to find welcoming homes. Avery leaned against the window; his heart rejoiced as his wife leaned against his shoulder.

They waved to their friends and family on the platform. Grateful to all of them, Avery was filled with a storm of emotion. He was happy, but he was sad saying goodbye to Dr. and Mrs. Simpson, who'd provided him with a home and friendship for five years.

Dr. Simpson has had a profound influence on my life.

Dr. Simpson waved his hand, and Mrs. Simpson wiped her eyes with her handkerchief. Retired General Geoffrey Keese saluted Avery through the window.

The general kept me safe in the war when I was so young. Avery saluted him. *There's Timothy staring, seeing only darkness just like many other soldiers who've passed through my life in these last five years. They couldn't see me change from a boy to a man, but they trusted me as their doctor.* Aunt Caroline blew him a kiss. *Aunt Caroline is looking so pretty and happy . . . a part of my childhood. There's little Phoebe, strong and ready to face all the challenges confronting her, just like many discharged into a changed world to learn*

to live in their own complicated places. I think the only thing that hasn't changed through this war is Gunner.

"Avery? Are you all right? What are you brooding about, my dear husband?"

"Standing there on the platform, they look like the final page of a history book, like the ending of a chapter." A tear trickled down to his chin. His wife wiped it dry with her little handkerchief. And then she dried her own.

"I'll need to make some new ones now," she said, looking at her little embroidered monogram. "They will say *CMB*." She smiled happily and kissed his cheek.

The whistle blew, and the train lurched forward. Everyone waved; soon the platform was out of sight, and they were chugging west to West Virginia. It was a day he'd dreamed of for five long years. The war was really over. Claire sniffed.

"Don't worry, Avery. These are happy tears."

The newlyweds talked and listened to each other amidst the noise and confusion of the crowded train. Avery laughed, "Does this remind you of the hospital?"

They both laughed.

"Where are we going, me darlin' Avery? Somewhere the war didn't go?" she said dreamily.

"I own property, Claire."

She looked surprised. In her heart she knew Avery would always be surprising her with things he said. She loved that about him.

"I have the deed. It's between Grafton and Alexandria. I think we could farm it. It has a good barn. Little else. An ancient pear tree. There's nothing for miles. But it's ours. We might want to think about farming that sometime."

"Mother says Wheeling is getting to be a big city now, and Charleston too. Good places to start a medical practice. There's a hospital; I could work there, too, you know."

"Or you could be Dr. Bennett's private nurse."

"What a wonderful idea, Dr. Bennett! Maybe Parkersburg, Avery. It's close enough to visit our families, and there's a church there. And a hospital."

"This is a big nation, Claire. A nation without war. We can go anywhere we want. Imagine that. But I'm not really a city man. I'm more farmer."

"I think that's true for me too, isn't it? Irish lass that I am, a tater for goodness' sake," she laughed. "We should live near a river so the busy doctor might find a quiet moment to fish and relax."

So like her, Avery thought, *to be so practical and to think of that.* He began humming softly "Shall We Gather at the River."

In the stable car Gunner rolled over on his back and stretched happily. Fan stomped her foot and swished her tail. Rose tossed her head, whinnied, and her merry mane rippled.

When daylight appeared through the train windows, Avery and Claire moved their stiff bodies and brushed the wrinkles from their clothing. They stood in a long line for the toilet room and held their noses. They walked around a bit, ordered coffee, and continued their conversation from yesterday.

Around midday they chugged into the Grafton station. For the next few hours they walked around looking at the old town with new eyes. There were no soldiers lingering and signing up for duty. There were no broadsides begging to be torn down by new recruits. They watered their animals and let Gunner have a run. The next stop would be Parkersburg.

When they settled back into their compartment, a man joined them. He didn't ask if it was okay, and Avery hoped he wouldn't be staying long.

"I saw you out with the dog back there," the man said. "Is your name, by any chance, Avery?" Avery shot him an interested but suspicious look.

"Maybe." He waited for the man to introduce himself. Instead the man reached out for Claire's hand. Avery quickly retrieved her hand and kept it gently in his own.

"Might I ask who you are, sir?" Avery was slightly irritated.

"My name won't mean much to you. You knew me as Cockroach."

Avery stared at the man and slowly the recognition moved across his face until it was a big smile.

"Well, what do you know," Avery said. "This is my wife, Mrs. Bennett."

"Bennett," the man snapped his fingers. "Now I remember. Avery Junior Bennett. I sure did remember ol' Gunner though. Avery and Gunner, I'll never forget the two of you. Though I wouldn't have recognized you, Avery, without the dog. You were a skinny knee knocker when I knew you. Lawsy, I remember them shoes tied on your feet with the toes hanging out . . ." The man laughed and slapped his knee, shaking his head. "Now here you are and married too. Whooee, look at that," he said good naturedly. "Nice to meet 'cha, ma'am."

They reminisced about where they'd gone and what they'd done during the long years of the war.

"One thing I never figured out," asked Avery. "Why did your cook, Richardson, hate me so much? I never crossed him, but that man just didn't like me at all."

"You never knew? He's the man who stole your horse. He didn't know that at first, of course. But something about the dog spooked him. He thought he'd seen him somewhere before. Then one night around the campfire ol' Gunner showed us his tricks, and Richardson knew. You told how Gunner had tricked the marauder with his dying trick, and everyone laughed and made fun of the marauder. That's why he hated you. Then when Gunner found your horse, whooeee! Was he mad!"

"Well, what do you know. I never knew that. Makes sense. Richardson had no character or honor."

The man visited a little longer and left to smoke his pipe.

"How about that," Avery said shaking his head.

"I can't wait to hear this story," answered Claire.

"Parrrkkkeeerrrsssbbbuuurrrggg," bellowed the conductor melodiously.

"Wonder what our new life will be like, Mrs. Bennett?"

"Peaceful, Dr. Bennett. It will be peaceful."

CHAPTER THIRTY-SEVEN
THE HOMECOMING

They stayed around Parkersburg for two days, "trying it on for size," Claire said. They purchased a new family Bible. In the center of the book on decorated pages, they wrote their names on the top line of the family history along with the date and place of their marriage.

"This will be in our home forever, Avery," Claire said, hugging the Bible to her chest. They rented a livery wagon, loaded up their few belongings, and took the road to Kanawha Valley. Gunner was in an excited frenzy and seemed to know exactly where he was going. The closer they came to Kanawha, the more he ran, circling and barking as if to say, "Hurry up! Can't you go any faster?"

"I feel that way too, Avery. I'd like to run and twirl and bark. But I'm also nervous. How will we tell them? What will we say? What will they say? Where will we stay?"

Avery looked at her and smiled.

When they turned off the road and started down the Bennett's farm lane, Gunner took off like he was chasing a rabbit, barking all the way. He was out of sight before they were halfway down the road.

"I guess surprising them is out of the question," teased Claire.

It was a Sunday afternoon and his mother would be at home, probably reading or praying, perhaps tending her herbs. His father—oh . . . his father would not be there.

The livery wagon bounced along the road on ruts his father would have smoothed. The trees in the orchard needed thinning; he and his brother had been taught to do this as young boys. No one was pruning these days. There was a new house near the edge of the property, and they saw small children playing nearby.

"They must be the children from South Carolina that Aunt Caroline brought here."

In front of them stood the Bennetts' house. "Needs some whitewash," mumbled Avery, surveying loose shingles waiting to blow off in the next storm. Chickens clucked around the yard. His mother's herb garden and vegetable garden seemed smaller than he remembered them.

"I learned a lot of doctoring and a lot of farming in those little gardens," he told Claire.

Walking toward the house, Claire said, "Oh, Avery, I'm ever so nervous. What if she doesn't like me as the daughter-in-law?"

Avery smiled and squeezed her hand. He wasn't worried.

Gunner came from behind the house tail waving and legs bouncing with excitement. Behind him came Avery's mother. Avery ran and embraced her. She laughed and hugged him back.

"Oh, I'm so glad to see you! Why didn't you tell me you were coming? I could have cooked something; my goodness, you are so tall and handsome, just like your father. And you're the picture of health. Isn't it wonderful the war is over?"

Hugging her, Avery looked down on his mother's head. Her hair had turned to gray.

Peeking around Avery, she noticed the girl looking nervous and slightly familiar. "Hello," she said, "welcome." She looked at her son, now holding the girl's hand, and waited for an introduction.

"Mother, do you remember Claire McDougal?"

"Oh, of course I do. Now I can place you, dear. So you two did manage to meet in Alexandria, did you? I'm sure it was a comfort to you both to know someone from home."

"Well, you could say that," Avery said awkwardly. His voice squeaked. "Claire got to be my best friend." He choked a bit and squeezed her hand for courage.

"Actually, Mrs. Bennett, Avery and I worked together side by side for three years. We were—are—best friends. Last week before making this trip together, we were married. I'm Claire McDougal Bennett." She extended her hand to Sarah. "I hope you don't mind."

Sarah looked at her son and bypassed Claire's extended hand, pulling her into a firm embrace.

The next morning Avery and Claire set out on horseback across the field into the next holler to the McDougal's potato farm. The field workers stood up and stretched their backs, watching the strangers riding up the road.

"Looks to me like Da's done a great deal of growin' in four years, doesn't it?"

The newly raked and furrowed fields were bustling with workers hoeing and picking bugs and caterpillars off the leaves and dropping them into buckets of water. It was a prosperous farm, much larger than it had been four years ago.

As they came into the yard, two red-haired taters, looking identical, peeked around the corner of the house, eyeing the riders suspiciously. Claire winked at them.

"It's Claire!" They both shouted and jumped up and down gleefully. Within minutes Colleen had joined them, followed by Sam and Molly McDougal.

"You've grown, Colleen," said Avery.

Colleen blushed. "Hello, Avery."

"And these two leprechauns are Sean and Seamus, the McDougal double trouble tater twins." Claire laughed and hugged the little boys.

"Hello, Sean, Seamus." Avery was delighted to know that all the taters had real names and weren't all named Tater.

Laughter and excitement followed with everyone talking at once, asking and telling at the same time.

"Avery, how nice it is that you've brought my daughter. You're good at rescuing the McDougal taters, eh? Did you find her lost at the train station then? How've you been? Come in, come in." Sam McDougal had his arm around Claire and led them into the cozy kitchen. Avery had been here once, but he hadn't known Claire yet.

"I've been fine, sir. Good to be home." *This will be interesting.*

"Avery, will you join us for supper then?" asked Molly putting on the tea kettle.

"Mam," Claire said, taking her hand. "Sit down with us. Don't fuss. We don't need a thing, really. We didn't just get off the train."

The family sat down, realizing Claire had something to say. "Avery and I, uh," she stammered. "Well, we . . ." she looked at Avery. Her tongue stuck to the roof of her mouth.

"Actually, Mr. and Mrs. McDougal, Claire and I have been working together since she arrived in Alexandria. We liked working together, and when it was time to close the hospital we didn't want to be separated; we wanted to travel together and be together always. So I hope you don't mind, but we—"

"We just got married!" blurted Claire. "It's official. At St. Mary's in Alexandria. He's my very own husband." She sighed.

"We hope you'll be happy for us," added Avery politely.

It was silent for a few moments while the family absorbed the news.

"Well," Molly began, "I had hopes and dreams for my forward and modern-thinking daughter, as any mother would. And there isn't a man alive I'd rather see side-a-side with me darlin' Claire than it be you, Avery. I'm so happy you found each other. You're well suited, you are."

"God bless you both, and praise to God for a blessing such as this," said Sam McDougal. Molly sniffed and dried her eyes, and Sam shook Avery's hand and then hugged his daughter.

With much relief and happiness, Claire and Avery later returned to the Bennetts' farm, where they were staying in the new room Avery's father had added to the house for Aunt Caroline and the baby a few years ago.

After the Sunday meeting the community surprised them with gifts of pots, plants, seeds, hammered spoons, embroidered tea towels, goose-down pillows, tools, baby chicks, an apple tree graft, and a lamb.

"Thank God, the war is finally over and you are both home safely," the neighbors all said.

CHAPTER THIRTY-EIGHT
FAMILY REUNITED

Summer in the Kanawha Valley was just as Claire and Avery had remembered it from their childhoods. Days began at sunup, and evenings were quiet.

"The difference is that now I'm the grownup, and I'm drying dishes with my very own husband."

Avery smiled and put the dish in the cabinet, remembering that his mother and father had looked just like this years ago.

"I always looked after the babes for Mam, so she could help Da with the fields. So I didn't learn too much else," Claire explained. "I never did all this homemaking before. It was a complete job looking after the younger ones, feeding them, and keeping them out of mischief. Now I'm learning cooking, gardening, canning, and preserving. Your mam and Maize are so patient with me. I do think I miss nursing though, Avery."

"Mother says since she's teaching a half day all summer, she appreciates your help. There are never enough hands on a farm. Banjo and I are mending fences tomorrow. I showed him how to prune the orchard today. We'll repair the roof and whitewash the house as soon as we can get to it."

"Oh, Avery, did I tell you Maize is a good poultry teacher? She's teaching me to tend the chickens and the domestic geese. But I think Gunner would be happy if he never saw another goose." Claire giggled.

Gunner lay under the table listening; his ears pricked up when he heard his name. He peeked out under the bench, and when Claire spread her arms and honked, Gunner shot out from under the table, out the door, off the porch, and ran to the barn. Claire doubled over in laughter.

"What was that all about?" Avery watched Gunner tearing to the barn.

"Oh, Avery," Claire caught her breath. "It's so funny. The geese have it in for poor Gunner, and the dog is terrified of them."

"You're telling me that the battlefield dog who's gone against rattlesnakes, thieves, gunfire, cougar, and who's been goose hunting since he was a puppy, is afraid of barnyard geese? What's gotten into him? The old boy's going soft."

"No, Avery, don't be hard on him. The geese are vicious; they are. They spread out their huge wings and run directly at him, honking, making a terrible racket. They pinch and nip him and run him right under the porch. The poor dog stays there half a day. The geese walk sentry back and forth and refuse to let him out. Maize says they could peck a dog's eyes out, so he's smart to stay hidden. And he *is* smart, Avery."

Once a week they went to the tater farm. "I've dug more potatoes in a month than I've dug in my lifetime," Avery groaned, rubbing his sore shoulders. "Your Da's got a big business going over there. I'm happy for him; they've worked hard at it."

Maize tried to teach Claire how to weave a basket, but it wasn't a craft that came easily to Claire, and she finally gave up. Maize created a beautiful gardening basket and a laundry basket, which she gave to Claire.

"For your new home," she said.

"I wonder where that will be?" Claire said aloud.

Maize smiled at her. "You don't worry 'bout that. The good Lord, He got a plan somewhere in His mind for you, missus. Just wait and see if that ain't the way of it."

Avery met Danny, who was in the middle of the seven taters. He was quiet, but Avery didn't find him to be shy.

"Danny likes being with you, Avery. What do you two do together?" Claire asked one evening. "He rarely talks to anyone, but he chatters away with you."

"I don't know. Danny's a bright boy. I talk to him about what he's reading. I've only seen him at his chores in the field and reading. I'm not sure if he does anything else. We like to walk to the river and back and just talk; nothing special. I enjoy his company. He looks like all the rest of you, but in the long row of taters, Danny seems to be invisible."

"Oh, my darlin' Avery, that is so like you to notice Danny. I love you more every day. And lucky Danny has you for a friend."

The white summery clouds blew overhead day after summer day—rain, sun, wind. Gunner enjoyed his civilian freedom. Avery and Claire walked through the orchard in the evenings, holding hands, listening to the whippoorwill. Sometimes they stopped on the hill and visited the grave of Avery Bryson Bennett.

"I'm sorry Father missed out having a daughter-in-law. He'd have loved you, Claire. And you would have loved him. He was a fine man."

"I know." She swung in his old swing that still hung from the walnut tree. They shared stories from their childhood and learned more about each other every day that quiet summer of 1865.

"Who would have thought we'd ever hear such peacefulness again? Sometimes when it's all quiet like this, my ears think they hear the cannon roaring off in the distance. As if they can't tolerate the absence of that noise. Does that happen to you, my love?"

"Yes, it does. I hear cannon and gunfire in my head too. Makes me appreciate this quiet even more. Sometimes I'm startled from my sleep at night; I think I hear a soldier crying out in pain. I'm glad to find you beside me and the house quiet."

CHAPTER THIRTY-NINE
HEALING TIME

Word spread throughout the valley that there was now a doctor in residence. Soon wagons were rolling and bouncing up the road, throwing dust in billowing clouds. Avery hung a notice at the post office that the doctor would be open for business three days a week in a small cottage he rented at the edge of the town of Kanawha.

They cleaned and scrubbed and made some repairs. Claire washed the windows; Avery built a medicine cabinet. At Claire's suggestion, Avery built a cot frame for an examination table that was as tall as his waist. They stacked cotton batting on the top and covered it with oil cloth.

"Now you don't have to bend over all the day and come home with a sore back."

Avery remembered his long days in the hospital bent over the low cots.

"You've always had the best ideas, Claire. And now it's time to go to Parkersburg and pick up supplies for our clinic."

The clinic opened and in came pinkeye, gout, poison ivy, canker sores, headache, tooth decay, diaper rash, earache, rheumatism, and blurred vision. They saw a colicky baby, a child with odd behavior, a man with a whiskey problem, and a woman with head lice. Gunner lay on the step and greeted every patient coming in. At the end of each day the three tired practitioners would climb into the wagon and let the horse pull them home.

"Avery, you mustn't think of me as ungrateful, but we have to talk about this. It's true many of our patients cannot pay with

money. Lots of people are short of money. The war, you know. The baskets of fruit and sacks of vegetables are helpful, of course, and I'm grateful, but our rent can't be paid with eggs and butter. We're paying our rent with money from our savings, and soon we won't have enough left to buy a home. What should we do?"

"Lucky for me I have such a practical wife. I hadn't thought about that. We can't turn the poor people away, can we? I guess we'd better find a place to buy soon or we won't have enough money left. Let's go look around on Sunday afternoon."

Avery, Claire, and Gunner took a picnic and a fishing pole and went up the road toward Avery's favorite fishing place. Claire lay on the moss under a willow tree reading while Avery fished and Gunner sniffed and hunted. Avery stared up the river, remembering all the times he'd fished here with his brother and his father. Squinting into the sunlight, he saw silhouettes of farm buildings. *They weren't there before.* He wondered.

"Claire, let's take a ride."

"Fish not biting?"

"I want to see something."

Their small wagon bounced and jiggled as Avery took it across the fields. Gunner ran along, staying clear from the bouncing wagon wheels.

Avery pulled the wagon up to the recently built buildings. They went through the gate and called out, but no one answered.

"It's empty, Avery. It has no curtains, and the windows are all closed up."

Avery walked into the empty barn.

"This seems very strange. Everything is new, but it has never been used." Claire said.

Gunner tore past them chasing a rabbit. They walked around the property and discovered they could look down on the river that flowed behind the house.

Quietly they returned to the wagon and followed the road back to town.

"I'll ask about this," Avery said.

CHAPTER FORTY

THE COUNTY FAIR

The leaves were beginning to yellow and the days were growing shorter. Soon Sarah, Maize, and Claire would be cooking pumpkin and preserving it in glass Mason jars. Avery planned to sizzle the seeds over the fire, and the children would have a fun treat to eat. In a week or so when most of the crops were in, school would be all day once again.

Avery decided the family needed an outing. "Sorry, Gunner. You'll keep Fan company today," he said to the sad dog. In the early morning fog he packed the wagon. At the McDougal farm, Sam was doing the same. The wagons from the two farms met on the road to Parkersburg for the County Fair.

"This is the most wagons, horses, and people we've ever seen in one place," commented Sam. They wanted to see all the exhibits and all the animals. Keeping track of everyone was a full time job for Sam and Molly.

For Maize and Banjo, the freedom to walk around, looking and touching, having money to purchase things, was a new experience. Their experience as slaves had been much better than most as they'd had benevolent owners who treated them with dignity. But they hadn't been free. Now they were, and it made all the difference. Their well-behaved children enjoyed all the sights and sounds of the wonderland called the "County Fair."

"Look, Claire, a memorial exhibit dedicated to all the soldiers from West Virginia, both Union and Confederate."

"It's made of flowers. Oh, look, Avery. The flowers make a waving flag with a cannon beside it. Isn't it pretty?"

The couple looked at it silently, immersed in private thoughts. Avery noticed that when the loud and excited fair goers came to this exhibit they were quieted. *Everyone has their own memories*, he thought. *And probably their own losses.*

Sarah enjoyed the educational exhibits and gathered some ideas for her school. She looked at the quilts, flowers, canned goods, and new inventions.

Avery invited Danny to come horse shopping with him. Danny was overjoyed. He was soaking in everything, looking side to side, up and down and all around. Avery didn't rush him. He let him stop and look at everything, and Avery answered his many questions. He watched the boy making mental notes about things. *Like me*, he thought.

The horse barn was a huge building with an auction ring in the middle. There were walkways around the barn where prospective buyers could see the horses moving and check them out in good light. Avery was shopping for a Morgan for Claire.

"Claire's going to have her very own horse? I didn't know girls could own a horse," commented Danny.

"Sure. Claire needs her own horse. She'd enjoy one, and it would be useful to her."

Avery wrote down the location of the first two that he liked. He and Danny were admiring the third one, while Avery instructed Danny what he was looking for. This horse was gentle, muscular, and seemed to be in excellent health. The information on the stall said the horse belonged to a Union soldier who had no further need of it, and he wished a kindly home for it at a fair price.

"What do you think of this girl, Danny?" Avery asked him.

"She's a good horse," the owner said, coming around to join them.

"Looks like she is," answered Avery and turned toward the man.

"Well, glory days!" the man exclaimed. He reached up to Avery's shoulders and put his hands on them. "You remember me, Doc?"

Avery stared at the man, gradually recalling his face.

"My name's Ezra Sanders. You took care of me for many months. Looky here," he said and pointed down to his pant leg. "Looky here." He thumped around in a little circle. "You remember me? My leg got shot up in the Wilderness Campaign. You tried awhile to save it, but then took it off. You and your nurse made me an iron leg. Remember that?"

"Of course, Mr. Sanders. Ezra. Forgive me, sir," Avery said, shaking his hand. "In the past five years I've seen thousands of soldiers and sometimes I forget names. I'm grateful you remembered me, and helped me to remember you. It looks like you're getting on very well with that iron leg. This is my brother-in-law, Danny. Danny, Mr. Sanders."

Avery had to help Danny with the handshake. Avery's father had always introduced his sons to his associates and adults even as small boys and had taught them to shake hands firmly. Avery knew many children in the valley were not to be seen or heard, nor would they be introduced to adults. For him to include Danny was just natural for him, but probably not for Danny.

"So you are horse shopping, then," said Sanders.

"Yes," said Avery, "I need a nice, easy, and reliable ride for my wife. I, uh, I married your nurse, Claire."

"Don't blame you for that," Sanders laughed. "Good for you! I think Maribelle here would be exactly what you need. A gentler soul never was. Smooth gait, easy ride, and on top of good health. And for you, my life savin' doctor, I'll offer you a very good price. I'd like to just give her to you for all you've done for me, but I need to get a bit of a price for her."

"I would never expect a free horse, Ezra. I wouldn't let you do that. I'll give you a fair price. You name it. What do you think, Danny?"

Avery began to point out some features to Danny. Sanders joined in, and Danny got a thorough education on buying a horse.

"I'd like Claire to make the final decision; it's her horse, after all."

Ezra scratched his head in puzzlement. "Horse trading's a man's business," he mumbled.

Avery and Danny started out for the food barns to find the women. They found them watching a demonstration of a new meat grinder that could make sausage meat in half the time. Sarah was considering buying it. Avery bought Danny a sausage and took Claire back to meet Maribelle. He didn't tell her who the owner was.

"Howdy-do, ma'am," said Sanders.

"Hello," Claire said, looking at him oddly. "Do I . . .? Have we . . .? Are you . . .? Oh, my goodness! Sanders, isn't it? Avery this is—"

They all laughed, shook hands, and enjoyed their reunion. Claire and Maribelle took to each other right off, and Sanders saddled the horse. He had a McClellan saddle just like Avery's. He expected Claire to ride sidesaddle as ladies should. He was surprised when she spread out her skirt and straddled the horse. Avery was so used to Claire, he didn't think about it, but Sanders looked a bit uncomfortable. Claire walked and trotted the horse around the barn with many onlookers staring and looking offended. Claire paid them no mind. Avery helped her off the horse, and they paid for Maribelle. Sanders insisted that she take the saddle as well. "I've no need of it, and it suits you fine. It would just sit in my barn and rot. Please take it and use it in good health." They would come for Maribelle at the end of the day to take her to her new home.

Maize and Banjo bought themselves a young heifer that promised to become a good milk cow. This was the first thing they bought together for their new homestead as free people. Maize won some blue ribbons for her baskets which she exhibited, and with her prize money she purchased a pair of geese.

Claire bought a quilt at the exhibit and a little parasol that was rubberized for the rain.

What a good idea that is, Avery thought. *Very practical.*

They ate some delicious sausages and tried some exotic foods from faraway places. Claire wondered how they could grow a pineapple. "It's wonderful," she said. "It's sweet and juicy and pretty!"

But Avery thought the most wonderful thing he had was hot blackberry pie, just made. He bought a hoop of cheese to take home. Sarah bought some sweet treats for the boys on the trip home. She thought that might give Molly and Sam a rest. If the twins had some sugar candy to suck on, they might be quiet.

As the sun was getting low in the sky, both families collected all their purchases of the day and loaded up their wagons.

"What an altogether wonderful day, Avery, thank you so much for taking us all. And thank you for Maribelle," Claire said, and she nodded off as they drove down the dusty road to Kanawha.

CHAPTER FORTY-ONE

A LUCKY BOLT OF LIGHTNING

"This weather feels strange today, Avery. I believe it'll rain. Or maybe storm. We might both be glad I've brought along my little rubber-coated parasol."

They rode cross-country through the hollers and onto the road to Parkersburg. They stopped along the way for a picnic and watched the migrating geese heading south, following the Ohio River and all the tributaries. Honking in their formation, they never failed to captivate Avery and Gunner.

"Your mother says the mallards stay all winter with her, did you know that?" Claire asked.

"I did. They always have. It's nice, isn't it?"

" 'Tis, Avery. Maybe someday we'll have a pond," she dreamed. "Maybe we'll have mallards and geese too."

"That would be nice," he agreed. "Maybe a fishing stream." They rode awhile longer, and Avery checked his directions that he had copied from the broadside advertising the property.

"This has to be it," he said. "It seems much more than the ad describes. Claire, we've been here before. Remember? When we went fishing, we came this way. Remember?"

"Yes, I remember. New and not used yet. Where is everyone?" The wind was picking up, and the temperature was dropping. "Told you, we'll get rain," she said.

Avery went into the barn and looked around. "Nice," he said.

They walked the horses in and dismounted. They looked at all the buildings, and the rain started to come down. Claire put up her little parasol, and she and Gunner ran up on the porch of the house. "The little parasol works just fine," she called. "Come to the porch, Avery, out of the weather."

But Avery stood in the yard, feeling the rain come down. The wind began to blow, and suddenly Claire shouted at him, "Avery MOVE!" She beckoned with her arms, but it was the tone of her voice that moved him. Not a split second after he ran toward her, a searing bolt of lightning struck the very spot where he'd been standing. With a tremendous crack it hit the ground, spitting dirt and soil high into the air. The grass caught fire.

Avery was stunned. His heart was beating wildly; he knew he had just narrowly missed death. Claire looked pale and scared. He wondered if this would be the second time in her life that she would faint.

"Sit down," he told her. Her legs obeyed, and she crumbled. He dropped down beside her, shaken. They sat under the porch roof quietly and watched the rain beat the fire out in the grass.

When the storm ended and the rain stopped, the sky lightened up and a rainbow appeared in the sky. Gunner was the first to notice it. He lifted one paw, whined, and cocked his head.

"Oh, Gunner, you're so right, it's beautiful!" said Claire. Avery got off the porch and walked to the burned earth. There was a hole with dirt blown out, and the grass and weeds were scorched to ash.

Why here? Avery wondered. He felt around the hole and pulled his hand back when he touched something sharp and jagged.

"What's in there, Avery?" Claire was looking down the hole.

He kicked around a bit with his boot. They carefully removed some dirt and discovered what seemed to be metal lying just under the soil. "Why would anyone bury metal here?"

"It's a mystery isn't it," Claire said.

"And one we can't solve, since this isn't our land," said Avery. "What do you think of this place, Claire? Mystery and all."

"I think this little farm would suit us well, Avery. The house is dear. It has a wonderful barn, a potter shed, a kitchen, a wood shed, a pump, and that little house over there is just perfect for your clinic, don't you agree?"

"It's close enough to town that people can get to us. When we have enough money, we'll buy a proper doctor's buggy to make house calls. It has a river and a pond. But I don't think we have enough money, Claire. It's got much more than what the notice said."

When they got home, Avery wrote a letter of inquiry; and when the reply finally came, they learned the land agent was very anxious to sell the place. The soldier who owned the property had the buildings built while he was at war. He planned to take a wife and come here after the war. But he never came back, and now the land agent was stuck. He was selling at a low price just to get it off his hands.

Avery and Claire worked on their finances and finally agreed they could afford this property. Avery signed the contract and insisted that Claire sign it as well.

CHAPTER FORTY-TWO
THE HOMESTEADERS

Their first official visit to their new home was with a shovel and hoe. Avery dug and dug until he hauled up a big sheet of metal with the melted hole in the center.

"What could this be for?" Avery wondered out loud. He continued to dig until he hit something solid, buried deep—a large metal trunk. It appeared to be very heavy, and Avery didn't see how he and Claire could possibly get it out. He made the hole large enough to stand beside the trunk, and then he rounded up Banjo, Sam, and a couple of the farmers. They came with ropes and draft horses, shovels and levers. After several hours they were successful at raising the trunk out of the hole. The tired men had never seen the likes of it and wondered where it had come from. But it wasn't their business, so they took themselves back to their farms and their own work.

"Whatever could it be?" asked Claire. She tried to wash the dirt off the trunk so they could see the rusty opening. Avery used every tool he could find to open it, but the lid would not budge. The next day he talked to the blacksmith in Parkersburg who loaned him a metal tool. Eventually they were able to bend the hinges back just enough to see inside and reach into it.

"What's in it, Avery, can you see?" asked Claire anxiously.

"Whatever it is, it is covered up with rich cloth."

"Let me look," she said. She peered in and slid her hand inside where she confirmed that the material was soft velvet. "Whatever can it be?" she wondered.

On the third day the lid to the mysterious trunk finally gave way. Claire lifted the velvet cloth and revealed bundles wrapped in fine cloths.

For several hours Avery and Claire unwrapped the bundles and saw before them heaps of gold, silver, jewels, chains, coins, and a beautiful tea server in silver with rubies around the middle. There were beautiful plates and goblets and mugs; ancient books written in a strange language. There were other items which must have been of value to be placed here, but they were unknown to Claire and Avery.

"Where has this come from?"

"Who does this belong to?"

They put the articles back into the trunk and dragged the heavy chest into the barn. Avery filled the hole. When they went back to the Bennetts', he wrote his brother a letter.

By Thanksgiving Mr. Yoder had made a fine little table and benches for their new home, and before the snow fell he had finished a beautiful bed. Sarah made them a gift of a new feather tick. Mrs. Simpson had mailed them a wedding gift of nicely embroidered linens. Claire made the bed and topped it with the quilt from the fair.

She began to work on the "little house," the guest house. It would become the doctor's office. A trip to Parkersburg netted her a cabinet and a small table, and she bought a rain barrel for collecting pure water. She hung the embroidered picture of Gunner and the doctor's diploma on Avery's office wall, and he installed his tall examination table in the new clinic. Just before Christmas they were in their new home with furniture, a braided rug on the floor, and curtains at the window. Gunner had his favorite spots already picked out.

Avery posted his notice: *Doctor Avery Junior Bennett, MD, graduate of the Medical College of Virginia, has moved his practice to*

County Road 7 between Kanawha Valley and Parkersburg and will see patients daily in the mornings.

"I have an idea, Claire, about those patients who can't afford to pay for services. They pay with food they need, but we have plenty of food. The one thing we need is a larger clinic. So here is my idea. Patients who have no money can bring a large stone for payment. We can make a pile, and when there are enough, we will build an addition to the clinic. Everyone can help. They'll feel proud they helped with their payments of stone, and we'll have the building supplies we need. What would you say about that?"

"That's perfect, Avery, just perfect. How clever of you."

CHAPTER FORTY-THREE
CHRISTMAS JEWELS

The Christmas card from Clayton and Elizabeth accompanied a long letter from Clayton. He had researched the items that Avery had listed, and according to the many sources Clayton had checked, none of these items had ever been recorded as stolen. No owner could be identified.

A museum curator suggests they were family treasures buried before the Revolutionary War to prevent them from being stolen. Another curator believes they may have been buried before the Spanish-American War, either as hidden booty or to prevent theft. He believes the origin may be Portuguese or Spanish. A Harvard historian believes the books are Portuguese.

At any rate, dear brother, the trunk and the contents now belong to you. That is how the law of the land is written. Congratulations, you have obtained some wealth!

With love and Merry Christmas and a Happy New Year.
Clayton

"Well," said Avery. "It looks like we've a bit of a nest egg on our little farm, Claire."

On Christmas Day they went into Parkersburg for church, and in the afternoon Sarah came to attend Claire's first prepared Christmas dinner.

"Oh, Avery, you must help me. I'm just hopeless at this," Claire fussed.

The goose Avery and Gunner brought in was grand. The potatoes, of course, were perfect.

"This is my mam's own recipe of Tartan Taters," Claire told Sarah.

Dried peas and beans with Avery's help, Sarah's corn bread, and Mrs. Mikesell's Molasses Cookies made a perfect Christmas dinner.

"Perhaps next year I can learn to make a pie," said Claire hopefully. "I might make a good cook after all," she said.

That evening when they were alone, Gunner lay by the fire on the new braided rug, and Claire handed a small package to Avery. It was wrapped in velvet and tied with a small ribbon. "This is our fourth Christmas together, but only the first one married, of course. Here. I hope you'll like it," she said.

He looked at the velvet cloth and thought how handsome a gift for a poor farmer and country doctor. "I like it already," he said. He opened the gift and found a gold pocket watch on a chain. "Claire!" he exclaimed. "My darling, this is very fine, a wonderful and beautiful gift, but we can't afford such as this. Can we?"

She shrugged. "It's not so expensive. I traded the jeweler some of the pieces from the trunk, Avery. He made the timepiece just for you. Do you like it? It really cost us nothing, just some little trinkets from the barn. Read inside, Avery."

He opened the little watch case and read the words inscribed on the gold case. *I am grateful every minute of every hour for you. All my love, Claire. Dec. 1865*

He pulled a small box from his pocket and handed it to her. "Our first Christmas without the war."

She opened the box and gasped. "Avery, this is so beautiful. It's wonderful."

"Do you like it? It's *just a trinket from the barn*," he laughed.

She held the comb in her hand. It had gold teeth to hold it into her hair. On the band across the top, jewels were set into the gold.

"Turn it over," he said. On the back was inscribed, *The blessings of rainbows. Always, Avery.*

He took the comb from her hand. He pushed the little comb into her tangle of curls, and the firelight sparkled on it.

"Thank you, Avery. 'Tis altogether beautiful, and I'll cherish it always," she said.

That evening they talked about all the things they could do with the treasure in their mysterious trunk.

"That trunk is a great mystery, isn't it?" said Avery. "I wonder if we'll ever know all of its secrets?"

That night the rain turned into snow. By New Year's Eve the homestead glistened like diamonds on a blanket of pure white silence. When Avery went out into the cold dark night for more firewood, he paused and looked up into the velvet sky filled with sparkling gems.

Inside Claire lit her beeswax candles. They flickered peacefully inside their glass hurricane lamps, gleaming like crystals. Gunner watched her pour their coffees and cut the cake she'd made. He rolled over on his back.

"I know," she said, "you'll just die if you don't get some cake, you old actor dog, you."

This is more than I ever could have dreamed, Claire thought. *This is more than all the treasure in all the trunks in all the world.*

"Do you remember this night one year ago, Claire?"

"I do, Avery. I do."

"We must always remember what that moment was like with all of us singing and praying for peace together, when all of us sang for our united country. And I'll never forget how it felt to be in love. This is the first of many years for us, my darling Claire."

"Happy New Year, Avery."

Gunner sighed contentedly and dropped his chin to his paws. He tucked his bone under his paws for later.

"Happy New Year, Gunner," they both said with grateful hearts.

EPILOGUE

JOURNAL ENTRY BY DR. AVERY JUNIOR BENNETT

December 31, 1899. The Eve of the New Century.

How interesting it is to look through all these old journals I've kept all these years. When Mother died four years ago, and Clayton and I closed up her house, I found my early journals that I never guessed she had kept. Some were made from used paper that I cut and folded and tied together with boot strings. Some were cloth, sewn together, and some were gifts. The earliest one I found was made of all kinds of paper. I was twelve years old at the time, and I wrote between the lines and in the margins about my new puppy that Father gave me for my birthday.

Old Gunner lived to be sixteen years old. He saw me through all the growing-up years. He was my friend and my army buddy. He made rounds with me and house calls on the old buggy all over these hollers. He was at Claire's side when we delivered our first child. Oh, how I miss that old hound dog. When I go in and out of my office, I always pat the embroidered head of Gunner that hangs in my office. Claire made that so many years ago. It means a lot to me.

When Mother died, Clayton and I divided the property. We gave Banjo and Maize a quarter of it where they had lived and worked all these years. They were a great help to Mother. We gave them plenty of land to share with their children and have some room to expand. I believe Banjo's family was a gift from God to my mother at exactly the time she needed it. We are grateful for that.

The second portion we gave to the county for the school with some land for future expansion. Mother's school sure did

grow over the years. Nearly everyone around can read and write now. The school has six licensed teachers. I sit on the school board, though I'm not sure I'm much help. These teachers today are very well educated.

The rest of our parents' property we sold to establish the Bennett Foundation for Education. With Clayton as our lawyer and Geoffrey Keese as our investment banker, there will always be some money available for deserving Kanawha Valley children for education and training, regardless of their color or financial means. Mother and Father would approve of using their resources this way, we believe. Education was always important to them both.

Clayton and Elizabeth are comfortable and have a happy life in Wheeling, where Clayton sits in the House of Representatives. They haven't any time for farming, but they live in a town home and have a lovely garden.

Their firstborn son, Clayton Bryson Bennett, Jr., lies at rest in our family cemetery, which is the last quarter of the property. It takes in the hill in the old orchard. We have a fence around it, and Claire weeds and tends it. Mother's bench is there. Baby Clayton lies there with Father, Mother, and Gunner. There's plenty of room for us all when the time comes.

Looking through the journals, I can see how many things have changed and how many things I've learned through the years. I always did enjoy learning new things. I wrote pages and pages of new things through the years.

The field of medicine has changed. In the years following the war, 1865–1868, the germ theory of disease revolutionized the entire world of medicine. And what I learned about it was that my mother had it right all along!

There are many medical schools available now for young men and even some that will take young women, as it should be. I was certainly fortunate. Of course the students today must go to school much longer than we did before the war. There is so much more to learn now. The compendium is now in two volumes, and the students' textbooks are wondrous. I would love to be sitting in their classrooms today.

Epilogue

Doctors today have some wonderful tools of the trade. I have a stethoscope, and I can hear the heart rate and hear the function of the lungs as clear as a bell. Why, I can even hear the tiny heartbeat of an unborn baby. Who would have ever thought that could be? In the 1870s we were able to see bacteria with microscopes. Imagine that? Now we know what causes anthrax, tuberculosis, and cholera. Isn't that a wonder? We should all be so grateful for the lives we can save.

Five years ago a man by the name of Roentgen discovered a new miracle called an x-ray machine. Many folks are still frightened by it, as you can actually see the internal organs and bones of the body. Some folks think it's the instrument of the devil. It is quite eerie really, but I think it has tremendous potential for the field of medicine. Can you imagine being able to look at a broken bone and knowing exactly where to mend it? We sure could have used that in the war.

Oh yes, I think the next few years will bring even more wonders to medicine. I am so grateful to have been a part of it. I think how different it would have been during the war to have known all we know now. How many more lives we could have saved.

But one cannot look back. We are all charged with doing the best we can with what we have and know at any time in our lifetime. And I believe we did that. History may be kind or unkind to us; only God can judge us.

My own practice here in the holler where I grew up has kept me busy for all these years. We quickly outgrew the "little house" as we called it, and the day came that we announced to everyone that we would build on to it, using our huge pile of stones that our patients had contributed. What a day that was! Neighbors came with food and drink, windows, fine hinges, shingles, and flooring. And, my goodness, what a fine clinic went up that day. Made of stone, it will outlast us all. And I've been privileged. In our holler Claire and I delivered new life and closed the eyes on expired life.

Phoebe is teaching at Gallaudet University now and is being courted by a young man who is also deaf. She writes to us

often. I think I'd like to go visit them in Washington, D.C. There I was for five years, so close, and I never visited the nation's capital. That might be something I regret. I don't have many regrets.

Timothy returned to the valley, and Caroline financed his shoe-making business. She found him a good location in town; he's very successful and respected. We're very proud of Timothy. Life is more difficult for him, but he does well with what he's been dealt. Many soldiers had to learn new ways to live after the war.

Danny went to the land grant college in Columbus, Ohio. He studied and earned a degree in animal husbandry; he always had a nice way with animals. He studied medicine, too, and now he's a professor of veterinary science there at the college. He has a nice wife; he's a good honest man.

We never learned the secrets of our land hidden in that trunk. Sometimes when the children were young we took turns making up tales about the history of this place. We filled Mason jars with arrowheads, bones, shards of pottery, buttons, chains, and things we couldn't identify. Some of the stories were simply entertaining, but I think some just may have bordered on truth.

I keep checking my little gold watch to know when it's midnight. Claire thought I needed this little watch when I opened my practice here, so I wouldn't miss appointments and I'd know what time it was. She's pleased when she sees me open it. She thinks I'm checking the time, and I let her think that, but I rarely check the time. Farmer's know when it's morning, midday, supper time, and bedtime. I open it a lot because I like to read her little inscription. It still delights me. Tonight, however, I really am watching the time.

In just a little while it will be a whole new century, and this old man of fifty-three doesn't want to miss it. I'm going to go kiss my wife, my best friend for all these years, and say "Happy New Year, 1900."

Avery

Notes from the Author

WHAT'S TRUE AND WHAT ISN'T

Though Avery and Claire and their families are complete fiction, they are a representation of the many good early-American families who settled places like the Kanawha Valley.

The siege of Petersburg and the fall of Richmond were both horrible times in our American history. In this story both are told from the viewpoint of the *Richmond Dispatch.*

A Bread Riot occurred in Richmond as well as in other cities on April 2, 1863. Poor harvests and foraging armies, both Union and Confederate, set the stage for this act of desperation.

The Emancipation Proclamation and the Gettysburg Address are both historical documents.

Glandular fever is still around today. It's better known to today's students as mononucleosis or mono. This was Dr. Simpson's diagnosis of Avery's illness in Chapter 8, "The Doctor Is In."

The emergence of a new disease, called Soldier's Disease, was the beginning of our understanding of narcotics and their use and abuse.

The greenback dollar was the currency offered by the Union soldier in Chapter 1, "Odd Communications," and it was the currency sent to Avery by his parents to purchase his graduation clothes in Chapter 7, "Commencement." Until 1862, money in the United States was silver and gold. After one year of the Civil War, the money was running out, and people who had silver and gold were hoarding it. So the United States government began printing its own money that wasn't backed by silver and gold and had absolute value by itself. People were skeptical and thought the

money would be worthless. It was called greenback because one side was printed with green ink. It fluctuated in value with the progress of the war.

The Confederate Chimborazo Hospital did exist and is accurately depicted, based on photos of the tent wards and museum documents. Dr. James McCaw was really in charge.

The Mansion House Hospital of Alexandria existed and can be seen today as the Carlyle House Museum. You can also visit the Hollywood Cemetery. The Mansion House Hospital is depicted in the book as closely as possible to the original, with a few sidesteps into my imagination. It too is based on museum information and old photographs.

General Abner Doubleday was a real Union general, and he did visit this hospital. He's believed to be the inventor of Bases and Balls, known today as baseball. Some experts believe it was invented by his cousin, whose name was also Abner Doubleday. Perhaps it was both.

The Medical College of Virginia in Richmond was the only medical college in the country that did not close during the war. That's a fact.

The Ladies Seminary School is an actual place, also known as Powell's School. First Lady Edith Wilson attended this seminary in 1889 and 1890. This was the destination of the boys in Chapter 6, "Boys on the Town."

The Gypsy Vanner, the horse Avery named Rose, is a real horse breed.

The Clad and Sons Candy Company of Philadelphia was real, and the description of the candy is accurate.

Shape note singing became popular because as the settlers moved westward, musical instruments became a luxury. Shaped notes allowed everyone to learn to read music easily.

"Shall We Gather at the River" was written by Robert Lowry in 1864. The soldiers sang it, but it wasn't actually published on paper until 1865, when the war was over. It's still a popular hymn today.

Shall we gather at the river,
Where bright angel feet have trod,
With its crystal tide forever
Flowing by the throne of God?

Yes, we'll gather at the river,
The beautiful, the beautiful river;
Gather with the saints at the river
That flows by the throne of God.

—R. Lowry

CLAIRE'S TARTAN TATERS

1 pound of potatoes
1 small onion is sufficient for a pound of potatoes
salt and pepper
2 oz. fresh butter
4 egg yolks, boiled hard

Peel and slice potatoes very thin into a pie dish. Between each layer of potatoes put a little chopped onion, crumbles of egg yolks boiled hard, and a sprinkle of pepper and salt. Put in a little clean water, and cut about two ounces of fresh butter into little bits, and lay them on the top. Cover the dish and bake for about an hour and a half.

To my friends, family, and readers:
I wish you rainbows always.